CYNTHIA ROGERSON

Stepping Out

SALT

LONDON

PUBLISHED BY SALT PUBLISHING
Acre House, 11–15 William Road, London NW1 3ER United Kingdom

Salt Publishing 2012

Printed in the UK by TJ International Ltd, Padstow, Cornwall

Typeset in Paperback 9 / 10

ISBN 978 1 907773 20 4 paperback

1 3 5 7 9 8 6 4 2

for Christopher, Brett, Caitlin and Nick

CONTENTS

ACCIDENT

□ □ □ □ □

A DANGEROUS PLACE

Sheila is getting used to the heat. The way the air doesn't go anywhere, but just sits mid stream, slightly stale. A whiff of salt from the bay, eucalyptus from the hill, exhaust fumes from the freeway. Something else underneath. Maybe the smell of things rotting. The air tastes used.

She bought clothes for their move for California, but the Marks and Spencer dresses stick to her skin and she's recently taken to wearing cotton shorts and sleeveless T-shirts from Macy's. Not flattering, over her dimpled thighs and upper arms, but vanity is out the window. All that matters is being able to do the shopping, the cleaning, the cooking. She moves in slow motion.

One mystery. Though it is baking hot there are no places to hang up clothes. Every house has a dryer in the garage. Pronounced gaRAUGE. Sheila can adapt to most things – she's here, isn't she? And they are not short of a bob these days. But she is not going to spend good money drying clothes with electricity when the sun can do it for nothing in half an hour and leave her clothes smelling sweet. So one of the first things she does is make her husband drive her to a hardware store to buy a clothes line and pegs.

Her new line hangs between the lemon tree and the pole her sixteen year old son Jamie hammered into the ground for her. She watched him do this from their kitchen window, his narrow frame tensed, sweat coating his freckled nose and sunburned ear tips. As poignant, in his clumsy metamorphosis to adulthood, as a toddler emerging from infancy. Such a brief appearance, this version of Jamie. A matter of months, the blink of an eye.

He could have used some help tying the line, she could see he wasn't quite able take the strain. But she stood and watched, her hands absentmindedly drying a dish with a tea towel. She saw that he didn't want help. A proud manliness had come over his face.

She has three sons; has the hang of boys by now. Pretending they are better than they are, is the only way to keep them getting better. Confidence is all. So she patronises them, even her Murdo, her fat, red faced, puffing husband. She patronises him, always says what a winner he is, and look where he is now. A transfer to the San Francisco offices. A very long way from Inverness.

Jamie is her baby, the older two are still in Scotland. Jamie might have left school if they'd stayed there, he is old enough and he hates school enough. But here, in this strange and lush place, he is only a sophomore in high school, has another two years before he will leave. This is good. This place slows down everything. Even childhood lasts longer, and god knows, thinks Sheila, everyone could do with a bit more of that.

It was a good move, coming here. Good for everyone. Isn't this the place everyone dreams of coming? You can't do better than California.

Yet she has to keep checking, keep justifying it to herself. Such an awful risk you take when you stop living the life you were raised to live and try living somewhere else. You can't know in advance if it is the right decision.

Jamie only had a few friends in his old school, but here he is popular. When he opens his mouth to speak, blond girls with tanned legs in short white skirts, stop talking and listen. Smile. Say things like:

'Oh Jamie, I love the way you talk. Are you coming to the beach later?'

One Saturday night, some boys come to his house. One of the boys is driving his father's car, a big blue Buick. Sheila thinks he looks too young to drive, has to remind herself the legal driving age here is younger. You can drive five years before you can drink in a bar.

'Wanna come out, Jamie? Maybe head down the point. There's a party later at Paula's.'

Jamie checks with his parents, who gladly say:

'Oh yes, go, son. Have fun. See you later.'

They watch him jump in the car with the other boys and drive off. Murdo notices the garden hose left lying on the lawn. Says:

'Lazy kid never puts anything away. Useless. Tomorrow morning he's doing it properly and cutting the grass too.'

'What about the baseball game? Don't you have to make an early start for that?'

'He'll have time. I'll just get him up early.'

The boys are in a good mood. It's July 15th, smack dab in the middle of summer, another six weeks of no school. Still hot, but bearable. The windows are all down, the breeze delicious on their bare arms and necks. Straight white teeth flash in almost continual smiles. They drive down the point by the bay, stop and drink a few beers from a twelve pack. They laugh hysterically at silly things.

An obese man in bright pink Hawaiian shorts and no shirt comes jogging down the beach. He passes in front of their car. Jamie laughs with the boys. He doesn't think the man looks funny, but their laughter is contagious. They laugh their croaky adolescent laugh, and then one of them says:

'How about this party then?'

They start off again. It's not late yet, only just after 8:00, the sky just starting to darken, the horizon a haze of pink sundown. They drive back up to the coast road, head south.

They get behind an old van.

'Pass it, man.'

'This guy's going nowhere. Come on.'

The boy driving swings out to overtake it, straight into the path of a cement truck headed for the quarry. The truck driver doesn't even have time to step on the brakes. All he sees is one second's worth of blue car as it flies off over the embankment.

Sheila and Murdo are watching television when the phone rings. They're watching a doctor show, the same one they used to watch in Scotland. They're drinking Earl Grey tea, and a plate of imported Mr Kipling cakes sits on the table between them. Their bubble of normality. Murdo answers the phone. Sheila turns the sound down.

'Yes. What? What? How badly? Oh. Yes. We'll be right there. Yes, I understand. I know where.'

Sheila is shaking her head, just tiny movements, but quick.

'What is it? What's the matter?'

'There's been a car accident, Sheila.'

'Jamie.'

'Was thrown from the car. He's at hospital. Where are the car keys? Quick. I'll get the car out.'

'Oh no, oh god, Murdo. Stop. Are you sure it's Jamie?'

'I'm sure. Sheila. He's not dead. We have to go now.'

He gives her a little push towards the door, then turns off the lights and television. Watches himself doing these things. In the car he hears his voice from a distance.

'She couldn't say how bad it is. I asked. She said they couldn't say yet. I don't think they know. She just said to come. The nurse. Or whoever she is.'

They arrive at the hospital and park. Start to walk, then run in. Sheila is shivering. They ask at a reception desk and are told to go to the third floor. In the elevator, she shuts her eyes and fights an urge to sleep. Odd, but she could sleep at the drop of a hat. A big, grey cloud of oblivion, that's where she wants to be. In a rain cloud, breathing familiar damp air, her babies asleep upstairs.

A nurse is with him, checking the tubes running from his arm and mouth. Sheila stares, startled. Jamie looks as if he's been here hours, all tucked in, clean and bandaged. As if this evening contains two Jamies, one they have waved goodbye to, who is spending this evening doing what carefree American boys do on Saturday nights. While another Jamie has lain here, tended to, his heart monitored by machines.

The tiniest fluke has incurred this. Surely such a tiny fluke can be reversed, proved wrong, inappropriate. Time travel on a grand scale is out of the question, Sheila knows, but surely travelling mere minutes into the past can be managed. This boy should be at a party. The other driver should've taken his time with his dinner earlier, not rushed it, not been exactly in time to hit a blue Buick driven by a child.

Anyway, how can this have happened without her knowing about it, not felt the smallest flicker of alarm? Just watched television and drunk tea. Something is very drastically out of kilter. Maybe to do with the dislocation of being in the wrong country. Her radar has not functioned and now this. Her son's lanky body, tucked tight under a hospital sheet.

'Jamie, Jamie,' they both say in low voices.

'One minute,' says the nurse, and presses a buzzer. A doctor appears seconds later, a young man, maybe thirty. His eyes take them in. He speaks slowly, looking from Murdo to Sheila, back and forth.

'Your son was thrown though the car windscreen. He's in critical condition, we're just stabilising him, then taking him to the operating theatre. He had his student card in his pocket, that's how we knew where to phone you.'

He pauses. They both speak at once.

'What's wrong with him? Is he going to be alright?'

'Why is he asleep, have you put him to sleep?'

'James was in a great deal of pain. He's been sedated. It's better if he's unconscious till we know more about his condition. I'm sorry I can't tell you more. I'm awfully sorry. You must be very worried. We're doing all we can. We're taking him in a few minutes. There's a room you can wait in.'

'Doctor, what about the other boys. In the car.' Sheila almost whispers.

The doctor shakes his head unhappily, exhales loudly through his nose. Opens his mouth to say something. Closes it, then opens it again.

'We're still trying to reach their families.'

Sheila shuts her eyes a second, absorbs this. Then picks up her son's hand. Soft and limp.

'It feels clammy, Murdo. Touch it.'

Murdo looks at the doctor, then lifts Jamie's other hand. Feels the flesh, but cannot say to himself this is my son's hand because a sense of unreality has fallen on him, heavy and powerful. He has to keep breathing normally and not shout and run. He has to remind himself to breathe.

'Yes, it does feel a little chilly. It's probably the air conditioning.'

'You don't think he's cold?'

'I don't think so. He's asleep Sheila.'

'He's deeply sedated. I'll talk to you as soon as we know more,' says the young doctor, and he turns and leaves the room.

They watch Jamie's face a few minutes, lean towards him. Below the bandaging covering his forehead, his eye lids flicker, as if he is dreaming. His lips press together. He has thin lips and pressed together, they disappear, make a pinched slit under his nose. His skin is white and the sunburned skin is obviously that – dead cells temporarily still attached to the pink living skin underneath. He is breathing, they both notice. They keep checking that his chest rises and sinks.

The waiting room is brightly lit, with a coffee machine, but no tea. Sheila makes them both coffee, but after a sip, neither drinks it. They sit across from each other in plastic arm chairs.

Sheila has rehearsed this scene. The way every mother waiting up for a child to come home imagines the phone call with the bad news. The sudden violent rip in the fabric of her life, a glimpse of darkness and chaos. And that is the strange thing. When she has imagined it, she has always reacted the same with a pounding heart and tears ready to flow. But here she is, living the reality, and it isn't like that at all. She feels cold and frightened, trapped inside herself. Her head feels squeezed. She is acutely aware of all the details in the room. The posters persuading pregnant mothers to give up cigarettes, a dark stain on the carpet, the tinny ticking of the clock.

'He'll be alright, you'll see Sheila. I've heard this is the best hospital in the county. Jamie'll pull through.'

She manages a glancing nod of agreement.

'Kids put you through it, no doubt. They all have.'

'But this is the worst, Murdo. Nothing like this ever happened before.'

'There was that time Ian needed all those stitches.'

'No. That was not the same.'

I've never been here, she wants to say. They are silent a while.

Each privately considers praying. Sheila, who has been very religious, shuns it, except to urgently offer a bargain to whatever powers might exist to never again take the lives of her children for granted, should Jamie be spared.

Murdo, though, thinks praying might be a good way to fill the time. He says all the prayers he can recall from childhood. He says them silently several times, his lips moving. He knows he is not a subtle man, might miss things. He likes to hedge his bets.

They look at the clock. They sit up every time footsteps come near their door. Once Murdo says:

'Sixteen is an insane age to be driving. I knew it was. It's crazy.'

And later,

'If I find they'd been drinking.'

But Sheila doesn't answer, only sighs. Paces sometimes, to the window and around the room. Out the window she can see their car in the car park. It's the middle of the night and the car park is almost empty. She can't open the window. She sees a light in the sky, maybe a star. Maybe first star, a wish star.

She has a clear sense of Jamie, of who Jamie is, how he feels, separate from his body. The thought of him has a certain shape and weight and colour in her mind, wrapped round by the soft vowels and consonants of his name. Shutting her eyes, she wills this Jamie to stay inside his skin, his blood, his bones, his cells. Inhabit yourself, she begs silently. Do not leave. She opens her eyes and tries the window again, but it won't budge. She longs for the sound of crickets and frogs, the lukewarm air and sense of over ripeness. Then in a sudden surge, she is drenched with longing for that other landscape. Home. Damp air hitting the back of her throat like a drink of water, the smell of coal fires and wood smoke, the sound of voices speaking with her own accent. She literally feels the floor and walls receding, all of California fading into nightmarish unreality.

Yet when she pictures their home in Scotland, she has to really think. Remind herself of the wallpaper pattern in the sitting room. So much has just slipped away.

She doesn't want to think of Jamie anymore. Jamie is in a very dangerous place and if she does not let her thoughts summon him, he might be safe. He needs to be alone now, not fragmenting into her mind. He needs all his strength. Her job is to hold her breath, mentally. Put everything on hold, so he won't have missed anything when he revives.

But again she sees him putting up her clothes line. Leave me alone, I know I'm not the strongest sixteen year old, but

I can do it. The man he would be, wanted to be, simmering impatiently beneath the surface. But still a child, still recognisably her boy.

'Should I go and try to find the canteen, see if there's any tea?' asks Murdo, coming to an end of a round of prayers.

'I don't mind, Murdo. Go, if you like. Go on, stretch your legs.'

And when he returns, he asks:

'Would you not be more comfortable if you took your cardigan off?'

And later,

'Maybe you should slip your cardy on again, you look cold.'

Once a nurse pops her head in, but by accident, and she has no news for them. Then a man comes in, looks at the magazines, looks at Sheila and Murdo. Eyebrows raised in a question.

'We're just waiting. For news of our son,' says Murdo.

'He was in a car accident, he's in surgery so they can see how badly injured he is,' says Sheila.

'Ah,' says the man.

'We think the other lads all died. He's lucky,' continues Sheila, almost whispering.

'How terrible. Terrible.' He frowns, then chooses a car magazine and leaves.

'He didn't want to know, did he, Sheila. Oh well, can't say as I blame him. Dreadful business.'

She says nothing.

'Are you sure you don't want me to get you something to eat or drink, love?'

'No thanks, Murdo.'

She knows what he needs. He needs the gift of her helplessness. Her collapsing in his arms. She may never give him this. While Jamie is in danger, she must remain remote and focussed. Active worrying is what she is good at. She's had years of practice and now she hones all her ability into concentrated hard fretting. This is what Jamie needs his mother to be doing. Not comfort seeking. She keeps busy looking out the window. Walks to and fro, in brittle movements. Moves her head jerkily from clock to magazine to window. Not to Murdo.

Murdo begins to feel strange with the effort of not crying. There is a pain in his throat, a gasping tightness in his chest. All his life, he has been able to fix things. He is a first class trouble shooter, but this is something else. Jamie's injuries lay outside his ken. Unlike Sheila, he allows himself to sense the possibility of losing Jamie and he sees it clearly. There it is and though he knows he can do nothing about it, he can not stop wanting to fix it. Frustration wells up and his whole body tingles. He thinks he might faint. He stretches, takes deep breaths camouflaged as yawns. Fidgets by emptying his pockets. Money, keys, two baseball tickets.

He turns his face to the wall and begins to cry. He rocks and cries quietly, while his wife looks out the window. Searches in her bag for a clean hanky to give to him.

The driver of the truck that hit the blue Buick sits in an all night diner. He orders black coffee and a donut. He is tired and dirty. Dirt clogs the pores of his face and the creases in his hands. His nails are short but still grime has found its way under them. He ignores the donut and lights a cigarette. His boss has said he can have tomorrow off, but he doesn't think he will. A day at home alone, thinking, is not what he needs. He runs over the evening's events again. He can't stop doing this.

Leaping out of his truck and hurtling down the embankment to the car. Seeing bodies through flames. The grass beginning to catch fire, sparks crackling on dry manzanitas. Clambering back up to the road, seeing the boy flung in the bushes. Checking for breathing.

'Jesus fuck, you're not dead, you're alright, what a smart kid you are, not dead, good boy, you good good boy.'

Scooping the body up, letting his broad chest and shoulders take the weight, carrying him up the slope. All the time talking to the boy. The boy whimpering, flinging an arm, not opening his eyes. Carrying him to a near-by house. Opening the door and hollering:

'Hey! I need an ambulance, anybody home? I'm phoning an ambulance.'

No answer. Laying the boy on a sofa, finding the phone in the kitchen, dialling. Getting some paper towel and dampening it. Gently washing some of the blood off the boy's face.

'Hey, you're going to be alright there guy, you're looking pretty good, have you fixed up in no time. You're such a good kid, everything's going to be alright.'

It doesn't take long for the ambulance to arrive. But all the time, saying things to the boy.

Jamie lies still while men and women he will never meet hover over him. Sheila loses sensation in her legs, giving Murdo the chance to do something. They lean against each other like felled trees, caught mid fall by lucky accident. Six thousand miles away, in a house where two other sons are eating their dinner, all the places where Jamie spent a lot of time – his bedroom, the soft chair by the television, the place in the garden that slopes down to the noisy burn, the flat ground where he used to kick the football – all these places might quiver if they knew. A light might flicker over them. Even in California, which has known him so briefly, there are places that might notice. The pole holding Sheila's washing line might remember his straining. It is hard to tell the difference made by one less heart beating. It is dawn. Outside the hospital, the crickets stop and the traffic starts.

THE ETIQUETTE
OF ACCIDENTS

There it is, without preamble or logic, as shocking as a hard slap – blue sky in February! And the air smells weirdly and nostalgically of summer. Four people, from various houses and lives, all decide to change their plans for the day and go up Ben Bhraggie instead. They come to this conclusion separately, in their own houses and lives and almost at the very same time. Charlotte, Morag and Rosh phone each other, and delighted to find an echo, drive to the Ben in a dark green Volvo estate, along with two dogs. Andy, nearly 28, drives too. A red boy-racer with dodgy brakes. His mountain bike is strapped to the back of his car. There is a sense of urgency and each car speeds. Hurry! The sun cannot last, can it? It's been a very long winter, very wet and dark.

The three women and two dogs unpeel from the Volvo and set off. It's called a Ben, even though it's not a mountain. It's a hill, and the sky is still blue, the air still sweet. The light is low, illuminating leafless trees and dead bracken. There are snowdrops and the women wonder, as they do every year, if the blooms are earlier than usual. Geese are noisy in the fields at the foot of the hill; no one knows if they have returned or if they never left for winter at all.

Andy arrives and also begins the ascent. He'd almost invited a friend to come, but decided to keep this pleasure for himself. It'll be better on his own. His gear is good. His bike is good. His muscles are good too, and he pedals uphill without effort.

Charlotte and Morag are old friends. Rosh is their recently acquired writer friend. They are middle-aged, and Rosh is not quite middle-aged. They haven't known her long enough to ask, but they've speculated. Not forty, they think. Maybe thirty-six. They are a little in awe of this published writer. They usually chat in an overlapping flow, but today there is a self-consciousness. They're showing off, a tiny bit. Sounding intelligent, yet witty and careless, isn't easy, and after a while they settle into comments on the gradient of the hill, the condition of the path.

Rosh the writer has never walked up a hill. She's known, at some level, that hills are walked up, and by humans. But she has never really assimilated what that means and she is finding the actual experience unbelievably painful. At first she thinks she might be having a heart attack, and shyly tries to conceal this by striding ahead, sweating profusely and panting. Her shoes are new. They look practical, but already the blisters are forming. Except, never having had a blister, she thinks her heels are having an aneurism.

Quite early on, she begins to feel wheezy, and clearly pictures her inhaler sitting by her bed. This image instantly makes her crave a cigarette. It's a nightmare. Who are these women and why is she here? Suddenly, she wants rain. Rain and wind and her old street in Leith. She pictures her bed, her faded duvet. The way she feels when a movie is starting, and the way the first cigarette always tastes. This woman's favourite part of each day is just after she wakes and lies there in bed, enjoying the softness of the duvet.

'Are you OK?' Charlotte asks.

'Aye. Just a bit out of shape. You go ahead.'

'You sure?'

'Oh aye. Please.'

The two women quickly walk past their new friend, politely

pretend they have not noticed she is winded, and are soon talking of demanding aged parents. Then without an obvious link, they begin talking about relationships. Charlotte is single, and she has finally had it with men after an episode with a married one.

'The worst part, is the way I feel such a fool.'

'But a fool is the luckiest creature on earth,' says Morag. 'You're brave! Passionate! You're really living!'

'Am I? I'm so tired. I wish I'd never met him.'

Morag is married, and she constantly pines for romance.

'Stay or go?'

'Stay!' says Charlotte. 'He is a good man, and anyway, all relationships are boring after a while.'

'But I want to be in love.'

'Yes. Well, being in love's a bugger to beat, alright.'

It's a popular walk, and there are other walkers and bikers, all with bemused and stunned faces. The sun! their faces say. The statue of the Duke of Sutherland, The Mannie, peeks at them from the top of the hill. The whole day feels as effortless as a happy dream, as the first day Prozac kicks in, as a ballet they can dance by heart. Even Rosh, alone now, stops and cannot help smiling because her skin tells her to.

Andy on his bike, a sleek seal in black lycra, is on a path that keeps intersecting with the hikers' path. He sees them twice, but doesn't really clock them; they're middle-aged women. Up and up he goes, rejoicing mindlessly. There was a time, not long ago, when he had to get off this same bike, and push it up this hill. Now he can go anywhere, do anything. He is very beautiful and young, but he's not aware of this. He simply pedals and breathes.

'Look, not far to go now,' the friends say to Rosh. They have stopped to wait for her to catch up.

'Almost there!'

At the same time she reaches them, Andy reaches the top of the hill. He's not interested in views, but pauses anyway and looks towards Dunrobbin Castle, which always reminds him of dreary Sunday afternoons with his parents. Having tea and scones in the tearoom. Scanning the dark oil portraits for some breasts, or at least cleavages. He takes a long swig of water, then straddles his bike, his steed. Launches himself gracefully back down the hill. Leaping off the first jump, he sighs: Ahh! There's always that sublime sigh, leaving the earth.

The women are nearly at the top, so close The Mannie cannot be seen. The only obvious track is also obviously a mountain bike track – steep ups and downs. Rosh, who has been gallantly pretending she is not suicidal, suddenly and with debilitating nausea, notices the height and feels a seductive pull to the edge. There is the North Sea and the blue sky, and all the empty air below her. If she does not drop, right now, to the ground, she will fall off this hill and die. Of course, she wants to fall and die. That is the crux of her vertigo – fighting a death wish. She makes small animal noises of distress, mouth closed, then collapses to the ground. There she sits, mute in her humiliating surrender. She is a beautiful large woman, and with her shaggy long jumper and closed-mouth whimpers, resembles something cuddly and prehistoric. One of the dogs, a cocker spaniel, manically digs the hill above her, and clumps of earth fall on top of her. It is hell. Hell! Her new friends console her.

'Don't worry. Quite normal to feel like that.'

'No hurry anyway. Let's have our picnic right here.'

Sky still blue. No wind. No clouds. They crouch with her, this red faced weeping figure, in the lee of a small rise, and he flies into them like an angel. Silently. A part of his bike – the right handlebar gear lever – sinks into Charlotte's arm. Punctures her skin and severs a muscle like a knife into butter, that easily. Her back was to him, and for whole seconds she can't comprehend why her arm is burning. She hunches into the hill, holding her arm, and wants her mum or someone to fix it – but something has happened to the universe and her own body. Besides her mother died eight years ago. And this sudden young man on the ground rolls with pain, and says:

'What the *fuck* are you doing here?'

Morag says simultaneously, with equal indignation: 'What the *hell* do you think you're doing?'

The dogs are barking excitedly. And Andy is not moving now, just moaning. He'd felt himself lose control the second of impact and let the fall take him, head first then the tumbling. That old surrender; the willed looseness to lessen breakage, the bladder weakening. Rock tearing through his skin and pounding his bones. Physical agony is old hat to Andy, but the fear is fresh each time.

'Fuck,' says Charlotte, who understands they have caused this accident, but is more aware of her arm and the cracking sound she remembers. No pain, but she will not move it. The sky is still blue and the air is soft, and damnit! She is furious.

'Fuck, fuck, fuck! Get the dogs away from him! Cover him up with my jacket. Call 999.' This is Charlotte, with the breaking heart and married man, and who drinks too much every night and thinks Morag's man is sound. She cannot separate Morag from Morag's luck, or her married lover from her ache, even now. It rides under everything and nothing can shake it. And Morag does what's needed, but guilt slows her. It is all, somehow, her fault. It seems to have weight, her guilt; weight and volume. Her limbs are heavy, and her stomach turns on itself unpleasantly. She covers Andy – Oh! The poor boy! – puts the dogs on leads and gives the leads to Rosh, still crouching into the hillside. Calls 999.

Rosh, who is allergic to dogs, and terrified of dogs, is now actually relieved, because this surreal turn of events means that she is asleep and dreaming. She almost smiles. Relaxes into the hill slope, waits for the dream to slide into another phase.

Andy is not moving now. He has done an inventory of his body, and knows his back and neck are not broken. He does not know if he is bleeding much. He is acutely aware of waves of pain, getting worse with each one, emanating from his groin area, and belly. He has never been hurt exactly this way. Jesus fuck, it better not be his balls! When the waves peak, he has to close his eyes and focus on breathing. He hates getting hurt, but in an angry way. Like he hates it when his bike frame gets bent, or the gears break. It means inconvenience and expense. But underneath his anger a slow fear begins to crawl. Literally crawl along his skin. Anatomical terms float through his mind. Spleen, pelvic bones, appendix. He is cold. What were these women doing on the cycle path? Stupid fucking menopausal cows! He's aware one of the women is talking on the phone.

'Yes, he's conscious. Yes, he's warm,' Morag is saying. 'No, he can't move.'

'They're sending a helicopter,' she tells them.

'Thank God it's not windy or raining,' says Charlotte.

'You OK? How's your arm?'

'Don't know. Hurt. You just tend to him,' feeling equally gallant and terrified. There is a warm wet feeling that must be blood, and that cracking sound must have been her bone.

Rosh, realising it is not a dream, begins to take mental notes. Hmm, she thinks: The physical manifestations of extreme fear, pain, anxiety. She used to hate this about herself, but since she can't help it, hating seems a waste of emotion. It is how she is. It also helps take her mind off the dogs. And her vertigo. And her blisters. She notes that the boy has freckles and they stand out in a way that may be related to his pain. That her appetite for sandwiches has gone. And Charlotte, who is usually quite pretty, looks . . . stripped away now. And something has happened to time. It's become thick and glutinous and wrong. Like a movie scene with the soundtrack suddenly out of synch. The blue sky is wrong now too.

There are not enough of them. She thinks she will add more people to this scene, if she writes this story. There will be some men with them, maybe two, and no writers. She's never liked stories with writers in them. One of their group will be a twenty-one-year-old woman, and the injured biker will fall in love with her. The distressed tearful way she fusses over him, will suddenly contrast with his wife's aloof competency. This is what happens when you think you might die: You fall in love.

That's quite clever, she thinks.

When the story is made into a film, that'll be the blurb on the posters. Though she knows it's not true. The really true stuff never sounds clever, sadly. It always sounds naff. Probably all you think about when you're dying is the same stupid stuff you think about all the time. Like what you're wearing, do you look OK?

And the boy really may be dying. This piece of information seeps into the old friends, not Rosh, who is still just imagining the boy dying. The boy may be bleeding internally. Are his pupils contracting? What do eyes do, pre-death?

'Talk to him! Keep talking to him!' says Charlotte to Morag, who then takes off her jumper and places it under Andy's head, still helmeted. Wonders what she can say.

'What's your name?'

'Andy.'

'Andy. I'm really so sorry.' She wants to say they are to blame, but they didn't mean to hurt him. It was an accident. This sounds defensive, so she just repeats herself. 'I am so sorry, Andy.'

'S'alright.'

He closes his eyes, as pain rolls through him. As if his injury is the epicentre of an earthquake.

If I don't die, he thinks to himself, the first thing I'll do is invite Julia from the shop out for a drink. That was a dead sexy top she wore. Red and tight.

'Do you want me to call anyone, Andy?' proud she has thought to ask this sensible question.

'My mum. But don't tell her it's bad, OK? She worries.'

This evidence of his kindness, and the thought of his worried mother, undoes Morag. She has a son about this age too. Has imagined getting a phone call like the one she will need to make. She imagines this woman in her day right now, unaware. In Tesco, maybe. Or hanging washing. This accident will un-tether her from all ordinariness. By the time she re-attaches to her life, she'll be a different person. They'll all be different. Or will they?

Oh, why are men so careless with their lives? Break your heart over and over, that's what they're good for.

Then she is busy. She checks on Charlotte's arm, the quivering Rosh, the dog's leads. The emergency services keep phoning, to ask how he is doing and to ask if the helicopter is there yet. The man talks just like they do on that telly show. ER. She asks Andy what he works at, and tells him about herself. Her name, her job. She touches his forehead, to see if it is clammy. It is not, but she notices, at the second of touching him, that he is handsome. It is less bearable, somehow, that he is beautiful. Her heart feels squeezed. She thinks of a boy she had a crush on when she was sixteen, a boy who died in a car accident before she even kissed him. She touches Andy's hand, wants to hold it. But doesn't – not sure, now of the etiquette of accidents. Let's face it, she wants to lay on the muddy ground with him, curl her body protectively round his. Stroke his face and whisper that it'll be alright.

She very much wants, suddenly, to talk to her husband, the man she has been so tired of. Ask him to hold her. It's been years. She can feel his arms, as she tells this tale.

Nineteen minutes have passed.

Rosh is thinking about the nature of accidents, and the way life seems to condense around them. No time to dissimulate. No artifice. Accidents force change, and then what? If life doesn't end, it goes on. Right away. No safe lay-by to sit in, until one's in the mood for living again. Life is many things, she thinks, but mainly it is fucking relentless. Soon, she expects she will feel exhilarated. They all might. She wonders if it's the possibility of accidents, the unexpected, the good and bad surprises – that makes people get up in the morning. If, despite all their alleged love of plans and control, everyone secretly rejoices in the random. And when they get everything they think they ever wanted, don't they usually proceed to smash it up?

Then, finally, about twenty minutes behind everyone else, Rosh reacts to the actual scene in front of her. This occurs with a fizzing sensation in her head, as if something is literally dissolving. The people are specific individuals, and the hill is not metaphorical.

'How is he?' Rosh asks. 'And how is your arm? Do you think it's broken?' She begins to cry, a sudden hot gush full of snot and salt water. What if he is dying, right now, in front of them? And what will become of them if the boy dies, or is crippled? How will they live with the knowledge they have caused this? Some good will need to come. Perhaps she will stop smoking. Write with less cynicism. Morag may fall in love with her husband again, and Charlotte might discover how to love a man who loves her back.

When the helicopter comes, at first it looks like a shiny new yellow toy. Bright against the blue sky. The tail has a perfect oval shape cut out.

Charlotte shouts, 'Hooray!'

Andy thinks *Thank fuck.*

Morag, moony-eyed with love, assures the boy that help is at hand.

And Rosh wonders what the oval hole in the tail is for.

HOMESICK

Izzy hates her mother. She has hated her mother as long as she can remember. It isn't anything in particular her mother says or does – it is everything she says and does. Izzy supposes there must have been a time when things were different. She has a vague memory of opening her stocking one Christmas morning to find dozens of miniature presents – fairy gifts – and she'd played with them for hours, weeks, months, till they were worn out, and still she'd not wanted to share them. Of cuddles she can remember none. This is odd, because there is plenty photographic proof of affection. And happiness. It must have happened, yet there is not a scrap of it left in her fourteen year old heart. Even the sound of her mother's voice, even the word *mum* coming up in text on her phone, has the power to set up little waves of repulsion.

So when her mother is killed at milk crate corner – a clear and cold October afternoon, with the blackbirds at the rowan berries and the geese all revving up, round and round – Izzy feels none of the things she ought to. Except surprise of course, because no one expects sudden death on sunny days. She feels intensely annoyed with her mother – stupid woman, what was she doing driving home just at that moment? Typical. Oh! Izzy is so angry! Angry, but excited at the same time, because whatever else this is, it is not boring. A shameful and secret joy twists with her hot irritation, till she doesn't know if she is coming or going.

She does not miss her mother one bit. In that place in her life – that continuous surrounding place – where she had become used to feeling repulsed all the time, witnessed all the time, there is now a resounding and resplendent relief. Izzy used to love to swim, back when she'd loved things, and this reminds her of diving into water deeper and warmer than the shallow chilly water she'd braced herself for. Sometimes the loch was like that, on a July afternoon after torrential rain. Mother-less, she is able to unclench now, and just be.

The evening of the funeral day, she goes out to find a boy who lives down the street, the one everyone calls that ginger haired loser from down the street. Still in her new funeral clothes, she walks over to the bus shelter – his home, basically – where he is smoking with his mates. She finds she is walking very slowly. All her limbs feel heavy, as if gravity has increased its pull on her. She asks for a puff of his cigarette and tells him: 'Hey, I'll do it with ya.' She says this in a flat, serious tone, and her eyes are dead under the orange street lamp. The ginger haired loser from down the street looks like he'd rather not, but then all his mates are watching, so he takes her to his uncle's empty place across the road. They both slide through the half-open kitchen window at the back. The window ledge hurts her belly, and later he hurts her too, but not much. The whole thing takes less than fifteen minutes. It is not at all like she'd expected. She can't understand what all the fuss is about. She is angry about that, too. She doesn't think she'll be bothering with that again anytime soon, thank you very much.

'Where have you been?' her father asks, after she walks in her own back door, with sticky knickers and aching thighs.

'Nowhere,' she answers.

Then her father says: 'Sit down and eat.' That's all he says, and he looks back to his own food. Izzy feels as if she's put her foot down hard on a step that is suddenly not there. Into this alarming void she falls. Thwump! And suddenly there is her mother's grating voice, loud and sharp: Where exactly is nowhere, and what do you think you're doing, worrying everyone on a day when they've enough to worry about, selfish besom that you are and always have been. You'll be at the washing up tonight, my love, because you've done nothing else all day but suit yourself.

Ears ringing and dizzy, Izzy notices all her siblings are already at the table. Not a lot of eating seems to be going on – mostly mash getting pushed around on plates. Becca's long blond hair has not been properly brushed in a week, and looks like cutting it might be the only solution. Steve's chin looks swollen where he has stitches from the big fall off his bike yesterday, and his nose runs right into his mouth. Rachel, the eldest, sits silently crying without looking any less pretty – a mean feat, impressing Izzy, who can't decide if this takes practice or if some people are born this way. Annie has always been perfect, her mother's angel, so probably it is genetic, and there is no way on earth Izzy is ever going to be able to cry prettily. Or perhaps at all.

Her auntie is sitting in her mother's chair as if she has a right to, and eats with great efficiency. Blow your nose, she tells Steve, and passes him her own cloth handkerchief. Izzy flinches at both the sight of her auntie sitting in that chair, and the tone of her voice. Even the fact of her proper hankie is appalling. They'd all grown up knowing ingenious alternatives to hankies.

Her father sits woodenly shovelling the steak pie in. His eyes look small and his hands tremble. He seems much older than he did last week, and he does not seem very substantial. Izzy wonders if perhaps both her parents were killed last Tuesday, but God has decided losing both parents is too much of a cruel shock for the family, and so has allowed her father back for a bit. She looks hard at him for traces of encroaching invisibility.

In the kitchen, the radio is on, as always. No one ever listens to it, but tonight no one is talking and everyone hears it. Who had tuned in that naff channel? No one ever thought about it. Like the way clean clothes and wholesome broths produced themselves. Now a man with a rich pouring voice sings about a pussy cat, and asks the pussy cat what is new. He keeps asking in a coy tone, as if he already knows the answer, as if he expects to be told that something happy is new. Izzy hurts down there, and she can smell herself now, in the warmth. Sweet, but rank too. The food in her mouth has no flavour, and takes great effort to swallow. She watches the clock on the sideboard slowly shunting the minutes. Something unpleasant has happened to time, and even the clock seems to know it. The sideboard itself is piled up with new toys, like Christmas. Izzy, who is too old for toys, feels a giggle rise up – the same laugh that's been riding around inside her for days. But the laugh is too big, way too big. If she let it out now, it might finish her off. She pushes her plate away and stands up.

'Where are you going?' her father asks.

'I'm tired. Needing a bath.'

'OK. Goodnight.'

Again, the plummeting feeling and her mother's voice: Aye, well that's a fine thing. Don't let us stop you! Don't feel you need to keep us company in our time of despair and grief. Just go on then! Hey, exactly where do you think you're going, young lady? You march right back here this minute and sit with us for a while. Who do you think you are? The Queen of Sheba?

Izzy locks the door and runs the bath. There's only one bathroom, and she knows she has ten minutes of privacy, tops, so the taps are on full blast, and she strips off and slips in while it's filling. The water is a blessing. She turns off the cold with her toes, and lets herself be scalded. She is stinging inside now, and her inner thighs ache and her mouth feels puffy. She tenderly inspects her body, as if it's been plundered while she wasn't looking. As if it is not even her own body.

The water slowly turns pink and she closes her eyes. Feels her breathing and heart beat slow, and slow, to almost nothing, and she thinks of all the things that have happened in her life so far that have led to this pink bath. The sequence of events is confusing, and she has to keep going back again and again as she remembers more. It seems important to remember it all, in just the right order. What had she last said to her mother? What had her mother last said to her? These words elude her, though she has a clear memory of shouting at her last Wednesday, about her red top that her mum had put in the drier and shrunk.

'I hate you, you always have to ruin everything.'

These were pretty much her exact words. And they were true. Everything was her mother's fault. Everything still is. Now, in the bath, she can still hear the kitchen radio, and it's playing a song she likes, one that she's liked since she was wee, about a yellow submarine. She knows all the words, and that's because they used to sing it on the long car journey to see her gran. At her gran's house, she was always put to sleep on her own in the attic room, which smelled of cat pee and had spooky wallpaper. She'd often woken with an ache deep in her belly, and also lodged in her throat – a sort of all pervading pre-tears angst. She'd creep down the stairs – *she'd forgotten this* – to the room her parents slept in. Her dad would never wake, but Mum would always wake instantly, pull open the duvet and in Izzy would slide. Hush darling, you're only feeling a wee bittie homesick. Scoot in here. Then her mum would yawn, roll over and her snores would lullaby Izzy to sleep. That had really been her mum, and that had really been her own self. She even remembers her nightie – pink daisies on blue, brushed cotton, and how she would curl into her mum's warm back and breathe in her mum smell.

Well!

Izzy closes her eyes, sighs deeply, sinks down under the water. She wonders for a second if you can be homesick for someone you hate. Impossible, and yet there it is. There is the same deep swollen ache in her belly and throat. And then, while she is worrying about this, as well as all the normal things that keep popping up as if nothing has changed – like what to wear for school tomorrow – there is a scuffle on the landing outside the bathroom door. Becca is shouting at Tom: 'Sod off, you wanker, that's mine!' There's the clear sound of a slapping hand landing on flesh, and Tom automatically shouts, in the summoning bark they have all used since the day they could call her: '*Mum*!' For a second, then another second, silence. Then footsteps and her father's voice: 'Bed. Now.'

RUBBISH DAY

I hate my life. After I lose my job, I have all this time to think, and I start noticing things. Like the fact Neal grunts now; he mumbles too. Not to his mother, who he doesn't hate, but to me. His dad. The person who played footie with him in all kinds of weather, who bought him the fanciest trainers in the shop, because I was *that kind of dad*.

We used to talk, but all I get now is the occasional indecipherable word, usually with the inflection of a question. Hupmhum? Mosetier? Polikmunday?

How can I answer these?

I feel flayed. My son has plundered my life. Traitor!

When I look around my house, I see that it too has been plundered; we have not been vigilant about keeping the decay at bay. The bathroom floor needs re-tiling, the walls need re-painting, the sofa needs re-covering, the damp spot on the ceiling needs . . . something. And I am instantly, *vividly*, struck with the image of the next family who will live here. They'll gut the bathroom, first. Then they'll take our cheap MFI kitchen units and toss them in a skip somewhere. I don't know how they lived like this, they'll say.

But why don't we do all these things? Why can I only see other people doing them, this other family whose children will be too young to be anything but physically exhausting? We don't fix these things because we don't care enough anymore, that's the truth. Oh well, we say. We're at the oh-well stage. Quite liberating, really. I blame Neal. Well, why not? He blames us for everything.

'You should have bought a decent car, not an old banger that won't stop in time,' shouts Neal when he crashes our car into a tree.

'You shouldn't have let me drive your bloody stupid new car,' he shouts when he crashes it into a ditch.

We may not be keeping the decay at bay like this other family will, damn them, but we are keeping the decks clear. We each have our little jobs, and no longer argue about who does what. I, for instance, am in charge of the rubbish. It's a man's job, and I am The Man. Six inches shorter than Neal and chronically, as they say, unemployed, I am technically still The Man. I can be trusted with rubbish, and what's more I enjoy it. Rubbish day is the ultimate bowel movement. Completely cathartic. Getting to the end of a tube of toothpaste, so I can make room for a fuller, neater tube of toothpaste – this gives me pleasure. The same with cereal boxes, bulky things that they are. I've even eaten cereal I didn't like, just to throw the box away. Neal, being impatient and undisciplined, opens new boxes before finishing old ones, so I have to do this end of box thing a lot.

Mondays might mean back to work and school for most of mankind, but for me, these days, Monday is rubbish day and therefore synonymous with domestic enema. Shopping day is the opposite and fraught with ambiguity, because the joy of replenished stores is offset by the sheer amount of stuff that now must be consumed and the remainder discarded. It seems like a lot of work. It *is* a lot of work. No, I much prefer rubbish day to shopping day. You know where you are on rubbish day.

Although lately it's been troubling me that every time I get ready for rubbish day, it seems like rubbish day was just yesterday. I watch myself lift the lids, toss in the black bags, the actions that punctuate my life, but it does not seem like enough time has passed to fill those bags.

Every day, a rubbish day.

Things like this worry me. A few thousand more rubbish days and I'll be dead.

I'm forty-five. An ancient poor sod, accuses Neal, as if this is my fault, and if I'd only been more careful I'd still be sixteen like him. I sit here at home, alone in the afternoon, and I swear I can hear myself aging. It's like a heart beating, only more insidious. Ba boom, decay decay, ba boom, decay decay. It's a cruel thing to happen to anyone. Cruel, cruel, cruel.

If Neal understood how cruel it is being forty-five, would he be nicer to me? Would he tell me how he's doing, for instance? Or one day, ask me how I spend my days?

I spend my days watching telly of course. Daytime television is vastly under-rated. Anyone who has missed *Kilroy*, for instance, cannot possibly understand the meaning of life.

'Christ Dad, *Kilroy*. That's for losers,' says Neal, but what he doesn't know is I could easily go on one of these shows. I could be a *Kilroy* star. My Son Hates Me and My Wife Hates Sex, they could title that day's show. I'd tell them how my sixteen year old accuses me of stinginess, seconds after I hand him a twenty. How my wife is so jaded with sex she doesn't even bother faking it anymore. 'Is that you finished, dear? That's nice.'

My wife thinks sex is vastly over-rated.

But then she thinks *Kilroy* is over-rated too.

She has no idea what it's like to have too much time on your hands. All I do, most days, even during *Kilroy*, is bloody think about my life. I hate it.

But tonight something happens. Neal goes out to some party. At three o'clock, I wake and notice my wife isn't in bed. She's in the kitchen, drinking tea.

'What's wrong?' I ask.

'He's not back yet.'

'Well, it's only 3.'

'Still, I couldn't sleep.'

I think she's over reacting and go back to bed. She's always been a worrier, right from the start.

I don't remember much from those early days, but there are one or two scenes that have stayed. One winter night, I woke because I was cold, found Neal cuddled up between us. They'd pulled the quilt off me. I could hear the wind screaming, and rain hell-hammering on the roof. Maybe somewhere close, trees were falling onto sleeping children, fires licking living room curtains, flood waters capsizing boats carrying fragile cargo. *And there we all were.*

'Are you asleep? How can you sleep?' asks my wife.

'I'm tired. That's how.'

'You. Are. Tired.' She has this way of spacing words.

'Uh. Yeah.'

'Neal is out there, god knows where. And you. Are. Tired.'

Another winter's day memory. There'd been a power cut since the afternoon. I lit the fire and candles. Our living room was shabby, but that night it looked cosy. We played Monopoly – one of those games you imagine you'll play a lot when you have children, but somehow don't. There was a lot of laughter and I thought they were so lovely, my family. They had a purity in the fire light; a luminous quality I hadn't properly noticed. My wife looked mysterious and I wanted to get to know her again.

I sleep till she wakes me again at 7.

'He's still not back,' she says.

'No? Maybe he stayed the night there.'

'I phoned the house.' Her voice is tight, like she has considered crying but decided it would distract from hard core worrying. 'They said he left at two.'

'At two? Two o'clock in the morning?'

'Yes, that's what I just said. He left. Alone. At two.'

'So where is he?'

'God! If I knew that, do I you think I'd be calling around asking people?' Adding hostility to her tone. My wife is skilled at expressing layers of complex emotions. 'I knew something bad had happened,' she says. 'I woke up and I just knew it.'

'Right,' I say, hearing the implication loud and clear. I get out of bed, get dressed. She hovers. Paces. I put the kettle on, try to join my wife in her fretting universe. Neal! Neal! It feels like inside we are calling his name over and over. Summoning him in some parental psychic way.

'He could be in a car crash somewhere,' she says, in case I need an image to get in the right mood. 'He probably took a ride with a bunch of boys who'd been drinking. Or doing drugs.'

I remember Neal's birth. He was red and angry looking. He gave me suspicious looks, that first morning – furtive glances when his mum wasn't looking. *He knew*. He knew I was waiting for the real father to come and take over this awesome responsibility. I was waiting for Neal to go away so I could *relax*. But by lunch came the cataclysmic love for him. It was like being punched hard, unexpectedly.

At ten o'clock, I say: 'Well, I'd better go shopping. We're out of bread and coffee.'

'What? Shopping?'

'Yeah.'

'Our son is missing. Really missing this time. Neal has never not called and told us where he was.'

'Yes he has.' I'm starting to feel angry with him now. Stupid thoughtless boy!

'I'm calling the police.'

'The police?'

'You don't get it do you?'

I obviously don't. The police come and they get it. They ask for a photograph.

I remember walking Neal across the road one day. When we began to cross, a car zoomed past so close we were pushed back by the wind it created. If I'd started across one second sooner, we would both have been hit. Did I really look for traffic, or did I just think I looked? It was terrifying to think that not only was Neal too young to look after himself, I was not up to the job either.

The police ask about his friends, his habits. They write in their notebooks. They mention sniffer dogs in ominous tones. I sit at the table, listening, stupefied. Neal, in trouble? In real trouble? Perhaps unconscious in some waste ground? Or bleeding in an alley? And within one millisecond, my mind produces vivid images from all those news programs. Kidnappings and murders, fatal car accidents, and worse – the faces of missing smiling teenagers. I am not an anxious person, yet I have stored these pictures.

Neal is dead. The chant starts up.

I will look back on this morning and remember every detail. This is how the horror began, I will think. What did I say to him last? Did I shout at him to pick up the towels, take his plate off the table? I find I have no memories at all of the last sight of my son. Nor of our last words. I look at the photo the policeman is holding. Not a flattering photo – his goofy grin, two pimples on his forehead. My stomach feels as if something primal is leaping out of it. My wife, of course, has sensibly arrived at this terrifying place hours earlier, and is now impervious to my sudden plunge into the abyss. Her face is white, thin lipped, business-like. She has moved on to coping. I can't help thinking: She's quite unattractive, really.

'You married the wrong person, Dad. Your whole life has been a waste of time,' said Neal once when I told him he'd wasted his study leave playing on his Playstation. For someone who usually mumbled, he always found clarity when he had something hurtful to say. 'Mum's the wrong person,' he said. 'It's true.'

I've always found, and even more so lately, now I'm doing all this thinking, that truth is vastly over rated. And besides, is it true? How can you pick the right person to marry, if you haven't a bloody clue who that person will be in 25 years time? Really, all you're choosing is someone who is lovable for the immediate future. Neal, genius son of mine, there is no right or wrong person for an entire life. A spouse that has grown less right, is like noticing your favourite clothes no longer fit, but what the hell – they're soft, they don't require much.

That's not to say I didn't notice that boring old Margaret Petrie next door, who used to be in love with me about a century ago, has recently become a dish. Margaret Petrie! Who would have guessed. *If only* s taste like coffee after tooth-paste. The only solution is just don't do it. Brush your teeth after your coffee, not before.

Secretly I think Neal knows that I look at the shape of my life and suffer minute but regular panic attacks. He knows I wonder if it's too late to change my life. That's why he doesn't respect me. I'm afraid of Neal.

I'm also afraid for Neal. He would be so easy to hurt. He is alone somewhere, and probably dead. I am imagining my son's funeral, if they ever find his poor body, if I ever have to identify it in some sterile morgue, when the phone rings and it's him.

'Cannapick mupatthbus?' he grunts.

'Course, Neal,' I say, hearing myriad doors shut on dread-ful fates.

My wife does not cry with relief, but I can see she has begun to breathe normally again. I imagine her perspiration smelling less of fear now, less sour. I wonder why I still feel terrible. Perhaps I am not just slow to worry, I am slow at the other end too. Perhaps the weight of Neal's possible demise has a momentum of its own. I go to fetch Neal home.

All the way in the car, I keep saying to myself I'll talk to Neal. Really talk. There are so many things I want to tell him. How I've thought and thought about my life but still can't come to any conclusions, except that *Kilroy* is under-rated. I want to tell him about rubbish days coming quicker and quicker. I also want to tell him this: It used to be easy to love him and now it is not. Some days I don't even like him. But still. If the world ceased to contain him, I don't know if I could breathe.

He is slouching up the pavement. I stop the car and he slouches in, along with a cloud of lager and cheap deodorant. 'So,' I say. 'You OK?'

'Aye. Fine. Head's a wee bittie sore.'

No eye contact, but I note less mumble and feel brave. Maybe this'll be it. We'll talk.

'We were worried, Neal. You should have called.'

'Aye. Sorry. Meant tae.'

'You know what Neal? I've been wanting for some time now to have a talk with you.'

Neal yawns.

'Remember how we used to talk Neal? We could go back to that, do you want to go back to that? Then we could tell each other things. I've got loads of things to tell you. I've been . . . thinking about things.'

Silence. I think he's waiting for me to begin telling him things, and my heart lifts.

But as I open my mouth the most god almighty snore fills the car. You'd think he was an old geezer the way he snores. Jesus, my son could snore for Scotland.

All the way home he snores like that and I notice his shoes are caked in mud, which is now all over the car floor I just hoovered yesterday. This irritates me in the old way. Neal is not dead. In fact, Neal is back to being irritating, and the world is shrinking back to its normal size. I've missed half of *Kilroy*, I don't have a job, I'm getting old, my wife hates sex, my son hates me. I love my life.

ELISABETH

□ □ □ □ □

THE BEAR

Elisabeth's having a great time with her new friend. It's August and they're in the Sierras, in the log cabin settlement where her grandparents spend every summer and her family spends two weeks. Dusty and pine scented and hot, but cooler than the valley they have escaped from.

Six old cabins are scattered along the creek. Watermelons and bottles of wine and beer lie half-submerged in the shallows. Inside the cabins is one dark room with a camping gas stove and table and plastic covered chairs. The tables are covered with red checked plastic. The screen door creaks. Built onto the front of each cabin is a sleeping porch. Screened windows and a few camp beds. Scattered everywhere, is all the paraphernalia each family finds essential for its comfort. Food, transistor radios, coolers full of cokes, swim suits and suntan lotion, comic books, and always, always the packs of playing cards. Everyone plays cards. Before swimming, after lunch, after dinner, someone is always shuffling cards. Expertly, without looking. Cascading pyramids.

In fact, that is what Elisabeth and her new friend are doing right now. They are playing Old Maid again, even though the old maid card is carefully marked by a crease, and no surprise is possible, only trickery and cheating. At six years old, they are old hands at this already. They are sitting on the porch steps, getting in everyone's way, dedicated to beating each other. Losing can make you giggle, embarrassed, but winning can make you hoot and dance and persuade the loser to play again. And the chance to finish the day as a winner is so attractive, the game just goes on and on. She has just lost, and her friend is full of gloating hospitality.

'Come on Lisabeth, another game, come on, you might win.'

'Nah . . . I have to be getting home. My mommy said it's bedtime soon.'

'Aw come on, it's not that late. I'll ask my mom for some Kool Aid. Cherry.'

'With ice?'

'Sure. You wait here.'

Creak and bang goes the screen door as her friend runs inside. Voices and dish-washing sounds drift out to her. It is getting cooler at last and she hugs her bare legs and rests her chin on her scabby knees. Her skin feels warm, still holding the sun it caught that day. Gradually she becomes aware of the crickets and frogs that have been noise-making for a while now. She wonders why she never sees them in the day. An owl flaps out of a nearby tree and small creatures dart for cover. Elisabeth imagines the chipmunks and red squirrels she feeds by day, running home now to Beatrix Potter under-tree homes, complete with matching china and rocking chairs and miniature fireplaces. Cosy, yet alien. Nothing in her suburban childhood has approached those illustrations, but she inhabits them, nevertheless, when she feels like it.

Elisabeth is not soft. She knows the chipmunks and squirrels do not really wear clothes and sleep in proper beds, but now and then pretending they do, especially when a huge owl is about to dig into them with his sharp claws, is nicer. Pretending makes her feel calmer.

Creak . . . bang! the door again.

'Here you are, Lisbeth.'

'Hey, this is orange.'

'Sorry. All out of cherry.'

'You said.'

'Well, I thought we did. Drink some. It's nice. Lots of ice.'

'Well, alright.'

They slurp.

'Want to play now?'

'OK.'

'You deal this time.'

'No, you won, your deal.'

'That's OK, you deal.'

A heavy crashing through distant bushes.

'What was that?' says Elisabeth.

'Oh, probably a bear.'

'Oh, shut up, there's no bears here.'

'Are so. Ask my daddy. Grizzlies.'

'Really?'

'Yeah. Don't worry, they won't eat you. Not unless they're really, really hungry. And my daddy says in the summer they get plenty to eat.'

'My daddy never told me about no grizzler bears. My grandad never told me neither.'

'Grizzlies. Well, maybe they don't know everything. That's a bear, sure as anything. Now, are we going to play or not?'

'Alright. My deal then.'

'Nah, my deal. I won, remember?'

'Yeah, but you said . . .' Whine.

A woman's voice calling Elisabeth.

'Who was that?'

'My mommy. I got to go.'

'Oh no.' Genuine despair.

'I know. I don't want to go. I'm not even tired. We never get hardly any time to play.'

'Hey. I got an idea. You wait here.'

She dashes indoors while Elisabeth listens to her mother coming closer, calling her. It is a pleasant low voice and for a moment, Elisabeth imagines her as a mother rabbit, with cape and bonnet and basket over her arm, calling to herself, a little bunny, to come home and have blackberries and cream. Then her friend is back.

'Listen. My mom says you can stay the night.'

'What?' Such a possibility has never occurred to her. She has never slept anywhere but with her two brothers and parents.

'You can sleep over. We have a spare bag. Tell your mom.'

She does, feeling grown up and excited and her mother kisses her goodnight and says she'll see her in the morning and walks back.

Elisabeth and her friend hug each other and giggle and forget to play cards. Now the game is sleeping over. They have only known each other for three days, since their vacations began, but it feels like years. They eat together and swim together and have been generally inseparable. Their parents have encouraged this. It is one less child to look after. And after all, what harm could come to them here? They are given freedom to run wild and they do.

They pull two camp beds to one corner of the porch and crawl into their bags. Elisabeth normally sleeps between her brothers, and it feels a little odd to be sleeping right next to the screened wall. They whisper a while, make plans for the next day – build a fort and a dam – and then they are quiet. Slowly it occurs to Elisabeth that her friend is now sound asleep. She checks this theory by a careful prodding and soft whispering of her name. No response. Well, then. She is wide awake and she is as good as alone. Not what she thought would happen. The grownups are inside, softly laughing, pulling beer taps and dealing out cards. 'Gin!' is triumphantly called out from time to time. She lays still and feigns sleep, when the mother peeks in.

Night noises are loud. She feels exposed, with no one between her and the screen, and for a moment she thinks of the bear. She tries to imagine the bear with dungarees on, fishing off an old bridge, while momma bear boils a kettle on an antique range. Then she drops off to sleep. When she wakes later, it is pitch black. Everyone has gone to bed. She notices her sleeping bag smells unfamiliar and thinks longingly of her own bag. Of her brothers' night time farts and snores. She is taut, listening out for . . . for anything threatening. A mosquito obliges, and she hides under her covers till it goes.

Still, she listens. And it isn't too long before she hears the bear's blundering footsteps. This bear does not wear dungarees. She stops breathing. She wills him to find the garbage cans and fill his belly on old fried chicken and hot dog buns. There is a silence in which she almost relaxes, then quite close by, a heavy scurrying noise. Maybe a racoon, who has also heard the bear.

She sits up. Her eyes grow used to the dark, and she looks around at the familiar porch. Her clothes on the chair, the deck of cards on the table, her friend softly snoring beside her. But they are not comforting. They are all strange. They're wrong. She wants her own bag and her mother and father. She wants her stinky brothers. She feels her life is in danger without them.

She creeps out of bed, pulls her clothes on quickly, and with a minimum of creak, opens the screen door and runs back to her own cabin. It is only twenty yards away, but it's dark and she has forgotten to put her shoes on. And the bear is watching her. And the owl is watching the helpless chipmunk. And the whole world is holding its breath till she is safe in the nest of her family.

ROOM

This is how it feels: At first, Elisabeth is all inside herself, feeling shy and strange about the new space around her. Alien walls and corners and ceiling and floor and a long window broken into eight panes. And the view – never before have they lived in a house with an upstairs! She sits on the window seat frozen inside herself and looks out at leafless maple branches and slated rooftops and smoking chimneys. Her breaths are short and shallow.

The boxes are eventually unpacked and the space shrinks. Alien walls sport familiar pictures and corners are obscured by her old dresser and bed. Things she has never thought of as hers – the Mother Hubbard rug, the Alice in Wonderland poster – are now called her things and deposited in her new room. Elisabeth creeps downstairs to see which, of their things, her two brothers have now been told belong in the boys' room. Checks to make sure she agrees.

Normality, up till now, has been the constant companionship of her brothers. They fight, of course, and are competitive – a game of cards can bring out the cheat in them all – but basically they get along fine. They've always shared a room in the many small apartments and houses, in the many small towns their parents have dragged them through. They've been the only familiar faces in an ever changing landscape of new schools and playgrounds. Home is each other. And now home will also be this particular house. Their parents have promised there will be no more moves. Unimaginable, but that is the plan.

It is very odd and lonely to be away from her brothers, in her own room, though she's begged for it, rejoiced in it. Regretting getting something she very much wanted is a new sensation, and a terrible one, but her pride stops her from voicing this change of heart. She is not a sissy. It's her choice, the bedroom in the attic. She'd wanted the novelty of an upstairs bedroom. Like a tree house. But there are also three cavernous storage closets on her landing, with ancient glass doorknobs and skeleton keys. These doors she keeps locked. Not even during hide and seek is she tempted to go into them.

At night, the room feels even stranger. She lays wide awake and hears noises and thinks about the dark closets. Wounded convicts crouch there, bleeding. Also bats and rats and crazy old women who like to kidnap children and, and . . . do AWFUL things to them. Sometimes she wraps her quilt around herself and leaps out of bed, to avoid the cold hand that will reach out from under her bed and grab her ankle. Quickly, quietly past the closet doors, then down the stairs into her brothers' room and onto the scratchy old sofa. Huddles there, relief in giant gulps of air, at her narrow escape. Then listens for and then to the comforting sounds of her brothers' night time farting and snoring. Off to sleep in seconds.

The new room is friendlier by day, and there comes the occasional afternoon when Elisabeth wants to be there, alone, rather than downstairs with her old cohorts. Solitude begins to slowly grow on her. Tentatively, she draws out bits of herself to hold in the private sunlight of her own space. She likes to read books about magic and time, and from these she develops a system. The walls and ceilings are knotty pine. If she touches certain knots at certain times in the right sequence, magic will happen. She wears thick pullovers when doing this in case she is suddenly transported to a much colder climate and time. This ritual takes a great deal of courage, since she fully believes in it, but the risk excites her. Repeatedly nonfunctioning knots do nothing to diminish her faith. She has simply not found the right sequence.

Having her own room allows her to unfold her secret self out into space. But it takes a long time to fill. Months go by. Then one day, home from school, she races upstairs, flings off her shoes and school bag, and there she is – she is everywhere. In the corners, on the walls, the ceiling, she fills the entire space. And only she fills it. Her brothers are downstairs and whether or not they fill their space is of no concern. She is just herself now, in her own room, and everywhere she looks is evidence. Her books, her curtains, her cobwebs and dust, her knotty pine walls. She takes deep delicious breaths of her own air.

ENOUGH ROOM

Everything is just fine – as fine as can make no memories, just a smooth line of days – until Robbie's dad gets drunk at the office Christmas party and drives through the concrete barriers down by the bay.

'Jim's in the hospital,' is the first phrase that's bandied about the neighbourhood – phones ringing and back doors opening, then whispering awed voices, drunk on the drama – a tiny edge of enjoyment to the announcement, there's no denying. They live in the suburbs and not a lot happens there. Then two days later the words are: 'He's dead. They couldn't do anything. He never knew, thank god, never regained consciousness.'

Elisabeth curls up on the sofa in front of the Christmas tree and listens to her mother explain it to her little brother. Billy is so stupid. And then, when at last he understands, he doesn't seem to care. Sam, her older brother understands what a big deal it is. She can tell because he keeps having to leave the room quickly, and isn't looking at anyone properly. But Billy? Dumb as anything.

'Well, when's he going to get another daddy? And what are they going to do with the body? Can they keep it? Can I see it?'

Elisabeth knows her friend's father is really dead, and that it is a tragedy, but the information still hovers outside of her. How can anyone be dead and it be Christmas at the same time? There is just not enough room for both. She sits very still and looks at the Christmas tree, but it is no good. There is a lack of shine coming from the tree. It is just a green tree with cheap junk hanging on it.

So what, she thinks. Mr Jensen is laying somewhere with his face under a white sheet and he will never again tweak her pony tail or drive her to the swimming pool or laugh his funny hiccupy laugh. Elisabeth suddenly realizes no one else in the entire world can make that exact sound. The air will be forever absent of Mr Jensen's laugh. In her life, not many sad things have happened. People get sick and sometimes they almost die. No one she knows has ever actually gone and completely died. Mr Jensen's death feels a little unfair, like getting away with bad manners. Like playing hide and seek and never letting yourself be found. Leaving town instead.

Elisabeth has a practical mind and she finds herself worrying about the Jensen's Christmas tree, which won't know there's been a change in the universe. It will still have presents under it to a man who will never open them up. It will still be expecting the Christmas orgy of torn wrapping paper tomorrow morning and a day of indulgence and a family drawn in on itself.

It stands there right now, in ignorance. Like going all dressed up to a party that isn't a party, but just some people hanging around in their jeans. And then not even realizing. Staying in your party dress.

She'll have to go and see him about it. Her friend, Robbie. She gets up and leaves the house. She doesn't tell her mother she's going because she hardly ever does when she's just going next door to play. She's eight years old after all, and allowed to do lots of things her little brother isn't.

She takes the well-worn shortcut between their houses, through the gap in the hedge, over the fence, and up by the greenhouse to the kitchen door. It's the same old path, but it's different because now it leads to a house forever altered. The house where Mr Jensen used to live. Elisabeth can feel the path, the sky, the whole world rearranging itself slightly to accommodate the absence of Mr Jensen. Even the atoms of the air she breathes seem to be juggling themselves, making her heart beat fast.

'Hey Robbie!' she calls into the quiet house.

'Hey yourself!' he calls back, from the living room.

She walks down the hall to see him and the Christmas tree. His mother is on the phone, sounding tired and bored. She doesn't seem near crying at all, unlike Elisabeth's own mother whose voice is all over the place. In Mrs Jensen's hand is a whisky tumbler half-full and the ashtray is full of half-smoked cigarettes. Whisky and smoke and her weary telephone voice completely overpower the tree. It looks like Christmas was long gone already.

'Hey, your tree lights aren't on,' Elisabeth says, dropping on the floor beside him. He's looking at a comic.

He looks up, then shrugs. Like so what.

'I'm sorry about your dad dying.'

'Yeah.'

'What are you going to do?'

'About what?'

'About Christmas tomorrow.'

'What do you mean?'

'Well, are you still going to have Christmas and everything?'

'Course. Why wouldn't we?'

'Don't know. Just thought, with your dad dying and everything.'

Robbie flinches, then smiles brightly.

'I got to open one of my presents already, you wanna see it?'

They go into his bedroom, messy as usual, and he shows her his new remote control car. They play for a while, crashing the car into his dresser and bed and walls, and she forgets all about Christmas and Mr Jensen. Then Robbie turns on the light and she looks out the window to the dusk.

'I better go home now.'

'OK.'

He continues controlling the car and doesn't look up as she leaves.

'See ya.'

'Yeah.'

'Goodbye, Mrs Jensen,' she calls out as she walks back through the living room.

Mrs Jensen is lying on the sofa, snoring slightly. Her glass has spilled and the rug is stinking. Elisabeth starts to tiptoe out of the room. Then she turns back and crawls under their tree to switch on the lights. The tree springs into life. It is lovely after all, full of secrets. Elisabeth stands and looks at it. She can look at Christmas trees for hours. Now she knows something the tree doesn't know. She knows its beauty will not be appreciated. She tries to admire it extra hard to make up for this deprivation, then backs softly out of the room.

Outside it's nearly dark. She runs down by the greenhouse, hops over the fence and creeps through the hedge. All is still different, but already, her second time on the path, it is becoming less strange. Less wrong. Suddenly her mother's voice calls out her name. She is standing on the back doorstep, a dark figure against the glow of the kitchen, cupping her mouth and calling.

'Elisabeth! Elisabeth!' Stretching out the syllables, like she always does.

Everything in her lurches towards her mother. It seems unbearable that her mother wants to see her and cannot. Still, she freezes a moment in the dark hedge. It is Christmas Eve. Mr Jensen is dead. Her mother sings her name like a love song.

HOME ON THE ROAD

Elisabeth is sitting in the back seat of the car. An old green Hillman. First she looks out the front window. But the low morning sun flickering dark bright dark bright through the straight rows of olive trees hurts her eyes so she turns to look out the side window. Concentrates on looking down each long row of trees. Focus, blur, focus again; a row a second. In and out. It's hard work but it keeps her busy and it's not as confusing.

Then her eye catches the first sign. It's a wooden placard of a fat Italian-looking woman, her black hair in a red spotted kerchief and a frying pan in her hand. She forgets the rows of trees and sits forward to look for the next sign. Her mouth has started to water in anticipation, and there it is – a thin wooden man in a blue striped apron, his hands on his hips and a string of sausages dangling around his neck. Yes. Then comes the sign with the single word Bill. That's her little brother's name too. He's beside her, picking his nose. Then comes the sign saying: And Kathy's. And finally: 2 miles.

'Anyone awake yet? No? Then we'll forget Bill and Kathy's and keep going.'

'Dad! Stop the car! Pancakes!' they both cry. She and her little brother.

And on the horizon, across from twin silver silos and surrounded by flat fields, is the familiar building – log cabin style, with old covered wagon wheels fencing in ice plants.

'Nah, let's go on to the Red Top. It's only thirty miles.'

'Daddy! Stop the car! Put on your blinker, put on your brakes!'

'What? Did you hear something?' No slowing down.

'Jack, cut it out. They'll be hysterical. She'll throw up.' The old weariness in her voice, so familiar it's the background noise they tune out.

'Mom's right. I'm going to be sick, I'm going to vomit all over the seat, stop the car!'

'You always go too far Jack.'

But he does pull over, stop the car and they all pile out. Sprinklers spray them lightly as they run up the path to the restaurant. Bacon and coffee beckon, but it's the pancakes they come for. Short stacks, tall stacks, five inches across, melting whipped butter and hot maple syrup. Sometimes the blueberry syrup. Every Easter and every Thanksgiving – the long drive up the valley to the grandparents. The early morning start, her father carrying her limp pretending to be asleep body out to the car, the ritual stop for breakfast at Bill and Kathy's. She eats it all, as usual forgetting how she will feel in an hour or so, when the morning freshness is gone and heat will move through the car in languorous waves and her car sickness will become the main reality. Yawning and swallowing and hanging out the window like a dog, all in vain. The pancakes will not stay with her. But she's nine years old and doesn't worry about the future. She enjoys her pancakes, in fact she finishes the ones her brother leaves on his plate too.

Back in the car, heading north again, the second phase of the journey begins. This is the first time her big brother Sam has refused to come. It feels strange without him. Four is not the right size for a family, is it? But already Elisabeth is enjoying the extra seat space. The valley is almost five hundred miles long, fifty miles wide, and flat as Kathy's pancakes. The straight road disappears in a shimmering heat haze. She squints her eyes and tries to see mirages. By eleven o'clock, she is bare-chested and the window is all the way down and the dust of the farms coats her inside and out. Up ahead at her grandma's, it will all be washed away in the shower in the cool basement, but for now it feels permanent.

And as they approach the heart of the trip, she realizes she is waiting. There is always a fight – she cannot remember a trip up the valley that did not include bickering, then loud bitter hurled words, then hours of adult silence. It's the core of the day. She is listening for its beginning. She doesn't have to wait long.

'Milly! Pull back, you can't pass that truck now.'

'Dammit Jack, you made me jump – don't do that! You almost caused an accident.'

'Stopped one, you mean.'

'Do you want to drive?'

'No. I'm going to sleep.'

'Because if you can't trust me to drive, maybe you'd better.'

'I'm not listening. You just want to argue.'

'I just want to be treated with some respect. When you're driving, do I continually criticize you?'

'Shut up Mildred. Just keep your stupid mouth shut.'

'No I will not. When you drive, I trust you, I relax.'

'I'm tired Milly.'

'I don't know why. It wasn't you that stayed up till twelve packing.'

'I loaded the car.'

'Which took five minutes.'

'Jesus look out, that Chevy's coming way too fast. Get back in the slow lane.'

This part of the fight goes on so long and is so familiar, she and her brother ignore it and play a languid game of naming the fifty states. They have fifteen more to go. She tries to visualize the pink geography poster in her classroom. What were the names of all those little states up in the right hand corner? Eventually, she dozes off, her mouth hanging open and her head jerking on the sticky seat back. When she wakes an hour later, she instantly wants to throw up.

'Stop the car I'm going to be sick.'

'Jack, stop the car.'

'I can't right now. There's no shoulder. She'll have to wait.'

'Can you wait a minute honey? Put your head out the window. Breathe deeply.'

She can't even open her mouth to answer, the sick is so imminent. She swallows convulsively.

'Jack, you'd better pull over.'

'Dammit!' as he swerves onto a rough embankment and someone honks at him.

She gets out of the car and leans over and retches. Nothing. Oh no, not again, she thinks.

'Has she been sick yet?'

'No. Come on honey, hurry up and throw up. Your dad wants to get going.'

'I can't.'

'What do you mean you can't. Just do it.'

She leans over and tries to trick her stomach into emptying by making the noises of vomiting. But the fresh air and lack of motion have had the instant effect of making her feel well.

'I can't Mom. I don't want to anymore. I feel fine.'

'Are you sure? We aren't stopping again for a while.'

'I'm sure.'

She gets back in the car and ten minutes later she wants to be sick again.

'Mom.'

'What?' Hot and cranky.

'Nothing.'

'She's not going to throw up, is she?' Her dad.

'Do you feel sick again, Elisabeth?'

'Yes. No. A little.'

'Tell her we'll stop at the next rest area. Ten miles.'

'Can you wait ten minutes honey?'

She nods and closes her eyes.

'Don't close your eyes. Look straight ahead and – oh my god. Stop the car Jack.'

'Goddamnit.' More cars honking. 'Did she do it in the bag?'

'No.'

'Why not – oh Christ, it's everywhere.'

'I didn't have a bag. Sorry.'

'Why didn't she have a bag Milly?'

'Because she didn't, that's why. Just shut up and give her your handkerchief.'

'Jesus, why am I always the only one to have a handkerchief in this family?'

'Because you're so goddamned perfect of course.'

Aside from the car overheating twice in the afternoon, and her being caught cheating on naming the states by looking at all the out of state license plates, the rest of the trip passes uneventfully. Her parents have used all the usual words with each other and have subsided into dulled silence. The space her big brother Sam took up is completely filled now with other things, and it seems far longer than six months when he last rode with them up the valley. Billy is asleep, splayed across the seat beside her.

By seven o'clock, it is not a lot cooler but it is not as glaringly bright and everyone feels more human. Home seems very far away and the world has shrunk up to the size of her mother and father and brother. The drive which always seems interminable now has an end in sight. On the horizon are the minuscule buildings of her grandparent's town.

'At last,' says her father. 'I can't wait.'

'Me neither,' she says. But all of a sudden she feels, as she always feels near the end of a journey, that she can wait. The wheels of the car are bumping over the heat cracks in the highway and the air rushing in her window smells of exhaust fumes and over-ripe fruit. Her nausea is conquered and her body is relaxed and alert. Like a sailor finding his sea legs after the first day out. Behind her is home, school, friends; ahead lies Easter and grandma and grandpa and Mass and inedible marshmallow eggs in shredded cellophane. But right now, just riding along in the car at dusk and not thinking of anything, just letting her thoughts float in the haze, this would feel fine forever. She decides to try not arriving anywhere, for the rest of her life.

SAM THE MAN

It's good he's getting married. It must be, thinks Elisabeth. It wouldn't be nice for him not to be married after a while, especially if all his friends were married and having babies and all that stuff. He won't share the bedroom with Billy anymore, but he'll still be her big brother. She understands the necessity of it. But when she looks at him, and their daily life together, his forthcoming marriage seems unreal. She can't imagine the world with a married Sam.

Just the same, she wonders how long it will take for all traces of him to disappear from the house and re-emerge, different somehow, she is sure, in his new house. After much thought, she bets his spare hiking boots reside in the back porch for years to come. And his old posters. They're not going anywhere.

After he goes to work, she creeps into the boys' room, vulture-like, wondering if she should take a memento of him now, while he's too distracted to notice. A tape, or a few books. The wedding is in two short days. It's now or never to grab a souvenir of a vanishing life. In the end, she opens his top drawer and takes a big white T-shirt, the one he some-times lets her wear anyway. It smells of fabric conditioner and old sweet sweat.

Later, she watches him eating dinner. She would make a good spy. She's looking for signs of her on him. In the way he chews, asks for the salt, in his laughter. But no, he is still only her big brother Sam, whom their mother adores.

'More meat, Sam?' her mother asks, before glancing at anyone else's plate. 'Here's a nice lean bit, honey.'

'That's great Mom, thanks,' in his own voice.

Eleven years old, Elisabeth is suspicious of all change. She doesn't like it. These days, she watches all the husbands she knows, young ones especially. Sam is not like them in the least. They are a different breed. Their shoulders sit differently; their eyes, never restless. They notice her only briefly. They might clown around and act like boys, but they're men. She sees them as men, and Sam is only a boy. In fact, he's not that different from Billy.

Lucinda, his fiancée, is already a grown up lady. She holds her cigarette so lazily and her laughter is hard and sometimes tired. When she talks to her, Elisabeth feels about five years old. It's obvious Lucinda has been a grown up for a long time. Why can't she see that Sam is a son, a brother, a boy? He's not a man-husband. But maybe she does know, and that's how she has tricked him into this charade. It's hard to say about Lucinda. She's not one of them. She's from an old family, grew up in the house her grandparents built. She already has an apartment full of heirloom furniture, old china plates, antique laces. An apartment in one of those large old Victorian houses, sitting behind old holly hedges, in the Berkeley hills. Where she comes from is all over her. The style of her clothes, her perfume, her hair, even her pale smooth skin. Most of all, there's her walk – graceful, sexy, and her dark eyes. She is casual and glancing with these parts of her body. Who she is, is well hidden.

Sam and herself, and everyone else she knows around here – well, they hide themselves from newcomers too. But with shyness, not poise. And never with each other. She can't imagine Lucinda losing her poise. She cannot see her in a wrinkled robe, shoving dirty clothes into a washing machine. Or putting the bait, still live, on the hook for Sam, as Elisabeth does. She has never seen Lucinda blush, and with her pale cheeks it should've been so easy. She is a foreigner. Sam is marrying a Martian. What will their children be like?

Elisabeth is a junior bridesmaid, and for this honour she has made the concession to wear a dress. It's been especially made for her, to match the other bridesmaids, other glam Martians from the Berkeley Hills. Pale yellow with hideous lacy hems.

Finally the wedding morning is here. She has imagined it so much, she keeps having de ja vu feelings, which she's heard about on television. She is floating, unreal, the arrogant child psychic. But the weather is vicious. Slap in the face January. Horizontal hailstones. She runs out to the car and trips and falls on a very sharp stone. This is unusual. She never falls. It really hurts and inside her jeans her knees feel warm and wet.

Inside, she inspects her knees, carefully rolling up her baggy jeans. By noon, just before the wedding, she is wearing two huge band-aids. Her dress stops short of them and she looks an idiot. As if the dress didn't do a nice enough job of that on its own. Billy looks pretty silly in his get up, but she looks like a freak.

Sam is nervous too – the first sign of change. He has not eaten the bacon and eggs, despite their mom's coaxing. She's almost in tears, as if his rejection of the last breakfast she might ever serve him actually means something. Like he doesn't love her or something. Watching her mom makes her stomach hurt and takes her mind off Sam, so she concentrates on what it must feel like to be her. She sighs with the strain.

'Hey, midget face, don't you think a few more band-aids on your face would help even things up? Here, let me help you,' as Sam trips her up, then catches her as usual. Feeling his strong arms and hearing his old teasing tone, she laughs hysterically, relieved. He is just Sam, and she instantly feels real again.

'What about the open gate, then – waiting for the cows to

come home?'

He looks down to check his fly, while she whoops with laughter and runs upstairs before he can grab her again. It's fun, but also a little disturbing. What if she had cried instead of laughed, which is entirely possible today. He wouldn't have known what to say. He probably would've blushed and teased her, and that wouldn't have been as nice as tricking him into checking his fly.

The last half hour before they leave for the church, time becomes a syrupy substance. She has a million thoughts, checks the clock and only five minutes have gone. She has to keep reminding herself to do things like go to the bathroom, and to breathe. The impossible is about to happen. The boy Sam, her big brother, is about to disappear. Berkeley is not a million miles away, but if you're a kid and your mom hates driving and your dad works away, it may as well be. She's pretty sure her mother understands what's happening, but she's not so sure about Sam. He is almost treating it just like any other day. For a moment, she feels the superiority of her sex. Boys and men. Don't they get it?

Then time accelerates and she is walking down the aisle, randomly scattering rose petals, knowing she looks stupid and trying not to care. Proud. Then she watches as the bride approaches her waiting brother. He is starting to look a little scared now, she thinks. Something in his paleness and strained smile. His eyes don't smile. She wills him to look at her, but he doesn't. It's not too late, she tells him silently. Just turn around and leave. Or say: No I do not. We can go fishing down the river, Billy too. Mom will make us some sandwiches and maybe we'll even catch a few and sell them at the cafe.

But his eyes are still fixed on Lucinda, who is even more gorgeous and womanly and alien than before. Wait a minute. Sam's smile is changing. He's really smiling now, from his eyes to his toes. He is a smile.

She closes her eyes, then quickly opens them again. It

takes seconds. First he is a boy, recognizably her brother. Then, turning to return down the aisle, Lucinda by his side, both of them beaming sheepishly, embarrassed to show so much happiness – now, he is Sam the man. She is stunned and stares and stares and tries to understand what is different. He is a husband now and he looks it. A spell has been cast and everyone has witnessed it. Her mother is crying without restraint. So are her grandparents and aunts and uncles. Everyone is forgetting all Sam's annoying habits and deciding to be wholeheartedly nostalgic for his childhood.

He is stumbling a little in his excitement, but mannishly, and looking about – he's looking for her! He catches her eye and her heart stops. Sam! she mouths, wistfully, then sends him a smile. Generosity she didn't know was in her. A smile to the new Sam, though he is deserting her and their old life forever. Without a second's regret. Just like a man.

SUMMER

Hot, hot. The soles of Elisabeth's sneakers stick to the sidewalk. A sky, fluorescent blue, and the sun a painful white ball. While waiting for the light to change, she picks at the peeling skin of her nose. Slowly, expertly, till a big bit comes off. Satisfied, she looks at it, then flicks it away. A little sting as the raw skin is exposed; a bit of spit helps. Then the light changes, and she crosses over to where Debs is waiting.

'Well, what do you want to do today?'

'The store?'

'Nah.'

'The beach?'

'We go there every day.'

'Well, where then? I'm boiling.'

'We could go up the hill.'

'What's up there?'

'What's anywhere? At least it'll be a change.'

'Larry saw a rattler on the track last week.'

'So we won't use the track. Come on.'

Too hot to think or talk, they sing Beatles songs in snatches. Sometimes in unison, sometimes different songs at the same time. Elisabeth likes John and Debs likes Paul. At the top of the hill is a eucalyptus grove, cooler and inviting. The leaves are camphor and warm cinnamon, and bark peels back in layers like the skin on her nose. They throw themselves down on the crunchy yellow grass and eat the Butterfingers

Debs has brought. They can see the city across the bay, two bridges, some islands, and housing tracts swarming around the waterfront. But the light is too flat, and while the view is spectacular, there is no beauty to it. Everything is what it appears to be.

'Hey look – isn't that the Giambastiani's car?' She points down at the shimmering ribbon of road. A pink station wagon winds along it. 'It is! Guess that's them back from Mexico.'

'Wow. Well, well. Charlie's back in town. Charlie pie.' Taunting, long and drawn out.

'Shut up.'

'You're blushing.'

'Why would I blush? You're the one – all I have to do is mention Patrick O'Do . . .'

Debs squeals and puts a hand over her friend's mouth.

'Oh, alright, alright. Forget it.'

Too hot to fight. Even teasing takes too much energy. There is no breeze and there's a humming in the air. Bee-like, but not bees. They are used to it and not inquisitive enough to wonder about it. The insect buzz is like the eucalyptus smell – background, nothing. In the foreground are boys, music and two more weeks of vacation.

Their families don't go away in the summer. Three months of relative freedom, but no change of scene. Elisabeth's older brother Sam is married now, and her younger brother Billy has recently seemed miles younger than he used to. He seems a baby, and she's mean to him, when she can be bothered even looking at him.

Elisabeth and Debs have been bad this summer, their fourteenth. Partly because they are bored, but mostly because their parents are strict and it is fun to do things they know they shouldn't. It is more fun than being good. It makes them laugh, the best kind of laugh – deep down and giddy.

They have snuck into the grocery store back room and ridden on the conveyor belt and stolen Hershey bars. They have snuck into the Episcopalian church and read the marriage manuals in the Reverend's office and signed the visitor book 'Ho Chi Minh'. They have written on public walls and bathroom mirrors with lipstick – *fighting for peace is like fucking for chastity* – which they heard somewhere and think is incredibly profound. They have tried hitchhiking, smoking grass in a water pipe, and drinking screwdrivers. They have endlessly hassled the boy with acne at the deli counter for salami heads – the greasy lumps normally thrown out – and taken them down to the beach, gnawing on them and getting bits of fat stuck in their teeth. They've practised swear words. Debs' mother says they are bad for each other. This delights them.

Now they are singing again. There is an oak by the ridge top and they decide to climb it. Bare arms and legs swing up its branches. They are both skinny and mosquito bitten, freckled and sunburned. Debs' hair has a green sheen from all the chlorine at the pool. Greenie McLeanie, she gets called at school.

Debs is short and she is tall. In fact, they are the tallest and shortest in their class, and perhaps that is one of the reasons they get along so well. They both have the distinction of being extremely something. They are not part of the *in* group. The *in* group are all about the same size, and they have tans. At least that's how it seems to them, as they watch from the sidelines. Sometimes wistfully, sometimes scornfully. When it hurts, they make themselves feel better by calling the popular girls shallow, immature and snobby, but mostly they watch with secret and consuming envy.

But it's summer now, and they don't care about any of that. The stifling sensation of sticking out has completely faded. They live near enough to hang out without parental involvement, which is good. In two weeks they start high school and then everything will be different. A huge school. Having a locker. Changing classes every hour. New boys. New. Boys.

'But the fool on the hill, sees the sun going down and the eyes in his head see the world spinning round . . .'

They are singing together now, perched on the most dangerous branches overhanging the gulley. They feel good. They think they sound great, and the song brings Paul and John together quite happily. Below is the strip of tarmac, then the housing tract where they live, then the bay. The bay is filthy, un-swimmable, but from here it looks tropically clear and clean. Even the gulls are sparkling white.

Elisabeth breaks off a dry twig and sends it floating down.

'I'm thirsty. Let's go get a Coke.'

'Got any money?'

'No.' A cranky voice.

'Well, I don't want to go home.' Stubborn.

A snort of laughter. 'Well, I'm not going to die of thirst because you don't want to go home.'

'Go on, then.'

'We could put *High Tide Green Grass* on Sam's old record player. He didn't take it with him when he got married.' Coaxing; she is too afraid of rattlers to walk down alone. Then she breaks into 'Satisfaction', letting go of the branch to play guitar.

'I know. Let's go down to the Giambastiani's.'

'What?' Hands back on branches.

'They must be home now. They'll give us a Coke.'

'You're a genius.'

'Come on,' she begins the descent, swinging like a monkey. 'Charlie's waiting.'

'Shut up about Charlie, OK?'

'Why?'

'Because he's mine, that's why,' says Elisabeth

Explosions of laughter at her daring words, since she's never done more with Charlie than share a bus seat. He is too cute for her to even look at without flinching. They only have the nerve to go to his house because they know his little sister. Down the hill they go, not on the track, but loping down the slope, easily balancing on the loose stones and dry red soil. Now they are neither girl nor boy, just graceful young bodies, aware of nothing but the sun on their backs and the crunch of dead grass under their feet.

All summer they have felt surges of energy, followed by flatness, then saved again and again by great drenching waves of optimism. Things will change. Anything, anything at all might happen. Their legs will get shapely, their faces will tan, their figures will emerge. Boys who have never met them will be stunned into silence.

JACK AND MILDRED

□ □ □ □ □

WAIT FOR ME, JACK

'Milly, hurry up! You'll make us late again!'

'Coming! Sorry. Ready now, let's go.'

'Jiminy Cricket, Milly. That's my sweater, you know.'

'Yeah? So what? Whose shoes are you wearing?'

'Oh alright. *Come on!*'

The two sisters run down the street, with five minutes to cover three blocks to the bus stop. They don't look at all alike but there is something sisterly about them anyway. Something in their clumsy tandem run, and their laughter. They both laugh in a helpless way, as if even now – as they run – they have to surrender to a delicious, mysterious mirth. Don't ask them what's so funny, you'd never get it. They laugh because the very thought of themselves late for the bus again, and arguing about clothes again, tickles them. They are laughing at the very idea of themselves as friends, when the obvious truth is they can hardly stand each other. See? Not very funny, is it?

The fog is dense but they hardly notice. They live by the Bay, where it's foggy every morning and every evening. But the fog horn is still magical to them. The kind of sound that valley people can't help but find glamorous. Romantic, even. The fog horn makes them love their new city home even more, as if they'd moved to a foreign country, like France. Just plain better, that's all. Every damn thing is better here. Especially the men.

The bus driver teases them by closing the door just as they reach it. It is part of the ritual. He is their age and half in love with both of them. Before they reach Market Street, the sun has broken through. A hard blue sky, no clouds.

'Gonna be another scorcher,' says Milly. 'Got your new lipstick with you?'

At Third and Market, her sister gets off the bus with a quick wave, and a 'see you later alligator.' Just before Embarcadero, Milly gets off the bus too and joins the throng of office workers. This is her favourite time of the day. Here I am, she thinks, the young secretary rushing to work. Her face has shut down despite her inner joy. Part of the joy is in blending in and she is surrounded by tired, jaded faces. Workaday faces. She heads up Post and is in shadow. The skyscrapers on either side block the sun and it is cool here. Thinner crowds, and more serious. Still the seagulls, though. Like the fog horn, valley people like herself can never quite take a seagull for granted. She knows they are like pigeons here, pests, but she adores them. Adores all the different squawks they make, like confused, emotional human cries. Nope, nothing melodic about a seagull.

Entering the Smithton building, she quickly dashes into the bathroom. Combs her hair again, curls the ends of her page boy with fingers dampened in the sink. Re-applies red lipstick – inferior to her sister's, but it'll do till pay day. But it's Friday! Pay day is today ! How absolutely wonderful. And tonight, Tommy Barkman. From Oakland, if she remembers right. Tall, blue eyed, a bit big-nosed, but great mouth. Her obligatory Friday night date. Milly has been in the city for nearly two years now and has only had three Friday nights without a date. Or was his name Timmy?

Jack is drinking a cup of coffee at the corner cafe. Henry's Hideaway. He lights a Viceroy and gets a little light headed. Love that first smoke of the day! He is 24 years old. Fought in

France, or as near as. Wore the uniform, ate the food, slept with prostitutes who had no pubic hair. Came back, went to college on the GI Bill, fell in love with blonde busty Bernice, got dumped by blonde busty Bernice, drank too much and decided to hell with Bernice. All that, but Jack still looks too young to be smoking, and a middle-aged women sitting near him glares disapprovingly. Tisks, stares pointedly at the smoke. Bit like the way his mother used to make a face at him whenever he swore, even moderately. Even *Oh God*.

He blows smoke her way, as if to say: What's it to you, lady?

'Cocky kid!' she says.

It's just a Market Street greasy spoon and the clientele tend to speak their minds. And then, because he's noticed that she's not all that old and she's wearing quite a low cut sweater and now that she's blushing with anger, she actually looks kind of pretty – he smiles at her. His heartbreaker smile.

'Sorry,' he says, and puts out the cigarette. 'Just, I'm a bit nervous you see.'

'Oh! OK, I get it. Trouble?'

'Nah. Just my first day at a new job. Bit worried.'

'Ah, but you'll be great. You will! Here, let me pay for your coffee . A good luck gesture, yeah?'

That's how charming Jack can be. And how much he needs even cranky ladies he'll never meet again to like him.

Milly is sitting in front of her typewriter, clacking away a mile a minute. She is not in the typing pool with all the other girls because Milly Ann Molinelli can type 60 words a minute *correctly*, take shorthand, and has the sweetest legs in the office. Not too thin, not too short or muscular. And a way of whistling or humming softly when she works that everyone finds entrancing.

'What's that you're whistling?' her boss asked her ages ago.

'Was I whistling? Well, I don't know. Probably *Dream a Little Dream for Me*. Was it?'

'Could be. Do it again, and I'll tell you.'

Milly's desk is at reception, so everyone can benefit. Customers, potential clients, employees, bosses. Look at her, with her knees together and ankles crossed so demurely. Hair sweetly pulled back with a barrette shaped like a bow. She is a work of art, displayed proudly. Today, this Friday in August, she is humming a Glen Miller tune she's forgotten the name of. Her fingers fly over the keys in time to the song. She is so good, she can daydream while she hums and types. She wonders what to wear tonight and remembers her birthday is next month and she'll be twenty-one. For heaven's sake, what kind of age is that for a single girl? Time she was choosing someone. Mentally, she reviews Chuck and Harry, John and Larry. They're all swell guys, but nope, nope, nope and nope. Chuck is a cook in a lousy joint downtown, not good enough prospects. Too like her high school quarterback boyfriend, who begged to marry her right up till the midnight before she moved to the city. Harry is an accountant, but a little fat and both his parents are very fat. The fat gene is not a good factor when one is contemplating making babies. John is not fat, and he has a promising career as a social worker, but he's just so . . . nice, so very nice. Milly, who hardly ever swears, always finds herself wanting to swear, or say something shocking in his presence. Larry is slender, well paid and also a good mixture of corruption and goodness, but – and this is a big but – the man cannot kiss to save his life. Dear me, she's tried enough times, but given up. A man sucking her tongue like a popsicle is enough to make any girl run a mile. And tonight's guy. Tommy, or Timmy. Well, she summons his face, and it is an alright face, not too handsome or homely, just somewhere in between. He works at a high school in the Castro. They're supposed to go out to a movie. She'll give him a whirl, she supposes. Time's getting on, and maybe she is too fussy. Her sister thinks so. There is no Mister Perfect, stupid. You just find a man who doesn't drink or gamble or knock a girl around, and then you work on loving him.

Clickety clack, clickety clack. All the time she's thinking, her fingers flying and the words appearing. Clickety clickety clack. She notices, not for the first time, how when you really think about it, typing sounds a bit like a train rolling down a track. A big freight train, one of those eighty car trains, with a caboose and a man standing on the back platform waving at the kids at the crossing. And the whistle sounding all mournful and excited at the same time. And the dust rising and the clickety clacking becoming deafening when it whooshes three feet from you. Milly is cursed with a vivid imagination. It will lead her into all sorts of difficulties later, mostly to do with imagining scary things. Many sleepless nights ahead! But for now, it is a constant movie in her head, and the soundtrack too – always the soundtrack. She occupies two realities. Her imagined reality gives the world a pretty good run for its money.

Jack is being introduced to his colleagues. They are almost all a lot older. Salesmen in suits, and slicked-back hair. Not much like his pals from college. He bets they don't read Penguins or shop at Brooks Brothers or listen to real jazz. But they are all earning good money, and Jack respects them for that. He's transformed himself several times since he left his parent's house – maybe he will again. From the shy polite son of a milkman, to an army good time boy, to a frat brat, to a university graduate, and finally now – a tragic rejected lover who smokes and drinks and laughs as much as possible. When he wakes up, he looks in the mirror and reminds himself he is a resident of the richest town in Marin, quite the opposite end of Marin County from his parent's shabby house. Never mind he's staying in his pal's basement and his degree is the most useless one.

'What do you think, so far?' asks one of his new colleagues.

'Fine, fine,' says Jack, offhand. 'What time is lunch?'

This is Jack's first job since graduating, and it came from

his first interview – so he is, perhaps, lacking the gratitude, the humility expected from a young managerial trainee. It has all come so easily to him. His tour of the building continues.

'The bathrooms are down the hall to your right,' explains his boss, 'and the cafeteria is on the third floor. And here, this is your desk Jack.'

This is the best news he's had all day. The desk is right by a window, and it is a big desk, with a pencil organiser full of brand new sharp pencils, and a cut glass ashtray. There's even a file drawer. He can see being happy here now. Jack McAllister – a serious successful man, making money for the company.

'Sorry, it's so far from my office. I'm on the top floor.'

Better and better. He will be unobserved, in his own little kingdom, right here, within the perimeters of this desk. Jackland. Truth is, Jack is not crazy about having a boss at all.

'You won't mind being down here, will you?'

'Nah, not one bit,' says Jack.

'Good. Good, I thought you seemed an independent type. Just what we want. It's not glamorous here, Jack, but it's a decent company. Been here thirty two years, and not complaining yet. Now if you need anything typed, or a cup of coffee, just about anything, just ask Milly. Her desk is down there, see it? Guess she's away now, but you'll see her later. Nice gal.'

Milly is delivering her typed letters to the mail department downstairs. This is one of her favourite things to do. So satisfying to take a man's messy handwritten notes, transform them into black and white documents with carbon copies, and then see them on their journey. Also, Marilee is there, running the franking machine. She's from the valley too.

'What are you doing tomorrow, Marilee? Want to go shopping?

'Nah, can't. Going home.'

'Not again.'

'Yeah. Mom's saying it's an emergency.'

'She'll try and make you feel bad about moving here.'

'Yeah, well. Maybe I should feel bad, Milly. I like it here fine, but it's not really home is it? Do you think it'll ever feel like home? Tell you the truth, even when I'm having fun I don't really feel like myself here. Not as much as I do back home. Know what I mean?'

Milly nods. She knows, but since she was not that crazy about the self she was back home, the idea of going home has no appeal. She's not had a moment's homesickness, not even a second's worth. The way Milly looks at it is this – there are two kinds of lives. The kind you are born and raised to live, and the kind that you are not. Which is virtually any other life, anywhere, with anyone. Or no one. She was raised to live her life in Chico, marry a nice boy from high school, live in one of those new houses near the tracks near all her high school friends, have a few babies, and sometime later, get fat, become a volunteer at the hospital, play golf, and die. Not very terrible, not at all. You knew where you were when you were living the life you were meant to live. You could get up in the morning, and know pretty much how the day was going to go, and all the years ahead, as clear as a straight flat valley road. Instead she is living the other kind of life here in San Francisco. Not safe, not known, and no guarantee about how she will end up. A wild, crumbling, twisting cliff-top track. She can almost see the bridge she has burned. She can smell it. It has a thrilling charred smell. But is she really so very brave? Here she is, in her new life, establishing routines and rituals as fast as she can, anchoring herself much in the same way as she'd been in Chico. What if moving only alters the backdrop, and her future is already mapped out no matter where she is? What if city boys are really just valley boys, with better clothes?

Jack goes out for lunch. He's peeked at the cafeteria, and it's lousy. Old people and the smell of old grease. In fact, now he thinks of it, the whole set up is a little stuffy. The furniture, the hair styles, the job itself – selling. He knows no one here, and so far, doesn't see anyone he'd like to drink beer with. Oh sure, it's good money, but for crying out loud, what's a man like himself to do? Bury himself in a place like this for years? Not likely. He's walking swiftly, feeling lighter with every step he takes away from Smithton Electronics. Maybe he won't go back.

Chinatown, and he decides to wander up Grant Avenue. Goes into the first restaurant he finds, and orders chop suey. Has a sudden need to use chopsticks, a newly acquired skill. An extremely pale and pretty Asian waitress silently serves him, with a shy smile, and he starts to feel alright again. Nice place, great food. Now he looks around, he notices he is the only Caucasian. No wonder the food is delicious. He suddenly decides to take a girl here. To hell with blonde busty Bernice, he could do lots better than her. Stuck up girl! He can see himself impressing some other girl now, bringing her here, being recognised and greeted, showing her how to use chopsticks. Hey, even the Chinese beer is good. He orders another, then looks at his watch. Goddamn it, he's going to be late from lunch on his first day!

Milly is at her desk, having eaten the dry baloney sandwich she'd made the night before. In her head, she is singing *I've Got a Crush on You*. She has stopped thinking about the looming disaster of Marilee leaving, and the dresses, shoes, gloves and hats she wants to buy. She's back to thinking about boys. No, not boys. It's a man she wants, not a boy. She has a clear picture of what she wants to happen in the near future. Her imagination has honed this idea so often, it's like a memory, not a wish. She has a baby in her arms, a pretty pink sleeping baby, and she is in a home that she owns, with a yard and walk-in closets, and somewhere near her is a man, faceless for now. This man is mad for her. It is such a soothing image, the three of them. She wants to be a wife, with the same fervour some women dream of being famous movie stars, international airline stewardesses, or missionaries in Africa. Making some man happy will be her life's work. She relaxes into her work, filing documents in the big metal cabinet. Humming very quietly, the tune to *You Belong to Me*.

Jack re-enters his new office, a little sweaty from rushing, and a little drunk from the beer. He glances around the room, notes the young woman with her back to him, filing manila folders in the old grey cabinet. Doesn't think much, except I hope she won't report me being late. He sets to his task, which on this first day, is the unchallenging job of phoning up potential clients, and introducing himself over and over again. At first he is self conscious, but that goes after the third call, and really – who is listening anyway? Not even the young woman with the dark hair held back with the bow shaped barrette.

'Hello, I'm Jack McAllister calling from Smithton Electronics, can I please speak to . . .'

The boss comes round and slaps Jack on the back, asks him how he is coping, and great to have you on board, soldier! Then he says:

'You've met Milly Molinelli, yeah? No? Milly, come shake hands with Jack McAllister. He's fresh from College. Going to take over the East Bay sales team.'

And over comes Milly, and she says: 'Hi.'

'Hi,' says Jack.

They don't shake hands. Hardly look directly at each other. Both look, instead, at the boss.

'Milly, get Jack a coffee, will you honey?'

'Oh, I don't want a coffee. Thanks anyway.'

'I don't mind,' she says. But no smile, no proper appreciation of his charming manners, which kind of irritates him.

'OK then,' he says. If she's not going to even smile, then she can damn well make him a cup of coffee. 'Black, with sugar.'

The boss is gone when she gets back with his coffee.

'Thanks.'

'You're welcome.'

She returns to her desk, slowly, with a little wriggle in her walk he swears is for his benefit. He clocks her. Just the right size. Small hands and feet, medium tits, darling legs, big eyes, sweet mouth. Half sexy, half wholesome. Nice.

Milly is typing now, her red lips pressed with concentration. He didn't know eyebrows could be sexy. She's thinking about her date tonight. Will he be the one? Terry. No, Timmy. No, Tommy. Tonight, anything is possible. He very well might be the one, who knows? She enjoys the thought of her own nebulous future. Like having a ticket to a foreign country, an exotic place she's only seen on postcards, sent by people who scribble indecipherable messages. Tragedy? Ecstasy? Please God, not tedium. Her passport is in her purse, and she is poised for departure, her heart aching for the big unknown. And how about that new boy? Jack. Cocky, that's for sure. Maybe a little dangerous, even though he looks about twelve. She swears she could smell alcohol on him earlier. And cigarettes. And no real smile for her. Just that smug look that said: Yeah, I know. You want me.

Not likely, thinks Milly. She's never had to chase a boy, there's always been a line of them just waiting for a chance with her. But he sure has nice eyes. Blue as the August sky, and his hair is as yellow as . . . well, as yellow as the inside of the Butterfinger, sitting inside her purse right now. Gee whiz, she's hungry.

The rest of the afternoon passes, with Milly typing and Jack phoning, and suddenly it's five o'clock.

'OK?' the boss asks Jack, on his way out. 'Be back Monday?'

'Sure thing,' says Jack. 'See you Monday.'

Jack tidies his desk, puts away the phone book, lines up

the pens, closes the drawers. Milly pulls on her sweater, puts on some lipstick, squints at herself in a compact mirror.

'Bye,' she says nonchalantly to Jack, and sails past his desk.

'Bye,' he says back, and clicks his new briefcase shut carefully, as if there is something important inside. Follows her down the stairs to the street. What sun! A wall of heat and light. He catches up to her, and as he is about to pass her, says:

'Hey, want to eat Chinese tonight? Know a really good place, not far.'

Milly doesn't stop walking, just turns and half smiles, pityingly. He has balls. Have to give him that. Poor guy. Dumped last night, she bets. He sees her look, has a flash of anger, almost says: Hey, just kidding. Instead says:

'Could have a few drinks first. It's early now. We could go to North Beach. Vesuvios.'

'Oh, no thanks. I'm meeting someone.'

'A date?' he says stupidly.

'Yeah.'

'Ok, no problem. See ya.' He smiles crookedly, hinting at a wealth of untold jokes, jokes she will never hear now. His eyes boldly give her the once over, and he turns on his heels and leaves her in his wake. Damn it! If he could, he would hit himself hard. Damn, damn, damn. Nothing like starting a weekend by making a fool of yourself. Not like him to act like that. So grovelling. And why did he check her body out like that? Like a lech. She'll hate him even more now. Never again. He takes a deep breath and expels the bad feeling. He is Jack McAllister, goddamn it. No girl is going to ruin his Friday night!

Milly, meanwhile, strides along a few more seconds, oblivious to anything but the loveliness of the evening sunshine, the prospect of her date later, the compliment of that new boy asking her out. Then she glances up to see Jack about to disappear round the corner of Larkin Street, in the shadow of the old Bank of America building. Lean, neat, an easy athletic gait, arms swinging like a man undefeated. Hair glinting gold. Into the shadows he goes, and his shoulders are half gone, and his torso and legs too. A beat of a second more, and he will not be visible.

'Hey!' she shouts to him, and because he is too far to hear her, she begins to run towards him. Something inside is lurching forwards, as if the sight of him is suddenly something she cannot live without. No idea why, or what she will say to him if she catches him. But:

'Jack! Wait for me! Wait for me, Jack.'

STEPPING OUT

If asked, Jack wouldn't be able to remember the first time he kissed his wife Mildred, but he'll never forget the first time he betrayed her. After 20 years of marriage, he'd imagined what it might be like with other women dozens of times. Flirted with some of his friends' wives, danced drunk at parties with them, even kissed a few. Not a single proper dalliance, and in some moods he was proud of this fact. Face it, he told himself when tempted, Mildred was still gorgeous, lots of men looked at her when they went to parties or restaurants. Not only that, but she was a loyal, good woman. The mother of his three children, all of whom were still messily and expensively in the nest. Sex with Colette was never on the cards. It was New Year's Eve, 1976. Their group always took turns hosting the party; this year it was at Joan and Johnny Sarcotti's house in Corte Madera. Earlier in the evening, when Colette asked him what his resolutions were, he immediately said:

'Get rid of my kids.'

'Jack! He's just kidding, Colette,' said Mildred angrily. 'Don't talk like that Jack.'

'Sorry honey. Of course, I'm kidding.'

As soon as she walked away, he got his naughty look and Colette gave him a quick tight hug, and said: 'Well, better mingle a bit. See you.'

They'd known each other for years. He'd always liked

her slightly gauche way of acting. Now he watched her spill her wine, while laughing a little too loudly at Fred's joke. It was so obvious to Jack that she didn't even get the joke, just wanted to blend in. Perhaps that's what drew him. Jack was a bit of a fraud too, at these gatherings. These were the people he wanted to be with, his tribe of choice, but he was not one of them and never would be. And neither, he realised now, was Colette. They shared a queer kind of loneliness, and more. A mask.

When midnight came, he conspired to be next to her in the shadowy crowded living room. 'Happy New Year, Colette,' and he kissed her long and daringly hard. Mildred was in the kitchen somewhere, completely sober. She would be talking to Johnny's father, a doddery man who drooled and adored Mildred.

Colette was an exotic name but she was not exotic in the least. From Idaho, she once told him her parents named her in a temporary mood of glamour brought on by post natal elation, and regretted it ever since. Their names were Neil and Anna Anderson, and they always called her Linda, her middle name. But she became Colette again when she left Idaho and met her first husband, the now defunct but wealthy Gerald Goldwater. Colette was what Mildred called *fast*. Not a compliment. But Mildred did not spot what her husband spotted. She only saw the too tight, too short dress, the too high heels, the exposed cleavage. And was Colette wearing a bra tonight? Didn't look like it, nipples clearly outlined. Not right, for a woman in her late forties. Not right for any age.

Kissing Colette felt numb at first, the loose kiss of drunkenness. But when he pulled away, she grabbed his hair and pulled him in for another deep kiss. As if they were suddenly alone, not surrounded by their friends and spouses. And indeed, Jack felt unreal for a few seconds, as if he was not himself, but someone else. The very young and optimistic man he was once, several decades ago. Did a police siren begin and people hose them off, and shout: *Stop! That kind of kissing is dangerous and life threatening and terribly against the law!*

Nope. So they kissed again, parted to kiss others, then came back to each other and dove straight back into it, mouths open, tongues deeper and deeper till Jack was afraid finally.

'Mildred, honey, ready to go home?'

She turned to him and smiled beatifically. God, she was something. The only un-blurry person in the house, and she was his wife. Straight white teeth, clear green eyes, adorable legs.

'Yes, ready when you are honey.'

And that would have been that, but Colette was determined to call his bluff. And a devil in him wanted his bluff called. It took another seven days of ambiguous phone conversations, laden with innuendo, and a bad mood brought on by his wife's extravagance in I.Magnins. Damnit! Did she think money grew on trees? She was such a child in some ways. Not like the independent Colette. Colette was a woman, alright. She knew what a man wanted. And she had his number in every way possible. As he drove to her house, he was stone cold sober, telling himself with every mile this was not a mad impulse.

As soon as entered his own house again, he knew life would never be the same. Everything was different. Of course his own body felt different, and it should, given where it had been an hour ago, but why should his furniture look odd, and his children's voices seem thin somehow, and his wife's expression seem . . . well, so unsuspicious? Didn't she know him at all? Couldn't she see the imprint of Colette on him? It was glaring, goddamn it, it was blinding. Another reason to betray her. His own wife was virtually a stranger, but a stranger he was tied to, someone he had to support financially. Not to mention the life's sentence of eating, sleeping and watching television with her. God! It was only just now dawning on him, what marriage was. To literally *be* with a specific other person until you were dead. The price of fidelity was quite simply, quite *obviously*, too high.

And then, of course, all his life Jack had been dishonest regularly in small ways. Had stolen candy bars from the corner store, neglected to inform the check out girl when she undercharged him, parked illegally in the staff-only slots behind the courthouse, told fibs about being sick when he was just feeling lazy, cheated annually on his income tax. Doing these things diminished his resentment; evened things up. This thing with Colette was not like that at first, it was too big. But as with the stolen candy bars, when he didn't get caught, he became accustomed to not paying and kept stealing. A bit more each time. After a while, it didn't even feel like stealing. And anyway, didn't everyone do it? It was human nature to want to get away with things. He was not a bad man, just a man trying to find a way to make his existence bearable without hurting anyone. It felt like getting drunk for the first time; discovering that intoxication made nonsense of his worries, and realising that while a bit naughty, it was also something that pretty much everyone else already knew about. Like opening a door to a room he hadn't really believed was accessible, and finding no need for even a key. It was unlocked and inside, a big crowd of partying people. *Hey, Jack! Where the hell you been?* Probably faithful spouses were just spouses without choices. Anyone in their right mind would be an adulterer, if the right temptation came knocking on their door. Within a month, he convinced himself he was actually a kind of saint. That Colette was doing his marriage a huge favour. That, given his wife's extravagance and his sinless marital track record, he was entitled to Colette.

Mildred didn't know about the New Year's Eve kiss, but she knew about Colette. Of course she knew. She knew her own husband, didn't she? He was in love, it was as clear as day. It began with the phone calls. His animated voice, the giggling. Jack was not a giggler, not unless she was tickling him. But all this would not have given the game away, if he hadn't lied so badly.

'Who was that?' she asked.

'Peter.'

With those two syllables, Mildred felt herself slip into a fearful place.

'Peter? What did he want?'

'Oh nothing. Just the time of the meeting tomorrow. You know Peter, so forgetful.'

Then he walked away, and a minute later she heard him whistling in the garage.

That traitorous whistle! That traitorous giggle that Peter would never have elicited. And if it wasn't Peter, why lie about it?

While her husband learned new ways to deceive, so did she. Furtively, she went through his pockets, letters, the credit card bill. She did not confront him, though at first she almost did. She rehearsed it many times, those early days.

Jack. I know, she'd say calmly.

Know what?

Don't play the fool with me. I know about . . . her.

She'd retain her dignity, her righteousness. She'd wear her Chanel red lipstick, her best skirt, her new pale pink blouse with the ivory buttons. She'd shave her legs, to tell her husband she knew he was unfaithful. Gird herself with the only real weapon she had – her looks. But something stopped her, and it took a whole week to realise what. She was overhearing him on the phone again, when he thought she was in the shower. (She'd left the water on, part of her new devious system.) The tone of his voice, liquid with sex, pouring into the ear of the invisible recipient. She stood just out of sight, and was more frightened than she'd ever been in her life. Indeed, this felt like a battle for her very life. For her children's lives too. Just imagining them the children of divorce was enough to make her weep. If she confronted him, he might leave. The end of the world.

Her own father had disappeared before she was old enough to have stored a mental snapshot of him, and no photos were ever offered to her. Dad was a faceless young man and Mildred spent her early years wondering what was wrong with her pretty mom, that she had lost her husband while all the other moms had managed to hang on to theirs. Even the really horrible ones were at least there. So careless of her mom! She remembers envying everyone who had a daddy married to their mommy. Having just a mommy at home was like wearing a huge red sign saying COOTIES, every single day. And she'd never missed having a father for any other reason, not until she watched Jack with their children. His masculine rough-housing, his tickling, comforting, teasing presence was like a belated reminder of what she'd been deprived of. Fathers and mothers were as different as pineapples and basketballs, and children needed both.

So she surreptitiously watched her husband, to not lose him. She often watched him watching something else. Television. The newspaper. Sometimes she caught him just staring out the window, but it wasn't like him to look at the view. She made a careful note of his decreased appetite, but made no comment on his half-eaten dinners. (She was losing weight too.) She noted the extra time he took in the bathroom, and the way he'd begun to grow his hair a bit longer. Did daily Canadian Air Force exercises. He appeared home with shopping bags full of new shirts and boxer shorts, and she bit her tongue when she wanted to remind him she usually bought his clothes.

Who was it? Really, it shouldn't matter, but it still preyed on her. Sometimes she felt quite nauseous with jealousy. It made her stomach clench and her brain stop. She forgot to buy milk, forgot to meet the school bus, forgot to flip over the pancakes when the bubbles stopped filling in. Who was it? She didn't have many close women friends those days

– her husband, she'd hoped, was her best friend – but this was the point at which she began to look at them differently. Was Helen really just wanting to come for a cup of coffee, or was that a suspiciously happy smile she gave Jack when he walked into the kitchen? And newly divorced Karen, with her sexy walk and nice clothes. Divorced women were dangerous, everyone knew that. Everything changed when one of their couple friends broke up. The husbands found excuses to pop over to the newly man-less woman, and the women drew back, making excuses not to meet for coffee in the mall. The newly divorced men were never single for long, and soon disappeared into the social vortex of their new women. They didn't count, somehow. Aside from evoking jealousy from the husbands, and a kind of maternal, half-scolding affection from the wives.

'Honey, I'll be away next Friday night, alright? We don't have anything on, do we?'

'What do you mean, away?'

'Oh, some silly staff training session down in Palo Alto. I really don't want to go, but it's compulsory. Team training garbage, but no choice.'

'Can I come? Just for the evening?'

'Fraid not, sweetie. Wish you could. No spouses allowed.'

'But we've never had a night apart.'

'Haven't we? We must have had. I'll miss you like crazy.' He smiled at her, and gave her a hug. Quite a nice long hug, but now it didn't mean a thing. Worse, it felt insulting.

A patronising hug. He felt sorry for her. She was a fool, an undesired woman, and he felt sorry for her. She wanted to kill him.

'No, we've not spent any nights apart,' she said into his shoulder. If you don't count the times I was in the hospital having babies, she thought. Oh, hard times, those were. God, desperate days. She could feel tears welling up. Damnit! Here they were, pouring down. She felt incontinent with self pity.

'Mildred honey, what's the matter? It's only for a night. I'll phone you and kiss you goodnight, OK?'

He looked so adorable, so sincere. Maybe she was wrong. Wouldn't it just spoil things to tell him her worries?

'OK honey. I'm being silly. Sorry.'

'Anyway, you'll be busy with the kids.'

'True,' she said, sniffing.

'Go get yourself a tissue. Come on, my Milly. Want to go out to a movie?'

'Sure,' she said, brightening. He hadn't called her my Milly in a while. She couldn't remember how long. When had she become Mildred, not Milly? And why?

'Or we could just stay in and watch a movie on television. Have a quiet evening.'

'I guess it might be easier. The kids.'

And the evening petered out, un-memorably. Except it was the night his first proper fling was spelled out in the air for her to read and re-read, and each time hurt. She was on a boat with a dead engine, and the rip tide was pulling her further and further away from land. She felt seasick.

Three months later, and Mildred couldn't remember a time when she was not aware of the affair. More time had passed, in a sense, than in the previous three years. She now lived with this invisible third party always present. For Jack, it was the same, so each – separately and secretly – had more in common than they had ever had before. They were each living a double life – Jack, with Colette, and Mildred with the idea of her husband's affair.

But all affairs have their life span, their own plot line, and finally came the climatic night. Mildred had been sensing an increasing urgency, coupled with an increased carelessness. Did Jack want her to find out? It seemed like it, with his openly flirtatious phone conversations, his coldness in bed, his transparent excuses for everything from a late night home to yet another overnight meeting in Palo Alto. It was a Saturday night, early July. A night that still had some of the heat of the day, and flies were buzzing in circles in the kitchen. No one noticed them usually but tonight Jack ran around with a fly swat, cussing and slapping. He tried to mend the screen door, but it still wouldn't close all the way. The phone rang. Mildred was standing right next to it, but before she could answer it, he ran inside and grabbed it from her, covered the mouthpiece and (forgetting to pretend) hissed to his wife:

'Do you mind? This is private.'

She was so stunned, she forgot to pretend too.

'What do you mean? Who do you need to be private with?'

'Work! It's Bob from work. All very confidential, he gets pissed off if he thinks anyone's listening. You don't mind, do you?'

'It's not a work day. It's Saturday night,' she answered limply.

She left the room, and two minutes later he went out too, saying offhandedly:

'I'll be back later honey, don't wait up.'

Impossible to be forty-five years old and feel this way, but here he was, driving like a teenager, heart pounding, head bursting, to his lover's house. She'd given him an ultimatum.

Leave Mildred.

Leave her and live with me.

Do you love me? You said you loved me. Come to me now. Or never see me again.

All he could think was he may never again in his life have such great sex, and he could easily die of this deprivation. He knew this sounded melodramatic, shallow, selfish, but he couldn't help it. If he said no to Colette, he would be saying no to life. He wanted her more than he'd ever wanted anyone, and all rational thought was foreign babble. With her, he'd been a better lover. Imagine if he'd never slept with Colette! He'd never had discovered how amazing it felt to do *this* to a woman, and have *that* done to him. And he used to scoff at D.H. Lawrence, think nothing was really that horny.

People didn't really act like animals, not in his experience. It was all pretty hot, especially in the honeymoon period, but even then there'd been no torn clothes, no begging for it in coarse vocabulary, and certainly no oral sex.

Colette called it love. He didn't have a word for it. Sleeping with Colette was like being stunned by a gunshot. Violent, thought-stopping, cutting to the bone every time.

He slammed the brakes on in her driveway, hurtled to her door, which was locked. Knocked loudly, indifferent to the neighbours. At first he thought the house was empty and he was too late. He stood there and called her name, with a world of wretchedness in his voice.

Six thirty in the morning, and Mildred heard the car. His decisive footsteps told her everything she needed to know, and without thinking she pulled on a coat – his rain coat, because she was too upset to see what she was wearing – and slipped out the back door, onto the deck. Huddled in the dawn, behind the barbecue, shivering.

She heard him walk in, switch lights on, use the bathroom. Then through the closed door, she heard his voice call her name. She heard her name in his voice, and it was like an executioner's voice, cajoling the prisoner to place his head in the noose. Indifferent. Impatient, even. Her bare feet were wet from the dew, and all she had on under the raincoat was her nightie. It was a midsummer morning, not a cloud in the sky. It was going to be hot later, hot enough for a swim, she thought. A mourning dove in the lemon tree sang those elegiac notes, high for one count, then low for four counts. LA la-la-la-la. LA la-la-la-la.

'Mildred? Mildred!'

She shivered. Held her breath. Inside the house was her life, her old life. There it waited, and she would not go in to say goodbye to it. She would not. More footsteps, more doors opening and closing. He'd wake the kids if he wasn't careful. Then she'd have to breathe again. Finally he called in a tone she recognised from way back. From those days by the Bay. Her dress with the yellow roses, and his Old Spice cologne. It was as if layers had been stripped off him during the catastrophic night and dawn, and here he was again at last. A skinny, shy kid who hated to be alone.

'Milly? Hon?'

LA la-la-la-la.

WINE TASTING

Jack is a sixty-five year old man in a pink shirt and khaki shorts, pedalling his way up the valley road to Sonoma. It's August – hot, and he's taking it easy. He's thinking about all the nice drinks of wine he's going to have at the wineries, and this keeps him going. He has a silly looking pink fishing hat on. He knows it's not flattering, but he's reached that liberated age that doesn't care. His self-consciousness fled quite a few years ago, in fact, and he is finally able to wear his favourite colour. Pink makes him feel good.

Cars pass around him patiently and curiously. He is eye-catching. Some teenage girls in a Mustang whistle and hoot at him. He smiles and waves to them. He knows they are laughing at him, but this doesn't bother him in the least, since he is also laughing at himself. What a funny sight he is and what a boring serious young man he's been. He has instant access to his own past – can be young again for a minute, and feel the anxiety and pressure. He thinks wistfully about his own young body, but prefers his current state of mind. I am free, he thinks. I am out of all that other stuff.

'Oh dear, out of cat food again,' his wife Mildred is saying at this very moment. She's eating her ham sandwich and the cat has jumped on her lap.
'Sorry Tom. I'll get some milk.'
She struggles trying to open the new gallon container, and

drops it on the floor. She cannot reach down soon enough to prevent the huge spillage. Her bare feet are wet with milk.

'Goddamnit,' in her soft valley voice, the vowels stretched out.

One of her eyebrows is permanently cocked in consternation, and so, not being exceptional, means nothing. The accident, too, is familiar. In fact, it causes no change in any of her bodily metabolisms. Mess and chaos is the norm. The phone rings. It rings twelve times by the time she finds it.

'Hello? Oh hello Don. Just fine. Uh huh. Sure, I'll just go and get him.'

'Jack. Jack. *Jack!*' The last time she calls, it is in anger. An eavesdropper would say it has poison in it, but no, it has nothing in it, the last shout always sounds like that. It is just the form of things.

'Don? I think he must be in the garage. I'll hang up and go and find him and have him call you back, OK? Oh Don, no trouble at all. Oh Don, I'm not, don't be silly.'

He is flirting with her. At 63, Mildred is still pretty. Men have always wanted to take care of her. She loves Don's attention, but has never known how to respond to overt flattery, which is partially why she married Jack. She is blushing as she makes her way to the garage. The dog nearly trips her up, then she has to stop to say hello to the neighbourhood children over the fence. Ten minutes later she finds herself at the garage door. She pauses, puzzled, peering into the shadows, then goes over to the washing machine and empties the clothes out and into the drier. Then she goes back to the house. It's boiling hot and she reaches the kitchen with relief.

'Tom, you bad cat.' Tom is lazily finishing her ham sandwich. She nearly slips in the milk, trying to hit him – an impossible task. Even the furniture seems to know Mildred is unthreatening. The phone rings, only ten times this time.

'Hello? Oh Elisabeth. It's you! No. No he's not, he's in the garage, I think. Oops, he's not there either. I went out to check, forgot to look, but now I remember, he's not there.' A girlish giggle. 'He left this morning on his bike for Sonoma. Oh I know, it is awfully hot. But he's got his hat on. Yup. I'll tell him. Bye now.'

She hangs up, sits down, and surveys the milky kitchen floor from four feet. She visualizes the trip to the broom closet for the mop. But Tom is licking the milk from the floor with a steady fastidiousness, so maybe the mop won't be needed. The only other sounds in the house are the flies buzzing and her sighing. Turning her head, she sees her box of stationery. She takes out a card and begins a letter to her sister.

> Dear Doris,
> Boy, is it hot! Jack's riding his bike up the valley. He wants to go wine tasting. You know Jack.

Jack is drinking some Beaujolais as she writes. He is sitting in a eucalyptus grove at a mossy old picnic table and before him are two bottles, a plastic wine glass and his pink hat. He has already done the requisite sipping and made the appropriate cultured noises. Hm . . . a little dry but a nice bounce. Now the facade has dropped and he is getting down to serious business. His face is sunburned and feels hot even in the shade, and his eyes are bright blue.

But this is not quite enough. Jack is a social creature and likes to share his pleasures. He wanders over to a small group of university students who are eating sourdough and jack cheese, and offers them all a drink. They hesitate, then one of the girls says 'Why not?' and holds out her thermos cup. An hour and a few more bottles later, the students leave, tipsily arguing about who should drive Ted's dad's Oldsmobile.

It is 4:00 by now, the nicest time of an August day. Still blue and shining, but a lovely aromatic cooling down. To the sun-sensitive skin on Jack's face, arms and legs, the slight breeze is a sensual caress. He is on the grass, his back against the grey trunk of a eucalyptus. He knows he is drunk and he loves feeling this way. He used to get drunk and not know it, and then feel slightly nervous about not being in perfect control. Now he is a completely happy man. He has goofy smile. But the pink hat, now fallen on the ground reminds him his bike is somewhere near, and home is far.

The phone rings just as Mildred has finally reached the broom closet. It takes fourteen rings for her to answer it.

'Hello? Oh Jack! You're where? Oh good, you made it. You're what? Drunk? That's nice dear. Oh. Well, sure. I'll be there in 45 minutes. Sure, I know where it is.'

With one last look at the kitchen floor, she goes out to the garage again and gets into their Peugeot and starts off down the road. At the first stop light, she sees the grocery store and almost pulls in to do the shopping, then remembers.

Jack is remembering Mildred's young self. He has never told her – of course not! – what a bluffer he is. Didn't she ever realize what a beauty, what a catch she'd been, and what a chancer he'd been? It is his secret. He married the home-coming queen and she married a fraud. He's had to treat her rather cavalierly so she wouldn't wise up and leave him. Thoughts like these are a certain stage of drunkenness he knows well – this momentary clear perception of everything. But goddamnit, she is still beautiful and she is his and she is coming right this very minute to fetch him back home. Then, as suddenly as a rain cloud in front of the sun – what if she has an accident? What if she dies before him? She can't. She cannot. He stumbles to the vineyard rose garden and picks six yellow roses.

'What are these for?' she asks when he presents them in the parking lot.

'For you, silly Milly.'

'Oh Jack, how sweet, you never give me flowers.'

'Let's go. I'm starving. What's for dinner?'

He rolls down the window and starts feeling sober. A nice

tiredness is in his bones. He'd like to tell her he loves her, but he can't.

At a stop sign he says 'What's that?' pointing to her chest. She looks down and he tickles her under her chin. Their laughter is that of children.

FIRST

Getting old – no, let's be honest here – being old definitely changed your attitude to your also old spouse. Jack felt this thought struggling to be expressed and he laboured to lug it out of the morass of his thoughts (all about little nothings, needless to say). All of a sudden, Mildred was someone about to leave after an extended visit, and he was concerned about her comforts and way too well mannered to mention any of her irritating habits and tantrums of the previous sixty years. After all, what would be the point? She'd be gone soon, or he would. In ten years – same world, same house, different people. He could bear anything for a short time.

Anyway, most of those irritating habits had recently become endearing, and proof that she was still marginally whom she had always been. A fussbudget and worrier and sulker and his wife. Oddly, this sanguine attitude of his did not seem to be shared by Mildred. In fact, she took advantage of his new placidity and attacked him with gusto whenever the urge took her, which was several times a day. As if she'd saved up bundles of grudges over the years and now with great abandon, pulled her arrows of complaints and let them fly to find their home in his wrinkled old skin. This puzzled him, but with his new detachment, he simply viewed her as a disgruntled soon to depart guest who was no longer bothering to pretend she liked the accommodation.

She acted as if his refusal to rise to her bait provoked her

99

further, but in fact she was having far too much fun loading her bow to care. She could say and do what she liked. At last. Finding the kitchen sink blocked brought her joy now, and the excuse to shout at Jack.

'The sink's blocked, Jack.'

'Is it, honey?'

'I never pour coffee grounds down it, you know I never do. You don't, do you?' Hardly able to suppress her cackle, for she'd seen him do it that morning, and for most of the mornings of their marriage he'd got off with it.

'Yes honey, it was me,' sighing and putting down his newspaper with a befuddled little boy grin. 'You'd better spank me very hard dear.'

Avoiding his eyes so she wouldn't give away her amusement, she continued in her shrew voice.

'Not till you sort out the sink, you lazy bastard. Why can't you pour them down the toilet, or throw them in the garbage, but no, that's too much like work, you want your coffee so you just pour them down the sink and to hell with doing the dishes later, which you never do anyway.'

Exhilarated, she snapped the dish cloth in his direction.

'You sit down now Milly, and I'll fix the sink and do the dishes.'

She sat down for a minute and then popped up and hovered around him while he was plunging, then washing and drying. He was so completely without punch these days and she was fascinated by unsuspected depths of sadism in herself. A very good thing he'd not been so mild mannered all along, or she might've become the total bitch. Not that it wasn't fun being a bitch now.

So near the end of their lives, both Jack and Mildred found a kind of freedom and ease with each other. To their children, he now seemed stupid and soft as an old golden retriever, and she as cranky and demanding as an old Siamese cat. They did not appear as happy as they actually were. But what their children thought no longer concerned them. As in the beginning of their marriage, they were a contained unit. Jack and Mildred, in their mid-eighties, snapped and growled and caressed and secretly watched each other. To see who would leave first.

It was Jack.

Dreaming of hot fudge sundaes and eating too much and the taste of salt water on hair and a tightness. Clutching onto Milly – it was her hair, in the bow barrette – and they were clinging together, thin again, jumping together into the estuary from the bridge and letting loose of everything, letting go of Milly long before he hit the water. Motion and rushing and nothing.

Mildred woke.

'Jack. The alarm. You have a dentist appointment at nine.'

'Jack!' in her nagging tone. 'Turn the damn alarm off.'

'Jack! Oh god, Jack. You'd better not be. Wake up!'

She sat up in bed, realizing the truth, frozen. Then:

'How dare you! Did I say you could? You get back here right now, do you understand?'

Jack had a half smile, still entering the water.

Mildred slumped, defeated. She carefully leaned over him to turn off the alarm. Then she got back under the covers with Jack. And without another thought, went back to sleep. She slept and slept and slept. Every time her mind approached consciousness, she slid back down under the safe dark cloak, where everything was as it had always been and she was asleep with her Jack who had driven her crazy all her life and could not be allowed to leave it.

Eventually cold and hunger and a painful need to urinate forced her to wake and rise and leave Jack alone in bed. She did not look at him. In fact, she had on her *You've really blown it this time, I'm not speaking to you* face and went to turn on the heating and make a cup of coffee. She moved stiffly but efficiently. It was the middle of the next night, about three thirty, and as she calculated this fact, she realized she had not eaten for thirty hours. She went to the refrigerator, got out the bacon, eggs, butter, milk and cheese and cooked an extravagant omelette, oozing with cheese and crispy bacon. She'd always had a greedy appetite. Then she dumped all the greasy plates and cutlery and frying pans into the sink for Jack to wash, because he was being such a bad sport, staying in bed and missing this midnight feast. Typical of him.

She curled up under the quilt on the sofa and drowsily watched the dark sky turn grey, then light grey. She'd almost drifted back asleep, when the phone rang.

'Hello?'

'Hi Mom. Did I wake you?'

'Elisabeth! No, you didn't wake me. Well, kind of. What do you want?'

'Dad missed his dentist appointment yesterday. I happened to see the receptionist who told me, so I made another appointment for next Monday if that's OK. Is that OK?'

'Well, I suppose so. Only . . .' she started a laugh.

'You alright Mom? I did wake you, didn't I? What's so funny?'

'Nothing. Really, everything is the absolute opposite of funny. I don't know why I . . .' and she was set off again, with a hard laugh that began in her gut and completely shut off the possibility of speech.

'Mom. Listen. Is Dad there?'

'Oh yes. He's here.'

'Can I speak to him?'

'No, I'm afraid not dear.' Sincerely sorry now.

'Why not?'

'Because . . . because he's . . . well because he's still in bed.'

Mildred took another day to learn how to say Jack was dead – she'd always had a problem with clichés. She'd avoided saying I'm pregnant three times, and just left baby name books and baby clothes out in obvious places. We're married now, had posed equal difficulties and she had just let people guess. Forming the sentence *Jack has died,* proved almost impossible, and she would've been content to simply sleep in the living room and avoid the whole issue indefinitely. But one of her sons was coming for dinner, and so she blurted out the truth on the phone, in a level voice. As if she was informing him that she was out of milk.

'Anything you want me to bring, Mom? Dessert? Beer?'

'No, Sam. Oh yes. Look. Sorry, but your father's dead, he died in his sleep. Come for dinner and we'll figure it out, OK?'

Mildred took to sleeping on Jack's side of the bed, and with her head on his pillow sometimes she took to imagining the dream that took him away so it could sneak her away too. She didn't know about the bridge or the river, but the letting go – she could rehearse that, almost. And wait for it. Then he'd catch it.

FRANK AND MARTHA

□ □ □ □ □

THE WORLD AND
THINGS IN IT

When people ask how are you, what have you been doing, I always say: Oh, you know, the same old things. Not much. I can never think of anything specific or special enough to mention. But my life is full of little happenings, and every day holds newness and minor miracles and tragedies. Really, every single day. I have never had a typical day in my life. And this day was no exception.

Emily and Tim had come for dinner, with their children, for the first time. I only knew them because some of our kids were friends of their kids and on impulse the previous week, maybe to atone for the fact I was late once again picking up my kids, I'd invited them for dinner.

They'd only been in the house ten minutes – my husband had nervously poured them wine, while the kids, less shy, all raced upstairs to embark on an evening of no parental shouting – when there was a knock on the door, and there stood Freddie, holding both of my cockerels upside down, with a sweaty and proud smile on his face.

'Here, hold one of these please while I do the other one in,' he politely asked me.

I'd asked him to come and kill the cockerels, but that had been weeks ago, and it took a few seconds for it all to make sense. The timing was not good. But then when is a good time to kill cockerels?

'Great, Freddie. Which one do you want me to hold?'

'Why don't you take the white one, this red one's so vicious, it's already scratched my arm. I just saw them roosting on the shrubs as I walked up so I thought it would be best to grab them both at the same time.'

'Yeah, you did well, Freddie, I couldn't have done it. Especially the red one. Mean old thing, he's scratched my legs twice. Through jeans.'

Freddie handed me the white cockerel. It was huge and heavy and not struggling at all, but hanging limp and perhaps frightened but more likely beyond fear, having been swooped up by something so much more powerful than himself. He was probably saying to himself this is not happening, and imagining himself out in the field in the corn, with all the hens gossiping around him. His legs were cold and horrible to touch and his stirrup claw was deadly. Like a lot of things that are lovely to look at, up close it was quite different. His red comb looked obscene and his eyes stupid and mean.

I stood there frozen, gripping this bird, with my mere acquaintance guests inside drinking wine with my shy husband and my dinner hopefully simmering nicely, and watched Freddie back away with the red bird.

'Bye bye red cockerel, it's been a nice year, but it couldn't last,' I mumbled inanely.

'Oh, I've said a prayer and thanked it for its life,' assured Freddie in his posh vowels, reminding me he was no ordinary poultry killer, but an upper class new-age poultry killer. I mentally mixed him with the dinner guests and winced. They wore matching Shetland jumpers and ironed jeans, while Freddie had a weakness for vintage waistcoats and earrings. Never mind, I couldn't be bothered worrying about all that social stuff. I looked away as Freddie made a twisting and jerking movement with his arms and the red cockerel made one last squawk. That startled my cockerel into action again. It frightened me by struggling.

'Quick, Freddie, I'm going to let go.'

Ever chivalrous, he immediately let go the red one, which did not act in the least dead, and came and took the white one from me. For no reason at all, I was reminded of the doctor's office, and the examination and the expressions on the doctor's face. Sympathy and concern barely veiling triumph. Probably his life was full of patients with nothing tangibly wrong with them and the effort of pretending he cared was exhausting and not at all why he'd wanted to become a doctor.

'Look Freddie, it's not dead.'

'Sure it is, it's flapping about a bit, that's all. I'll go find it and put it in the boot in a minute. First do this bird, though.'

'Freddie, maybe we should keep this one,' an idea which was new to me. Who was doing the talking here, I wondered, but suddenly it did not seem imperative to kill off both birds. 'Yeah, what do you think? This one hasn't flown up at anybody. Maybe he won't be a nuisance at all.'

'Are you sure? Now's the time, if you want to do it.'

'Nope. Let's not do it. White bird, your life has been spared.'

With that, Freddie released the white cockerel who flew off to join the white hen. They both perched on the gooseberry bush and fluffed their feathers and stayed perfectly still, maybe hoping that Freddie would think they were part of the gooseberry bush and leave them in peace.

I brought Freddie into the house, pulled off his camel hair coat and trilby hat and generally made a fuss of him. I insisted he have dinner with us, though not much insistence was necessary. As a newly single man, he was apt to turn up at people's houses around dinner time. No matter, he was a gracious and entertaining guest.

Some of the kids' screams sounded a little serious, so after stirring the soup, I went upstairs to see them. Briefly alone, I automatically checked it and it was still there of course, even through my jumper. A hard bit of an otherwise perfectly soft breast. A wee bit sore where he'd stuck the needle in for the biopsy, but no real pain. Results in two weeks. Well what's two weeks? Fourteen days of imagining the world without me in it. Tiny waves of self pity and occasional splashes of panic eroding my days. I told no one but Frank, my husband, who seemed not to have heard, so blank was his response. I was sort of holding my breath for two weeks and inviting near strangers for dinner to keep me on my toes.

I sorted out the squabbling, which was, needless to say, mainly from my six, and returned to serve up the dinner. It went OK, the rest of that evening. The loaf I'd put out was a little dry and the pie crust was too heavy, but the ham was fine and the wine got finished and by some miracle of social symbiosis, Freddie did not alienate my other guests and everybody pulled out fiddles and guitars and those funny round drums and stayed late enough for me to feel they weren't just being polite. I went to bed thinking well, that's another day done, and glad it was over. I'd been in bed when I first noticed the lump.

Before I even made the doctor appointment I had my husband remarried to a younger woman and my kids not recognizing old photos of me. I had the world turning on its axis without me on it. It floored me, realizing how little altered the world would be. But I kept my doom to myself, in a little cold dark room with just space for me, and I only entered it one or two dozen times a day.

The white hen went missing after that. Peculiar, because hens do not go missing, unless they've been eaten, and we've never had trouble with foxes or pine martins or dogs before. Hens do not run or fly away. They go round and round the same routes every day, no matter what. I got three new hens and the white cockerel lorded over them and continued to not act aggressive with me or the kids, maybe knowing he was on borrowed time.

The new friends invited us round for dinner and that was fine. One day the lump felt bigger, but it seemed smaller than ever the following day. I shopped, cooked, washed, cleaned, even managed to read stories to my kids, but not to myself. I was too busy chattering away to myself up there, to listen to any story.

'Heard anything yet, Martha?' asked my husband one day, so I guess he had heard me when I'd told him.

'No, not yet.'

'Well, no news is good news.' Always one for relying heavily on clichés to get words out, was my Frank. And it was not lost on me that he was looking at me slightly differently lately either. A touch fearfully, if you ask me. He probably has his own room in his head too.

Then one day Ian, our four year old, came running – I watched him run from the kitchen window and saw his face, urgent and excited – and he shouted:

'I found her, I found the white hen!'

'Alive?' I asked, doubting it.

'Yes! She's in the back shed, sitting on a hundred eggs, way below the hay bales.'

We all had to go out and see for ourselves. It was our first year of chickens, and we'd never had a hen go broody. Had given up hope. Sure enough, there she was, almost invisible in the shadows, and when we disturbed her, we could see the five tiny bantam eggs under her. We whispered good luck to her and tip toed outside. Chicks on the horizon, something to look forward to.

It was funny, her going broody the day after the red cockerel snuffed it. It was almost as if his genes were cocky and determined to survive even if he didn't. He'd always been a feisty bird – his first crow was long before we could even tell he was a cockerel, not a hen. He was just this brown ball of speckled fluff, flying up on a fence and pushing out his wee chest and making an adolescent creaky croaky sound. Letting the world know it was time to get up or time to go to bed or time to just do something for the hell of it because he said so. We all used to laugh when he strutted around, all self-important and cocky. His feathers grew in bright red and although he never got very big, the hens all knew who was boss and even I started walking around him instead of over him. The big white cockerel never competed for the brood and had become a loner.

More days passed and I began to think of them as days when I was still in the world. It began to snow, soft huge flakes that quickly quilted everything. We brought the white hen food and water. Although we never saw her eat or drink, it was always gone when we checked the next day.

TO DANCE

I used to watch people dancing and say to myself, I'm having as much fun watching them dance as they are, dancing. Later, of course, I learned that just isn't true. It's much better to dance. Thank god I learned this in time. I am such a slow learner. My whole life feels like the most agonizingly long waking up.

My wife Martha, on the other hand, is quick and has been forty-five – the most capable age – since she was eleven. She is fifty now, and shows no sign of doubt yet. Unlike myself, she has always known who she was, what she was capable of. Never treads water, does Martha. And she doesn't know what grey looks like.

Not that black remains black forever and white continually white. No. Once in a blue moon Martha can change her mind, but she puts the whole weight of her belief behind each opinion, as if the opposite view is a mere ball of fluff. She can do this with apparently no recall of what it felt like to hold the previous view. A remarkable achievement, if you ask me, and I admire her immensely.

She has been the backbone of the family. I'm much older, but I've always felt she is the grown up and I am allowed certain childlike behaviour provided I go to work every day and wash behind my ears. It's so relaxing having a grown up for a wife. I rely on her judgement totally.

'What do you think,' showing her the tie I bought.

'No. Won't do. Floral's not you.' Her tone flat, obvious truth needs no embellishment.

But how does she know I'm not floral? Why don't I know?

'Give it to Brian, he's needing a fancy tie.'

'Is he allowed to go to that do, then?'

'Definitely.'

'But it's thirty-five pounds, just for the dinner. He'll want fifty pounds for the night.' My beer money is ten pounds a week. I take a packed lunch to work.

'A boy like Brian needs to feel equal to that lot, meet them on their own turf. He'll not be stopping long here, Frank. Brian's off places. Give him the tie.'

And the minute her words hit the air, their solid truth is apparent. I am not floral. Brian deserves the do. So when she announced last week she was going for her annual scan, but it was just routine and absolutely nothing to worry about, none of us did. She drove herself and did the shopping on the way home. I remember she made chicken pie that night, not only because it was delicious and one of my favourites, but because cooking it uses a lot of saucepans and I do the washing up. I spent an hour that night cleaning the kitchen. Well, there are a lot of us. At least five, and often more, when the older ones are back from college. They bring their girl-friends and boyfriends home now. Yes, it gets a little rowdy sometimes. Martha's voice rises above it all when things need taking in hand. Only slightly harassed, she'll say: 'That'll be enough winding Annie up, now Kieran.' Or simply 'No more of that you lot, or you'll leave the table.' I generally eat silently, or read at the table, if I can get away with it. Noise disturbs me.

I never even thought to ask her how it went. Isn't that awful? But she's been going so long. The lump was removed eight years ago, and there's been no recurrence. I'd relegated that to the cupboard under the stairs, so to speak. She's had a wee limp the last six months or so, but that was from the time she tripped over the front step.

Yesterday she announced she'd been recalled for another scan. I was surprised. Again, she was not worried, convinced in her dogmatic way it was a mistake and not worth a second of worry. I took her lead as always and buried my worry under some garden work. I did all the hedge trimming and put in the potatoes.

That's something else I've come to learn late. How satisfying it is to see the earth as a fertile skin, to lift out big chunks with a fork, pull out what you don't want – nettles, docks, grass – and resettle with the seeds of what you do want. I used to be intimidated by gardening, feel I couldn't know it. Now I realize it is intensely knowable, whether or not you know the words for things. There is the dirt and there are things growing in it. Almost anything, even a five foot dock with a root like a parsnip, is ultimately destroyable, and with a little care, almost any plant can grow.

Note the word almost. I don't relish total control. I love to see the grass come up through my gravel path, the rogue poppy seed sprout by the lupins. It reminds me life thrives anywhere, despite complete indifference, sometimes despite intentional discouragement. Like that mean red cockerel, years ago, and the white hen hatching out his chicks after he was killed.

I like to think of it all happening – the slow motion changes, the secret lives of worms and beetles, blooms opening or silently dropping off – when I am not there to watch it. Moonlit nights with only the mice and owls hearing a breeze in the plum trees. I can't explain why, but I find it soothing. A garden is never still, and perhaps most alive when left alone. Imagine all those lost years before I discovered dancing and gardening.

I have a room in the loft that is just my room. No one else has their own room, but Martha understands I need it. The walls are lined with my photographs of the garden, the sky, the house. They are black and white because, frankly, I find the world in colour a little gaudy. Of course, I've taken thousands of colour snaps of the family. Martha is always saying: Quick Frank, get your camera! Holidays, birthdays, Christmas. But these are in the albums she makes, not in my room.

Today I'm pruning the roses when Martha comes out to tell me the news. It's Saturday afternoon. The doctor has phoned from the hospital. I'm surprised he didn't wait till Monday office hours, like they usually do.

'He said he thinks it's in my bones, Frank. He wants me to come to the hospital now.'

She says this in her normal voice, as if she is saying she has to go to pick up one of the children.

'What else did he say? How sure is he? Do you have to go right now?'

She literally brushes my questions away, like the silly useless noises they are, and turns away to go back in the house. I try for a minute to act as if the words haven't been said. I finish clipping one scraggly branch. An awareness that everything is changing makes me nostalgic. The minutes, hours and days before her words. But that is selfish. I go inside. She is putting some nightgowns in her overnight bag.

'What does it mean, Martha?'

'Just what I said.'

'Can they cut it out?'

'Cut out my bones?'

'Well, what then? What are they going to do?'

'Where are my slippers?'

I don't know how to answer this. She always knows where her slippers are.

'What can they do to cure it?'

'I don't know. Chemotherapy maybe. Maybe they can keep it at bay for a while. They're not in the closet. Look under the bed for me, will you?'

I kneel and look. 'Here they are. What do you mean for a while? What does that mean?'

'Heavens Frank, just what it sounds like.' She clicks her case shut and starts to leave the bedroom. Her back is straight and her step decisive as always, which is reassuring.

'Are you going right now? Hold on, Martha, I'll drive you.'

'There's no need. You stay here. I'll phone you when I know anything.'

'But wait a minute, I don't . . .'

'Dinner's in the freezer, a lamb casserole. Defrost it in the microwave before you put it in the oven.'

'That's not what I meant. But how long for? In the oven.'

'Two hours. On low. Mind you fetch Ian from the football at six.'

She starts the engine. I'm still carrying the pruning shears.

'Wait a minute Martha.'

'What is it?' She puts it in gear and begins the descent down our track.

'What's going on? Is everything alright?' I feel stupid.

'Everything's fine. I'm probably going to die sooner than I thought. I have to talk to the doctor about a few things.'

Then she's driving away, without so much as a wave.

I go back into the house, then out again to the shed to put away the shears. They hang on a hook up by the window and as I reach my hand up the bright sun shines through it. Momentarily I can see the blood veins and white bones. My skin, which normally looks quite worn and dry is almost transparent. I stop and hold it there and try to see my pulse, the blood coursing through, but of course I can't. Everything inside me is working and unaware of me looking at it. Hello hand, this is your owner, who gets a little philosophical about you sometimes. Oh, is that who you are, well I'm not really interested, says hand. You need me more than I need you.

I'm sixty years old. Of course I think about dying. Sometimes I wonder how I've managed not to croak already. A thousand million cells all specialized, it's so likely some of them will malfunction, so unlikely that I will wake up every morning and yawn as if another miracle has not just occurred. Because not only have all my organs remembered what to do yet again, but the earth, with its layer of top soil holding my potatoes, and all the layers under to the core, have all carried on spinning. At the same time, the very same time that the whole shebang is rotating around the sun. And none of it, not the blood cells or the rocky outcrops, care whether I live or die. So I have lived for some time expecting to die. I also expect Martha to look after me.

I can still hear her voice. She always knows what to do. How does she know? And does knowing help? Her calm, certain, weary voice. I leave the shed and get the washing off the line. After I've folded it and laid it in the stacks to be posted to various rooms, I go to the kitchen. I'm doing all this and I'm not thinking of anything. Breathing takes effort. I feel numb and off course. Unreal. The house is empty, they all scatter once they reach twelve. I put the kettle on, ignore the baby nettles that have sprouted in the geranium pot on the window sill.

And then I see it on the back of the chair. Martha's handbag. At first I think she must be back, be in the house somewhere. It's like a flag flying – I am here and I am taking care of things and everything is fine. Martha unattached to her bag is more earth shaking than her news. Then the phone rings. Her voice is distant and nervous or it may be the connection.

'Frank, is my bag there?'

'It's here. On the chair in the kitchen. You forgot it.'

'Thank goodness. I thought maybe I dropped it in the car park.'

'Are you alright, Martha? What's happening?'

'Nothing yet, I just got here. They've put me in a room and I've got my own phone.'

'I'm coming down.'

'Pick up Ian first.'

'What am I going to tell him?'

'Tell him to do his homework. Have you put the casserole in?'

'No. Don't worry about that. Are you sharing the room?'

'No, I'm on my own. There's three empty beds. Guess it's a

slack time of year.' A giggle. Definitely nervous. 'Come down after eight.'

'Listen, I'm coming down now, Martha. This is stupid.'

'The dinner, the kids . . .'

'Are hardly kids anymore. They can take a bus. Heat up a pizza.'

'Francis!' She hasn't called me that in years.

'What?'

'Hurry up, then.'

When I began to dance, it was such a relief. But it made me wonder what else I was wrong about.

THE TRUTH ABOUT
ROLLER COASTERS

Alton Towers is hell. Look at it! Miles and miles of relentless fun. I've come here because the kids wanted Alton Towers and I had no firm alternative ideas. I asked myself what Martha would do, but still came up with a blank. Instead of opinions, I've a nebulous blur at my core now. They sense this, but they've become mysteriously un-greedy, now they'd get pretty much whatever they wanted. I hardly ever shout, yet the three who still live at home tidy their things away more often, offer to unpack the shopping and do their own washing. Do they feel protective of me, now she's gone? I hope it's simply those long years of her nagging that have finally paid off. I try to remember to always acknowledge their good behaviour, but worry because that, too, is contrived. It feels like we are always tiptoeing around each other. What happened to the spontaneous free-for-alls, when they cursed and slammed doors and threw things? What happened to mutual disrespect? Some days our house feels ominous, in its cleanliness and calm. Maybe this would be happening even if she was still here, maybe it's just what happens as kids grow up. I have no idea. I'm certain my kids, ranging from thirteen -year old Ian to twenty-three year old Annie, know more than me, but that's not hard. I know less today than I have ever known in my entire sixty-five years.

To be honest, I was slightly dismayed they all expected family holidays to keep happening. They all expected me to . . . make it happen, like Martha did. Didn't they know, I was always the passenger, never the driver. Luckily Alton Towers loves visitors who don't want to make decisions. We are eating, sleeping, swimming and roller-coastering a la Alton. And here we are right now, an hour after our Alton Towers breakfast buffet, entering Alton Towers Theme Park itself. Hell. The sky is steel grey, the air metallic tasting. Breathing is close to drinking and my hair and face are moist. We hand over our extravagantly priced tickets to a middle-aged man with a fixed smile and dead eyes.

'Welcome! Have a nice day!'

I detect an accent. 'Thanks. By the way, where are you from?'

The kids glare. Martha used to be the nosey, chatty one. Maybe there can only be one nosey, chatty person in a marriage. The kids rush ahead. The man, after a guarded second, smiles as if a light has come on, and says: 'Bulgaria. I come from Bulgaria.'

'Really? What do you think of England? Do you like it here?' I have to ask.

He shrugs and smiles sadly again.

'It is not what I thought. It is . . . not how I thought.' He shivers.

'Colder here?'

'Yes, cold, and also not . . .'

I lean forward, eager to catch whatever glimpse he can give me of another man's reality. He looks about my age, he's had another life, and now he's taking tickets in a hellishly happy place. I imagine he lives in a small flat with mould on the window sills and carpet smelling of sour milk. He probably drinks as much as he can afford to drink, and is despised by the shop keeper, a Sun reader, in the Co-op below his flat. Then another family group approaches and he turns to them. The moment is gone, and I mouth goodbye and walk away. But not before I notice the family he's smiling at. A mum, dad, two small children. Very organized, by the size of the rucksacks. I bet she's put homemade soup in flasks, and they'll have a nourishing economical lunch later, while we sit in Pizza Hut. I bet he's remembered to bring his camera, and what's more, spare batteries. I left my camera at home. I've forgotten my camera frequently this last year. I used to want to record the world every day.

I look for my kids, and they're all waiting for me in a cluster by the entrance to the pretend high street, with jolly pastel shops and restaurants. How can I call them children? Even Ian is taller than me now. They're a gang of six sleepy-looking adults, scarcely recognisable as the children I used to know. Not that I paid that much attention to them then. Goodness, it was enough to remember their names. I don't really remember much about them growing up. That was her territory. They're huddled together, shivering slightly because it's August and no one has brought warm jackets. They don't look very excited, considering how far we've travelled to be here. But then I smile at them, an entirely false smile, and they seem released. They smile back and spring away in different directions. We arrange to meet up every hour or so, and off we go!

I've always craved solitude. But now, watching them recede into the crowd, I suddenly wish there was someone with me. A friend would be nice, but any adult would do. Someone to talk with about the hellishness of Alton Towers, or even just the weather. I remind myself of the times I used to yearn for Martha and the kids to vanish for a while. Home was often too loud, too loud *atmospherically*, for me, and I used to hide in my loft room with my books and photographs. Did she feel rejected, resentful? But I couldn't help it. And the kids, well they're nice enough but deep down I always thought of them as hers. I would have been just as happy living without children. Or even alone. So why do I feel lonely now?

I stroll, purposely pacing myself. My legs and feet need

to last for at least seven hours, and I have arthritis in my knees. I can hear distant screams of delicious fear, as well as music. The light is cruel, and I notice odd bits of rust, gum stuck to metal, litter under shrubs. Under one of the rides, I spot eyeglasses, a baseball cap, a child's sandal and several mismatching trainers. There's a general air of encroaching neglect and rot. Despite this, I have to admit, Alton Towers is a substantial and prosperous theme park. Then I turn a corner to find the original Alton Towers, an ancient derelict mansion, complete with lake and ornamental gardens. The air rushes into a brief flurry of rain, just a gentle slap really, nothing serious enough to warrant pulling my hood up, and then it is gone and the air is just damp. Compared to the old building, everyone here today is as temporary and ineffective as that flurry of rain. Whoosh! It was fun and scary and now it's over! Whoosh! This makes me want to take photographs for the first time in ages. My heart clenches in the old way, but I can't click the shutter, the camera is sitting on the kitchen sideboard. For no reason, I think of Martha's old blue scarf wrapped around her head, and her laughing and asking if she looked like a babushka. She didn't laugh like that very often. Then I remember the time the car broke down on the motorway and we bickered for hours about who hadn't renewed the AA membership. She loved nothing more than a good long bicker. I hated it, needless to say. Gave me a headache. But remembering that afternoon of her flinging swear words at me with such gusto, and the kids all whining, I find myself smiling. More, I chuckle to myself.

Then the mood passes, and I'm flat again, flat and tired. And that is why I keep forgetting the camera. I just can't care long enough anymore. Just the random flash of emotion, like a commercial break in a long-running badly made soap. Stop it, I tell myself. Find the kids. Or get some coffee. Find a newspaper. Buy a disposable camera. Talk to someone. Talk! She used to be the talker. Maybe there can only be one proper talker in a marriage. Now, there's a thought. What if she'd wanted to be the quiet, passive one, but I'd already filled that slot?

I bet you think you know yourself. Know what kind of person you are, what you like and don't like. If you are a joining-clubs person, or a bookworm, or passionate, or cold, or brave or cowardly. A lover of chicken madras, a hater of pea and sprouts. I can remember how that felt. Like I was a very old friend I mostly tolerated, sometimes loathed, and on occasion utterly loved. Nothing I did or said surprised me, and I took *who I was* for granted. I didn't need to think about things. I used to be a reader and a photographer. I spent decades telling myself I was a reader and photographer. A quiet, didn't like a fuss man. Now I need to introduce myself to myself, every day. Get to know who this new person is. Not too sure I like him much.

And as if summoned by my loneliness, I spot Annie and Ian in the queue for the new ride. Oblivion. What can please both a thirteen year old and a twenty-three year old, but plummeting to their apparent deaths? I can't help seeing it as a mockery of suicide. They gesture me over to join them, and I remind myself I have never been a roller coaster person. Ever. The world is divided into roller coaster people and non-roller coaster people, and to be honest, Martha and I always felt superior to roller coaster types. Are their lives so bland, they need to pay for intensity? Besides, it makes me nauseous.

What would Martha do now? Oh, not for me, but have fun! she'd tell them, laughing in that happy way she had. For a serious and practical woman, often exhausted, Martha was always surprisingly quick to laugh.

'OK, I'll come on the ride,' I hear myself say.

They're surprised and smile, then watch me fearfully, as if the prospect of a roller coaster-loving father is much more frightening than riding Oblivion. The ride is short, less than four minutes, and the queue is very long. While we wait, we watch the riders. Everyone is watching, not just the people in the queue, but all the people milling near the hole of dark oblivion. There's a fence around it, but you can stand very near, maybe only eight feet from the tracks, and watch. The riders sit, four abreast, and ride up a steep slope. Their faces are calm – like old hands, they smile and tell jokes, you can hear them. Then, just above where we are standing, their cart is halted at the very top of the drop. They hang there, hair and legs loose, and their faces begin to gleam with . . . what is it? They are all lovely for a moment. The fat man, the pimply girl, the skinny Chinese kid. It reminds me of religion suddenly. They are full of something similar to grace. Then the cart drops, plummets straight down. Screams are ripped out of every single one of these people – I watch group after group and no one is silent as they drop. Some have their eyes closed, some wide open, embracing every nuance. I assume they all scream because their senses have told their brain they are about to die, and previous knowledge to the contrary is over ridden. It happens too quickly. They scream as if it is the last thing they will ever do. They scream ecstatically. Dying is apparently fun. When they get off the ride, about half of them rush to the queue again. Dying is so much fun, they want to do it over and over again. What on earth am I doing here? This is not me.

The queue moves slowly, and when we get to the front, Annie and Ian want us to wait longer so we can get on the front car. They've been here several times already and know the score. Better to have fewer reminders that it's only a pretend death one is submitting to. So we finally climb into our seats, and I'm trying very hard not to think about what I am doing. There are four seats, and Ian leaves a gap between himself and me. I sit next to Annie, and try not to think of who is missing. Have you ever noticed how much more pleasing even numbers are, compared to odd numbers? Who wants to be odd? Aside from the obvious grief and inconvenience, I am quite pissed off about losing the number eight. Seven just sounds wrong. I wonder if Ian feels the same way about odd numbers. I try to catch his eye, but when he turns towards me, I look away and chat to Annie. She's always been the easiest to talk to, for me.

A young girl pulls down our safety bars and checks our belts. She's so bored looking, so tired. One of her co-workers shouts something to her in another language, and they both laugh hysterically. I wonder if they're both from Bulgaria, like the ticket man, and open my mouth to ask, but then she's gone. I wonder if she checked our belts properly – she did it so quickly, and she's probably getting less than minimum wage, and she may be hung over, or homesick, or in the early stages of pregnancy, or maybe she found out that morning that her visa is not being renewed and she'll have to go back to a rapist stepfather and a drunk mother and a job making ... babushkas. Why would she care if we die or not? My heart pounds. Stop it. Stop it now.

And up we go. OK. Annie and Ian are smiling. Well, good. I have made this experience possible for them, and they are happy. Good. Up and up we go, it feels like it is taking a very long time, and then we are at the top. This is ridiculous. We are dangled at an impossible height, and I look, then squeeze my eyes shut, then peek out.

Fucking hell. Fuck! This is insane. How has it happened? How did I allow myself to become a roller coaster person? Or a swearing person, come to that. What else am I capable of? I stop breathing. Then between one held breath and the next inhalation, we are falling fastfastfast, and my throat is hurting and a part of my brain tells me I am screaming and then it is blackblacksmokyblack, and then we are swinging up and around and then is it over and I am not dead I am alive. The same jaded girl releases our safety bars, and I've no desire to ask if she's from Bulgaria.

As I stand and walk carefully down the stairs, Annie and Ian rush off to join the queue again. Silly me. I never understood before, what they know already. Dying is not fun. Almost dying is. Perhaps we fight a death wish all our lives, craving oblivion and immortality in equal measure.

The world looks different. The sky almost looks like there might be some blue in there somewhere. Not today, I think, but it doesn't matter anymore. Popular rock songs from the sixties, triggering nostalgia, blare from concealed speakers. These songs, the soundtrack from my youth, overlap each other as I walk away from Oblivion. All around me, grim faced parents frown at their kids running full tilt towards rides that parody death. Their middle-aged faces are a familiar mixture of bewilderment and anxiety and exhaustion. I want to go up to them and whisper: It's not like that really. Get in the queue.

THE PURPOSE OF PHOTOGRAPHS

It begins like a sheer veil dropping. One morning I have to keep rubbing my eyes to try and displace this layer dimming my vision. Such a small thing, after all – I can still see, and yet it becomes so distracting I can think of nothing else. People's voices come from a distance and are irritating sounds interrupting my concentration. I walk to the shops as usual, I later cook tea and watch telly – all of it is possible, but difficult. It's as if a fine grey mist is following me everywhere, silently drizzling over the world.

The doctor says it's my age, but I'm only seventy-nine. He says to keep wearing my glasses. To rest. To not worry. I know that I'm going blind but I keep quiet and pretend to listen to the doctor. Infirmity can't be real to him, he sees too much of it. He closes my file and dismisses me from his mind.

And Betty down the road has hardly a second to spare when I imply my vision is going.

'Ach, well,' she says, in between mouthfuls of cream cakes. 'We're all getting a bit that way. Comes with the territory, eh love?' And laughs and lights up a cigarette.

Well, but what am I to do? I've always lived a healthy life and have no practice being frail. The world, my world, is disappearing before my eyes. It's been a month now, and every morning I notice a slight thickening of the veil. I've always preferred black and white photographs, but now I'm literally chilled as the colour goes. The red flock wall paper in the hall is beginning to look greyish maroon. My yellow roses are more white. My own face in the mirror looks dead. I feel like the world is receding, saying goodbye to me before I have left it. Wait, I want to say. I am still here, you will remain in full colour until I am ready to close my eyes. I used to fill my entire body, exist along my skin and shine out of my eyes. Now I feel huddled deep inside myself, at a faulty Calor gas heater, distant even from my own extremities. Shutting up like a telescope, as Alice in Wonderland did. And shivering.

I've taken to looking at my old photographs. Not the black and white landscapes I have on my walls, but the colour snaps of the family. Long ago, when I was middle-aged and had a wife who knew everything, I put up shelves for all the photo albums she made. Page after page of births, birthday parties, weddings, first days of school, last days of school, Christmases, Hogmanays, Halloweens, Easters. And all the holiday photos. You'd think we spent our lives on holiday. Mostly they're smiling like idiots in them. Smile smile smile. I took these photos, those smiles were for me, but strangely I hardly recognise these people. I've become as fascinated by their faces, as if I've only just now been notified that I am, indeed, their father. They seem so incredible, these babies, these toddlers and ten year olds, these teens. Beautiful, even, in a clumsy, vulnerable, metamorphic way. How did I not notice?

'Dad,' cries my eldest, Annie. 'Why did you take them all out of their albums? What a mess. Will you not let me put all these back for you?'

'Sorry, Annie. No. They're not going back the way they were. There's too many for me to look at! I just can't bear so many.'

'But they're my childhood, and Tom's and Bobby's and Kieran's and Ian's and Brian's. Please don't do that, stop throwing them about, they'll get lost. Mixed up. You'll ruin them.'

'Annie, don't worry. I'll let you have all the ones I don't want. Come back in a week or two.' Then she gets this face on her, I recognize it because didn't Martha used to be exactly the same? She's going to lie to me now, trick me into thinking she agrees, then later she'll come back and take away all my photographs. Protect them from me, her senile father. Listen, see if I'm right.

'Oh alright, Dad. You're right. They're only photos. Here, can I toss some around too?'

I hand her a bunch and watch her fling them into the air. Coloured blurs of smiling faces, falling over her upturned face. She laughs. She didn't expect to enjoy it. But she still doesn't understand what I'm doing. She's a granny now, but she's still too young, too in the thick of it.

After she goes home, I sit on the floor and run my fingers over all the photos. Weirdly, some feel warmer than others. When I look at them closely, I can still just make out what some of them were about. Kieran, in the jumper Martha knit him one winter. Ian with his friend, splashing in the burn one summer's day. Six sunburned faces, Costa Brava. Which are true enough to keep, which are not? As a whole, they're misleading of course. They don't record enough tears, boredom, whinging and arguing, the endless making do and shutting up. Just because I wasn't paying attention at the time, doesn't mean those times didn't happen. She just never told me to take pictures of the ordinary stuff. I wonder if there is even a single photograph of a moment I remember from those days? I want something that seems true. Something that will last.

On top of the panic I feel about losing my sight, I am panicking about being near my death. Some days it feels like I'm tiptoeing around a mine field, while my peers pop off with startled cries. I have to give myself a shake, shrug off that fear, because what is important is time, and fear is a notorious time waster. What I need now are illustrations for the stories I will tell myself. Isn't that really why I was snapping photos all those years? Martha certainly knew, that's why she was constantly yelling at me to get the camera out. Every time I clicked that shutter for her, I was making a brief stand against the rush of time. Against, well, death. What defines life better than its brevity? And what better weapon against brevity than the camera, which can preserve images forever?

There are people in the world who believe their souls can be stolen by the lens of a camera. This frightens them, but now I suddenly, fervently, want to believe my children live on in their photographs. Just an essence of who they were, however mute, to glint out for me to study. I want to get to know them now. Maybe if I finally got to know the children they were, I could have a crack at getting to know their middle-aged selves.

I remember I once took a photo of our house on a windy day, my family unseen inside. With the trees wild and leaves mid-air, the photo seemed to catch the house mid-breath, mid-heartbeat. I love that one! Another was taken at night, the cow field lit by a full moon, and the round bales look like hobbit houses. They're on the wall in this room, in expensive frames. But these family photos are in colour, I demote them by calling them snaps, and they've always been tucked inside the albums Martha made. Till now.

After a while, I notice the light is dimming and my knees tell me to get up. I creak and moan, stretch. Switch on the lamps, stoke the fire and fortify myself with a cheese toastie and cup of tea. Then carefully, I sit down with my provisions to sort the photographs again. I cannot keep them all, that is clear. I will sort them by . . . states of happiness. Not the posed frozen grins, but the spontaneous laughs, the involuntary expressions of joy. I want to experience those moments for the first time, if I cannot remember them. I want to distil the memories into an elixir, for me to sip when the world chills.

I have to squint, and I think my veil actually helps in this selection process because I am not distracted by other aspects in the pictures. I'm looking for purity and that is what should shine out. Nothing else. Not the sun on the sea, or the cake candles. I almost feel like a voyeur in someone else's quite intriguing past. I feel intoxicated, but dopey. Like those first floating hours of the flu, when the high temperature feels almost pleasant. So difficult to discard any photo! The trouble is, they all shine out. Faces can't help but reveal, even false smiles are touching in their intent to please. The wedding and holiday shots seem so desperate to prove we were close, we were not alone, any of us. But I narrow and narrow it down, and about midnight, these are what I come up with:

Annie with her eyes almost closed and mouth open wide in a huge smile, baby teeth and gaps and two permanent teeth all jostling together. I see her capacity for being uninhibited. Life has battened down those gates of freedom, but maybe the capacity is still there? She's the only one I feel comfortable with, to be honest. Dear Annie, always bringing me food.

Tom, at twelve, looking away from the camera, but with a sly smile. Self conscious, but evidently happy. Maybe the person behind the camera, me, embarrassed him? Yes, I do think he hated having his photo taken, but perhaps was pleased that I wanted to. Was he a happy adolescent? He was so quiet. Still is pretty quiet. The only one who never married. Computer analyst. Maybe he's just a slow learner like me, and taking his time settling into his life.

Bobby and Kieran, absorbed in their play, putting grains of rice into the back of tractor wagons, ploughing the living room rug. The photo catches them unawares and their obvious contentment gives me a feeling of peace. There was always something between those two, an affinity the others didn't have. I do remember, not this moment of them playing, but their self-containment. But was it really that simple? Perhaps there was an unwholesome dependency between them. Perhaps Kieran was exploiting Bobby's lack of self esteem. I can see Bobby's purple birth mark splashed across his face, while he drops the grains of rice. Maybe Kieran was simply too lazy to make friends outside the family, and Bobby was just grateful for a playmate. I wonder if they are still friends. Oh! I feel on the edge of knowing them. Millimetres from being close to them! And a million miles too. It has a flavour, this particular curiosity. Like hazelnuts, bitter and nourishing.

And here is one of Ian and Brian, in their kilts, on their way to their Christmas dance. Ian was in love that winter, I remember Annie giving me a blow by blow account. Ian never told me anything. I guess I never asked. Ian's smiling at someone out of the frame. He was Martha's favourite, she admitted once. Maybe he was picturing his mum? This might sound unbelievable, but I didn't really notice how they coped with her death. In fact, it's only recently I can even use that word in connection to her. For me, those times were lived in a cloud. Brian is smiling broadly at Ian. There's something so transparently tender and proud in Brian's face. Did he love his little brother that much? How wonderful! A son of mine that loved so openly and easily. Is any talent more remarkable? I want to ring up Brian right this instant. Ask him how to do it. Then I remember Brian died. In that little Ford Fiesta, on his way to an Oasis concert.

Ah.

And the last photograph. Martha, about 36 years old, an infant in her arms and a toddler balanced on one knee. She is looking at the toddler, mouth open, probably telling him to stop being such a wriggle worm. On either side, the four other children. Annie smiling straight at me. All of her brothers angled towards their mother, some smiling, some not. No one is not touching at least one other person. Five are touching their mother. I can't remember the occasion, but this photograph fills me with such . . . longing. There they were, and there I was. There I always was.

I take these five photographs and pin them to the wall above the fireplace. I take down the silly watercolour of Paris to do this, and shove it underneath the sofa. Who needs Paris when the veil is darkening daily? I scoop all the other photos into a cardboard box for Annie, who will no doubt be the family archivist. I make a cup of tea and consider them all. Martha, Annie, Tom, Bobby, Kieran, Brian and Ian. I mourn them. Only Martha and Brian are dead, but I mourn them all. I mourn them because there is no trace of them anywhere on earth. Except, of course, buried inside their adult selves, and it's too late. Too late. And then I have a good cry. I'm not a crier, and without the practice, it's a bit of an effort. But the veil seems to be helping. The tears feel nourishing to my skin and eyes. Ridiculous how good it feels. Then I go to bed and sleep a solid ten hours.

Today. The morning light is bright. I pick up the framed photograph of Martha that's been sitting on the chest of drawers forever. You know how it is with objects you live with, you just don't see them anymore. I wipe off the dust. I remember her telling me to take it, in hospital a few hours before our first was born. A before picture. She looks like a kid holding a Christmas present, ready to rip the paper off, see who it is. The contractions hadn't become unbearable yet, and she was flushed and unafraid. It was me, she smiled for. Though now I peer closer, it's hardly a smile. More a look of complete awareness that the show was about to begin. She knew the moment was historic. I suppose it was a gift she had, to know when to pay attention. Above all, nowhere on her face is the knowledge that she will discover a lump in her breast one night in bed. That she will one day freeze a dozen beef stews, knowing they will outlive her. I keep looking at her. And there it is. It feels like something trickling back into me. She had a certain smell. Like soap and sugar, somehow. And chicken broth. Safe, steady. Martha, aged forty-five, from age eleven.

And then I remember Annie on the phone last month, full of the cold.

'I feel eighty years old, Dad. I'm stiff, my head hurts when

I try and think. All I want to do is lie on the sofa in front of the fire and sleep.'

And the sight of Betty down the road, same age as me, giggling like a girl last week when she won a tenner on the scratch cards. She actually danced, I saw her toes. Light as a feather, flouncing out of the paper shop.

Do we contain all our ages from birth and is that what souls are? I pour the first morning whisky of my life and salute my soul, that fluctuating flame, and then I drink to all my children, at all their ages. I drink to their present selves, and wish I knew them better. I drink to their future old selves, dear people I will never meet. Doesn't seem right, they might finally need me then. It all seems rather a waste and maddening. Like arriving late at the best party ever, to realise the party actually ended an hour ago. Just took too long to put on my party clothes, I guess. I drink to Martha. Martha, Martha. I tried, my dear.

TRUE STORIES

□ □ □ □ □

LIKE SINGING

There came a time when Flora's world thinned and flattened. The children were still young then and it might have been sheer exhaustion. Objects and people lost a dimension, became doubtful proofs of reality. Her own voice entered her ears from a great distance and she judged her words and became shy. Decisions, both trivial and major, were difficult. Then the words of her brother came twisting around her, lassoing her, and she had no choice.

'Come this Sunday. Just to see. I'll fetch you at nine. You'll see.'

It wasn't what she'd expected. Not a church, but an old byre by the tracks. Two dozen people unfolding metal chairs and arranging them on the stone floor. One woman big enough to fill two chairs, a wee boy with open sores on his lips, two teenage girls with lace bras peeking through their nylon tops.

'Take a pew,' said her brother, enjoying her curiosity, his victory in her presence.

She sat next to one of the teenage girls and immediately a man her own age sat on her other side. He smiled so widely at her, she thought she'd missed something. That they'd known each other since childhood and shared an old secret joke. It was all she could do to smile politely, pretend for an instant she understood, before slipping back into herself and staring straight ahead. It was a mistake, coming here. Her brother was wrong. In front of her stood a table with a black bible on it. It was an office table, laminated wood with metal legs. The table and the chairs were all broken in some way, hard, modern, corrupted. Only the soft July light pouring in through the window and warming the stone walls felt right. Her brother strode up to the table and the room breathed in.

'Brothers and sisters, my fellow creatures in the eyes of the Lord, it is good to see you.'

'Hear, hear.'

'Praise the Lord.'

Her brother paused while he shone his smile on each face. Flora began to cringe, waiting for his eyes to light on her.

'God is exceedingly happy to see you all looking so well and I want you all to open your mouths and your hearts for a good loud song to show Him we are all happy to be alive, a miracle in itself. We love Jesus and Jesus . . .'

'Loves us!'

At that moment the sun shone brighter, shot a beam through the window. Everybody stood up and the room exploded with raucous song. Flora did not sing. She was not a singer. She stood frozen, washed over, assaulted by sound. The song went on and on. The words had no meaning, they were simply noises emanating from hysterical people. She stood, crouched deep inside herself, bombarded. Then she fainted.

When she came to, she was across the large woman's lap, her head cradled by an old man and her feet splayed across the knees of teenage girls. A sea of faces smiled down at her. She could see the sweat on their skin, the hairs on their cheeks, the fillings in their teeth. Their expressions were open, tender.

'Praise God, she's come back, the wee lamb.'

'Poor soul that she is.'

'We love you, God loves you.'

'You're not alone, not alone any more Flora,' said her brother, whom she now saw was kneeling level with her belly.

She had a second's memory of him coaxing her to school her first day. Don't be afraid, Flora, follow me. Trust me.

'God has chosen you, you are chosen, we saw the light, bless you for you are blessed. Rise now and thank the Lord.'

She was swamped, overcome. Every thought of her own was stopped and she filled up with these people and their words. She slowly rolled off the laps, still attached to their hands, and smiled a small smile. Everyone cheered like she'd come back from the dead. She felt giddy and took a little bow. Then something expanded in her and she gave a great smile, relieved to feel something at last. She was not dead. She was alive. Voices broke into song spontaneously. Something about Jesus loving you and taking you home. Later she found herself humming the tune, but could not recall the words.

She dreamt that night. She was a small child again and there was a fright of some domestic kind, a spider in the bath, a strange face at the window. Strong masculine arms held her. Don't worry, leave it to me, I'll take care of you, her father said, and she'd crept deeper into his embrace. She woke and considered it. A forgotten memory? She didn't know. It was a comfort and more. It was seductive. She longed to re-enter a dream where she had no responsibility.

Since William had left, she hadn't slept well. Something to do with being the only adult in charge of three sleeping children. She had to stay near the surface somehow, be ready. No one but she could respond to the sound of a hacking cough, a gagging noise, a nightmare, or even the sudden absence of breath. She tried to get back into the father dream, but sleep sucked her into the usual dark chaos of forgotten appointments, broken milk bottles, reaching for found money that dissolved, failing to scrub out blood stains. Dreams that left her old and sticky-eyed in the morning.

As a young child, early morning had always been confusing. Day and night were not clearly enough marked. Sometimes she would dream she had woken, got up, dressed, only to wake again and find herself still in bed, sometimes a wet bed. Or she would wake and think she was still dreaming, so shining and fantastic was the world. Once she saw her mother, pouring steaming water into the tea pot, as a scarecrow figure, almost transparent, with wisps of finely spun fibre spinning out from her and sizzling on the hot stove. She'd screamed then, to waken herself. Her mother dropped the water, scalding her own feet, and became her whole solid self again, only her dark circles and fine lifeless hair reminiscent of what Flora had seen.

It wasn't just early morning. Twilight could be a blurry time as well. She saw odd things, heard voices and music where there should have been quiet. Once she saw lush green grass shimmer through January snow, then fade. It wasn't till she was about eight she realised the things she saw were unusual, out of their proper place. Not seen by everybody. She kept quiet.

She was twenty-eight now, not in a caravan on the west, but in a council house in town. Still her world was unchanged. Fluid, unsteady, a mixture of domestic tedium and strangeness. Only the speechless communication of infant flesh to her own made real sense. She frequently buried herself in her children. Their bodies undulated with unconscious grace and brought her to grateful tears. But they would not stay, they would grow into adults. Meantime, when she was not overcome by their beauty, they exhausted her. Their dependence was strangling.

The week passed. Flora endured it. Eking out the money, trying not to snap at the children too much, cleaning bottoms, tolerating tantrums, carrying a heavy rucksack while pushing the pram against a gritty wind and trailing two squabbling children. The endless mindless tasks that can be balm or irritant, depending on each moment's mood. Moments of goodness. The taste of the baby's ear lobe, her soft babble against her own roughened skin. The sight of her son carrying his little sister, proud he had the strength. The taste of some fresh picked strawberries from a neighbour's garden. The occasional awareness that they were all alive, and more – they were healthy.

Sunday drew near and she began to dread her brother coming. Her fainting and subsequent flooding with joy had begun to seem an aberration, a frightening loss of control. The memory of herself being cradled by strangers and smiling, repulsed her. It was a trick, unreal. An illusion that caring could be impersonal. But she understood the attraction. The temptation to suspend disbelief, if only to alleviate loneliness. They were no doubt good folk, a ready made network of support. It just didn't feel true in the way that being alone did.

Friday night he phoned.

'You did right in the sight of the Lord, Flora, you gave way and He took you in his arms. You are on the way, the road to salvation lies before you. You've taken the first step. Now you're saying no? You're turning your back on all that God has to give you? Life everlasting?'

How could she answer that?

'I'm saying I've had a strange week. That's all I'm saying. And I'm not coming this Sunday. I don't feel well. Maybe another time.'

He paused, sighed in his most older-brotherly way for some seconds.

'I'll be by tomorrow, see how you're getting on. I'll bring Daisy to watch the bairns for you, give you a wee break. We could have a cup of tea at the Royal maybe.'

Sometimes when the children were all asleep and she was too tired to go to bed, she sat by the electric fire and watched the television. Her eyes stayed open but the screen was not perceived by them. She gazed at the box full of sound and images and emptied out. She did not think. Her mouth was slack, her hands limp. It was not a bad way to spend an evening. Nothing hurt. Sometimes she heard fluttering like bird wings around her. She would not have been surprised to turn and see the room full of purple butterflies or lime green canaries. The room sometimes fluttered and sometimes shadows moved in and out of corners, and up and down the stairs. They did not feel threatening. She did not turn. It was an old house; many families had lived within its walls. The previous tenants had been an old couple who had died within weeks of each other, in the bedroom upstairs. Probably many of the previous tenants of the house were now dead. Soft comings and goings did not disturb Flora. She sat, a husk, and did not care if they were spirits or products of her own mind. Nothing mattered but the basics. The bairns. Food, clothes. Putting one step in front of the other. Breathing. Occasional kindnesses.

'You'd better take a scone, Flora, you're looking like you need something.'

'No. No thanks. The coffee's grand, though. I'm not hungry.'

For a second, as she raised her eyes to his, he was an Alsatian dog, perched on the hotel chair, head cocked, ears pricked with intelligence and inquisitiveness. A blink of her eyes and he was back. He'd been an Alsatian many times, it was not a startling sight. She hadn't commented on it since she was six, and her mother had scoffed, Don't be a dafty, course he's not a dog.

'If you're sure, then.' He ate his own two scones with relish, leaving crumbs over his black jumper.

'I'm sure.'

'Listen, Flora. I'm not going to nag you about coming to church because I know you are going to anyway. Deep inside you know it's the right thing to do. And I wouldn't be saying this if I didn't love you. As a brother and as a fellow sinner in the eyes of our Lord.'

'Aye, I know. I know you mean well. It's just that, it's not for . . .'

'Of course it's for you, it's for everyone.'

A second's panic as he briefly transformed from a protective Alsatian to a hungry wolf, peering greedily into her, searching for her soul. Another tortured second as she beat her own wings convulsively to escape.

'Yes, of course. You're right,' she lied, instinctively hiding.

'I'll be by in the morning. I'll bring Daisy again to stay with the bairns. I knew you'd see the light. It's for your own good. You'll see, Flora, you'll see.'

The outing had broken up the day, but left her heavy-hearted. Again and again in her mind she came up against her brother's black certainties, his energy. The bedtime routines sapped her and as she lay down on the bed to send the youngest off to sleep, she slipped into sleep herself. She awoke cold, the curtains still open, herself uncovered. The moon shone into the room. The baby lay asleep, warm and limp. She dragged the quilt over herself and turned over to trick sleep back. Gradually she became aware of a presence in the room. Her thoughts, scattered to shopping lists and laundry, scurried back to note this presence. Someone was in the room. She lay very still. Kept her breathing regular. She noted that someone was near and she was not afraid. She was interested. Then the presence was a weight on the bed beside her. She lay, curled around the baby and someone lay down behind her. Warm, accommodating her posture. Then it didn't move. It didn't seem to ask for anything but space near her. She lay still, fully awake, listening to the clock tick, the baby breathe, the movement rather than the sound of the being's breath.

Who are you, she asked in her mind. How do you know me?

For she had the feeling it did know her very well. It was like lying next to her own self.

I am here, was its only answer, explaining nothing.

A faint whiff of something, wood smoke, relief.

Then it was enough to share this lonely hour. Her questions left her. She relaxed, slept.

When she woke again the room was full of grey light. She was refreshed, for once. When she remembered the presence, she automatically looked around for it, not knowing what shape it might take. She was accustomed to seeing all manner of things emerge and fade, but never before had she felt connected to them. A sense of loss cut through her as she recalled the comfort of meeting a like mind at last. Who understood, who offered no answers but this affirmation of similarity.

Who knew, too.

That the world was a mysterious place, shifting, unknowable, prone to accidents. Indifferent to frightened people spouting interpretations of old books. She could not believe in explanations. It was enough to notice the stars now and then, to feel her own blood course through her veins and stretch her muscles.

She found herself in the church byre again. She was weak against her brother.

'Ah, you've returned, praise God, we were all hoping to see you today.'

'You're looking better now you know Jesus loves you, because he does, lass.'

'All us sinners, he takes us in, sit down love.'

Again the sun shone through to the metal legged table and her brother fixed them all with his bright manic stare and shimmering smile. The light was behind him, shone through his thinning ginger hair. A furry red halo.

'Welcome all, welcome again to this poor house, poor in appearance but immensely rich with the presence of our Lord Jesus Christ. Watch us oh Lord, heed our cry. Heed our cry.' His voice pouring like liquid, slow and golden. His eyes now lifted high.

'Join us Lord, we are here again to be saved,' cried the man whose smile she remembered.

'Amen!' said the two teenage girls. 'Amen to that!'

'Let us begin by singing hymn 406. We Sing of the Glorious Conquest before Damascus' Gate. Page 114 in your hymn books.'

The congregation rose and the lusty singing began. So much expelled air must scour all the cobwebs from the ceiling, Flora thought. Again, she didn't sing. Could not even find the page in the hymn book. The words swirled around her head, meaningless and disturbing. Her own breath seemed to be swallowed by all the heavy inhalations around her, all needing more and more air to pump noise outwards. The sun baked the corrugated iron roof. Again, she felt she was leaving herself, a fizzing numbness at her extremities. This time she sat down before she fainted. No one noticed. She concentrated on the open window. Imagined the fresh air pouring in and took a little breath like a sip of cool water. Revived, momentarily hidden among the towering swaying bodies belting out bible themes. Noticed how joy made faces look vulnerable. Then the hymn ended. All the heads swooped downwards and hovered over her. She jerked back in her seat at the nearness of their outstretched hands, their teary eyes and glazed smiles.

'Rise up sister, rise and meet the Lord, he is here among us, come to feed our souls, our poor deprived souls, stand up Flora and give us your heart.'

Not just her brother's voice but it seemed all their voices, in echoing unison.

'No, I, please, no . . .' she choked as they wavered and became slavering hyenas, parched vultures. Shut her eyes against them.

She felt a hand unclench one of her hands. Not one of theirs, not insistent claws, but a warm friendly hand. Knew without looking, it was the presence from her bedroom. Felt a safe private space form around her. They could not harm her, consume her, alter her. She was herself, strange as she was, and she would remain herself. The hand tugged upwards, firmly at first, then effortlessly as it met with less resistance.

She found herself leaving her chair. Walking lightly towards the open door. She was aware of silence behind her. Looked back to see hungry faces, puzzled eyes. Her brother stared angrily. A sulky snarling Alsatian, cheated of his bone. She inhaled the sun, felt like singing.

BELATED LOVE LETTER
FROM A FAMOUS WRITER

Shortly after Sonoma Finch woke, she noticed she was not dead yet. So many mornings, and still – not dead. Maybe this would be the day. Well, it might. Her left knee joint ached, her tongue felt dry and sour, and the bed seemed to exert a gravitational force she'd never properly noticed. Is this the last day of my . . . my what? Life was both too grandiose and too vague a word. My visit? My grand day out? My chance to do lots of stuff, both sensible and not? She asked this question of the world at large, in an agnostic way, open to any version of a listening ear. She felt a small tingling at the back of her mind, the bottom of her stomach – an itching ache to find out what the final experience of her life would feel like. But how frustrating – no telling about it afterwards. Surely the most exciting bit of news anyone could have, and she'd be unable to bequeath it. The ultimate deprivation, having her mouth silenced. Worse than death.

Some clouds shifted and the sun suddenly poured through the old curtain above her bed, bathing her. She closed her eyes a second in case this was, indeed, the moment of her departure. The lighting seemed to indicate it might be – she might detach from this ridiculous form any second, and travel up this shaft of light, leaving her body conveniently, modestly, and even rather attractively, arranged on the bed below. She was reluctant to be caught out, to be surprised; she warily watched for her own exit portal, could not help but hope it was here in bed. She sighed and opened up her eyes again. If she was not going to die in the next two minutes, she would have to get up and pee.

On her way back to the bedroom, she picked up the letters, which the postman had slotted through the door earlier. An invitation to acquire a gold credit card, an invitation to acquire a platinum credit card, a bill from Calor Gas, and a letter in a square blue envelope. The handwriting seemed unfamiliar, yet caused an alteration of her heartbeat. It was in old-fashioned long hand, a strong masculine hand, yet with some feminine attention to appearance. It slanted aggressively to the right.

Dear Sonoma, love of my life.

What? She felt something flutter over her, slide down the skin of her exposed neck and arms. As if someone had just dropped a huge gossamer shawl from the ceiling. She shivered and sat down.

I'm glad you sat down. You are still susceptible, I see, to that swooning feeling. I knew you would be.

She scanned to the bottom of the short missive, and sure enough – there it was, clear as day. Hemingway again. Bastard!

I have to tell you, Sonoma, that I was wrong. Wrong, wrong, wrong! That night on the lake, when we were fishing and I was quiet, surly, and you kept asking what the matter was, and I kept saying I didn't know, nothing was the matter. I remember I said I didn't want to eat the food you brought, that I just wasn't hungry. That was a lie. I was starving. I had to make a point, be melodramatic.

I knew that! Arrogant boy.

I acted like you irritated me, and then I made us have a little argument. I told you I had taught you everything you knew and now you were full of it. Then I told you it wasn't fun anymore. Nothing was fun anymore. You asked if love wasn't fun, and I said: No, even love was not fun anymore.

Cruel! Cruel and untrue. I hated you.

Then you left, you just got in the boat and rowed yourself home, even though it was dark. I didn't care. I lay on the blanket and heard you cry and I did not care. Bill came later but I didn't feel like talking to him, and he went away too.

You were a miserable bastard, always were.

The next day, my real writing life began. I'd been waiting to do something I could really hate myself for, and then write about. You knew, didn't you? How could you not? You were the betrayed good wife in A Moveable Feast. You were the nameless wife in The Snows of Kilamanjaro, that masterpiece of bitterness and regret – 'I'll always love you, don't you love me?' asks your character – and I got to answer for the hundredth thrilling time: 'No. I don't think so. I never have.' And in The Sun Also Rises – you were Brett and I was Jake. 'We could have had such a damn fine time,' says Brett, her head on his shoulder in the dark taxi. 'Isn't it pretty to think so?' answers Jake, cynically. Damn, I loved saying that.

You would.

I wanted to write this letter because I want to thank you and also to tell you that I lied.

No, no. Truth, always, no matter how hurtful. That was your philosophy. No softness anywhere in you. You hated women, except in bed.

I loved you, especially in bed.

No.

I never loved anyone else. I never stopped loving you.

And who were all those wives and lovers, then?

They were all you, my other women. They were you and I had to re-enact our lake scene dozens of times. I hurt them all.

Why?

Don't ask me why Sonoma. Why doesn't matter.

Bastard.

Yours, Ernest

Sonoma Finch was not going to die today; there was nothing

wrong enough with her yet. And besides, she was only thirty. She stood up and crumpled up the letter. Threw it in the bin. Then took it out and tried to burn it in the sink. The matches were old – she'd given up smoking in an effort to extend her life – and would not light. Finally she smoothed it out and read it again. All those years ago, and she'd never left him. But that wasn't really her, he'd carried around in his head. No, not her at all. She found a piece of paper and a pen.

> *Dear Ernest:*
>
> *You never knew me, never knew the real Sonoma Finch, just used some surface bits of me, the bits you liked, and made the rest of me up so you could pretend you'd known someone like me. I bet you used my name too; I saw your eyes light up when I introduced myself. 'Sonoma Finch? Sonoma Finch?' you repeated, smiling, as if a name like mine was too good to be true, and certainly too good to be wasted on a non-fictional character. A person with an actual heart beat. But you didn't care to get close enough to notice my heart beating, did you? You writers are too frightened to get close, you much prefer your own distant version of things. Of people. You like to think you're so observant, so perceptive, so sensitive, when really you are shallow and cold and cowardly. You would gawp at a road accident, just to write about it.*
>
> *You thought you broke my heart. That was not the sound of me crying you heard on the lake, in the dark. I did not cry. It was the sound of your own crying you heard.*
>
> *Sonoma Finch*

But when she looked for a return address to write on her envelope, there was none. And when she went to look in a directory, she could not make out the words. By the time she'd blown her nose and found her glasses, she'd lost the letter entirely. Searched the house from top to bottom, flicked through all her manuscripts, and still no letter. Remembered he was dead and therefore incapable of writing. Later, much later, when it was almost not necessary, she got dressed and lived through the remains of yet another day of responsible citizenship, not properly loving anyone but a ghost.

PERSEPHONE'S PASSION

I'm beginning to suspect my squeeze is dead, but it seems rude to ask. Look at him, on his usual political rant, smoking like a chimney, black circles under his eyes. Like a cadaver on speed.

True, he's dead sexy but also – and I mean this – exceedingly ugly. The anti-Greek god. He's no good angles at all, even with wine and candlelight. He goes on and on about weird stuff, like unions for rowboat operators. Sometimes I'm fascinated by the depth of his fascination, as if he's not quite human. But mostly, when I look at him I think: What the fuck? Is this really the man I love? And the answer, of course, is an eternal yes. This doesn't stop him irritating the crap out of me.

'Arthur. Shut up for a few minutes, will you? I've got something to ask you.'

'Have I been going on too long again?' He puts his rollie out on the lid of the tobacco tin.

'I don't mean to be rude or anything, but I was just wondering why I've never seen you eat.'

'I ate that banana.'

'What banana?'

'This banana,' he produces a blackened peel.

'It's ancient. You been carrying it around all week.'

'I ate it,' he wheezes.

'When?'

'This morning, while you were in the bath.'

'That doesn't count. I've never see you drink anything either.'

'Fuck sake Persephone, what exactly is the matter?' He opens the tin and begins rolling another cigarette. His fingers are so yellow, they've their own little case of jaundice.

'And we never go anywhere,' I whine.

'We're here, aren't we?'

'Yeah, another hotel bedroom. How come we never go to a movie. Or a pub. You've never met my friends, or my parents. You'd love my mum. She'd love you too.'

'She likes bad boys?'

I snort. 'Like you're a bad boy.'

'You don't think I'm a bit, well, dark and intense and dangerous?'

'No.'

'But I *am* a married man. I'm a bit bad, right?'

He looks, for a moment, guilty. But I don't think he's married at all. The wife's a cover, because he's embarrassed about being dead. My lover is a chain smoking ghost.

'Arthur, there's always just you and me.'

'Usually horizontal,' he leers, sputtering Golden Virginia shreds on the sheets. Our beds are always covered in my sandwiches crumbs and his tobacco shreds.

'Yeah, well, I want some proof.'

'Proof of what?'

I open my mouth to say: Proof you are visible to someone not me. *Not dead*. But I can't. It sounds distrustful, somehow. I decide to say it anyway, but then he's kissing me and sliding his hand up my legs again. So what if he's dead, I think. It's not like he's a Jesus freak or something.

I'm beginning to suspect she suspects. Not that it's all my fault. I was happy, minding my own business – dead as

155

a doornail, of course, but still quite busy. You think being dead's a doddle? Think again. I'm in charge, for my sins, of the whole shebang. The days are never long enough. Moan, moan, moan, that's all dead people ever do. They think I'm some kind of God, that I can just magic their problems away.

So there I was, stressed, when a wave of electricity surged through my office. Fuck off, I said automatically. Just fuck right off, I'm a busy man, OK? But there it was still, pulsing away, so I had a look at the source. By god, I'm glad I did. Look at her! A pain the arse, with no consistency whatsoever, mood swings to beat the band, and lousy at blowjobs. But those aren't the reasons I love Persephone. No! I love her because I love her. I love her involuntarily. She's exciting as hell, but here's the mystery: When I'm with her, I relax.

She can accuse all she likes, but I wouldn't be here if she hadn't sent for me. Lonely people send out signals. Like a whistle only dogs can hear. I'd watched her a while – a perk of the job, the voyeur option – and she grew on me. I was interested in her ways of attracting suitors – not easy for her, given the scarily powerful parents. I know all about dysfunctional powerful families, believe me. Why do you think I moved so far away?

Persephone lit candles and wished on stars and left clear marbles under her pillow and joined match.com. I was puzzled by the lack of response. I took some time off – I still had the holidays I hadn't taken last year – and discovered a dearth of suitable living men for dear lonely Persephone.

What else could I do? Her yearning was like a Hoover to my heart; I was sucked up into her life. I first appeared on her computer screen. I pretended my name was Arthur. Hades is off-putting, don't you think? Too loaded. She's a writer, so a letter was the obvious tactic. I'm a writer too, as it happens. In my spare time I sometimes write sestinas about snow, to cool off.

'Your name's so long,' I wrote. 'Can I call you Sephonie? Or just Seph?'

'No.' She was such a flirt.

And she played hard to get. I emailed her on Tuesday, and she made me wait till the following Monday. Said she wasn't into married men. See, I'd told her I was married, to explain the need for secrecy. I sent her some Green & Black's ginger chocolates, with pomegranate seeds inserted. My own invention.

'What the fuck,' she emailed. 'Meet me at Hoots tonight.'

'How about Hotel Highland,' I wrote. 'More discreet.'

'Whatever.'

I knew, the second I saw her, I was toast. Soon after, the room lights fused, our watch batteries died and her mobile battery crashed too. We made an electric storm between those sheets. Damn, I'm hot.

And now I think she suspects the truth. What if she ends it? Never expected to fall like this. One gets beyond surprise, after the first dozen centuries.

Patricia, the palm reading psychic, promises it'll be alright. Patricia can't be her real name – she's Chinese – but what the hell. Bit like Arthur's name – it seems wrong somehow. Sometimes whole seconds pass while I try to remember. Arthur, Arthur, Arthur, I chant to myself, but nope. It will not stick. Anyway, I asked the psychic pretending to be Patricia about love, to see if she was the genuine article. She wanted £20. Then she held my hand and stroked it, turned it over a few times.

'There is a man,' she finally said. 'He love you very much, this man. But there is another woman. She does not love him like you do. You must not contact him. For two months. He will return to you.'

Then she gave me a piece of printed paper that had been ripped at the top, as if getting rid of someone else's name. It said that Mary the mother of God spoke through her, and she was happy to answer questions regarding love, work or health. Even by telephone. She took Visa.

I found it all pretty spot on. How did she know there was a man? I could have been a lesbian, for god's sake. And it summed Arthur up. The confusion, his so-called wife, his love for me.

'Wow, how do you do that?'

She smiled enigmatically, like a proper psychic.

'Two months. He will return to you.'

I wondered if she actually understood English, or had just memorised the lines about love. But I hate cynicism – there's just not enough time to wonder if people are telling the truth. So I thanked Patricia and left. She'd confirmed what I suspected. He's either married or dead, which is the same as married. I'm not prejudiced, but I never heard of anyone marrying a ghost. I want to get married, so that was me, screwed. I would try the Patricia way.

'I'm not going to contact you anymore, Arthur, and I don't want you to contact me either. I'm tired of secrecy – not my style at all. More of a shout it from the rooftops girl, me.'

'Ah, don't be like that Persephone. I'll be yours one day. You *know* I will!' His cigarette was unlit in his fingers, he was that upset.

'I don't know any such thing, my darling man that I adore every molecule of. It's over.'

'Please don't be so cruel, sweetie.'

'Please don't be so married, dearest wreck of a man. Goodbye.'

Of course, this was pure bluff. I'm already in deep withdrawal. It's been four weeks, and it's not getting easier. I think of him all the time. Even when I'm dating match.com teachers from Killiecrankie. I think of the way he feels when he comes into bed, all lovely and cool, and the way his fingers slide into me, and the way he wheezes when he laughs. The way he holds me when we say hello or goodbye. He always squeezes me so tight, head to toe; seems to lock into me somehow. He fits me and my mind shuts up.

I miss his emails and texts. I've deleted his number but not his old messages, which I read when feeling weak. I found one of his rollie butts the other day – no idea how it ended up in my pocket, but there it was. I keep it in my desk drawer, and it smells like his mouth tasted.

He will return to me. Patricia said. Four more weeks to go.

I can't believe this place is so boring. Why did I never notice it before? And hot as hell. Shower all day long, and still sweat like a pig. I tried swimming in the river Lethe, renowned for enabling forgetfulness, and the lamenting river Coxytus, hoping to run of out of lament, but no luck. There's no answer to the missing of Persephone.

I tell Dougie my dilemma – he hanged himself, broken heartedly, so understands – and he says: 'I dinnae understand what you're on aboot, man. Why do you not just marry the lassie, and have done with it?'

'Dougie.' I love Dougie, but he is a bit slow. 'Persephone is alive, are you not listening?'

'Ah. But I wouldna hold that against her, man. She cannae help that.'

Then Dougie does this little jig, punches the air and shouts:

'Beauty! I've got the answer, man! We'll job share. You can spend half the year with Persephone, up there!'

It's like cool delicious sleet running down my whole body.

'Jesus Christ Dougie, but you are a genius!'

Then my heart sinks again. 'But she'll never go for it. Persephone wants to be with me 24/7. Six months a year will not be enough.'

'Sure, she can come down here for the other half, man. Fair's fair. She's a feminist, right?'

'How do you know about feminists?'

'I keep up with what's what. What, you think I just sit down here, stewing in my own juice?'

Dougie, it suddenly occurs to me, would make an excellent best man. He's already got the kilt.

Eight weeks to the day, and he jumps out from behind the rose bushes while I'm gathering a bouquet for my mother. Like a Heathcliff psycho, he doesn't bother explaining or apologising. Just grabs me and gives me this enormous snog, then off we go.

I'm not telling my parents. No way. They'd hit the roof. Mum especially. As it is, she'll probably go into a tailspin. Go around switching off lights and turning the central heating down. She goes like that when she's sad. Just sits in the cold dark, watching old reruns and swigging port. But I'll be back every spring, like clockwork. With what's his face. Arthur.

HERMAN'S NIGHT OUT

Everyone has wet dreams, right? And they always seem so real. But this one was different. There was me and Gary, husband of my friend Fiona. Of course, you know how these things usually go, with your subconscious fancying all sorts of people and never even letting you know. Well there we were in a room in some kind of theatre, not the stage, more like a backstage room with a bed and low lighting and we were doing it and it was pretty OK, but then – and this is where it started being different – suddenly we weren't doing it. I was disappointed, I don't mind telling you, but I pretended it didn't matter, just like you do. He sat up and looked at his traitorous appendage and said: 'Naughty Herman, you shouldn't quit so early.'

I thought it was an odd pet name for it, but since I don't know of any satisfactory name for it, I simply murmured: 'Never mind Herman, another day, it was fun while it lasted.'

I woke up and lay there, quietly so as not to wake up my husband, feeling a little frustrated and pondered it. I'd never thought about Gary that way before. It was absolutely like him in the dream. He's always blundering and having a resigned sense of humour about it. As if he expected to blow it, but was never too worried about it because he was only a human being anyway. Well, the day intruded and all the days after and I'd forgotten completely about the dream until one day when I was having lunch with Fiona, wife of Gary. I hadn't known her that long, but she's one of those people who take about two seconds to get down to basics. Which that day was her son's un-descended testicles.

'I took him to the balls doctor yesterday and do you know what he said? That he'd need an operation if they don't come down before he's five. Can you imagine? A knife coming anywhere near his dear little Herman, I die just thinking about it.'

'What did you just say?'

'They might have to operate on . . .'

'No, I mean what did you call it? Did you say Herman?'

'Oh, yes, it's silly isn't it, most boys just call it their willy, but Gary,' (giggle, giggle) 'has always called his Herman for some reason. So Ralph does too. Has to be like his daddy, you know.'

I laughed, and turned to cover my blush, because the dream had just come flooding back to me. It made the kitchen seem a little unreal as I stumbled around making us a cup of coffee and trying to act normal. But it must be a coincidence, I thought. And calmed down till I simply forgot about it again.

I rarely saw Gary. Husbands just don't enter into most of my friendships. Stay at home mums visit other stay at home mums while their husbands are out working with other out working husbands. That's my life, this phase.

Then there was another dream. This time we, me and Gary, were on a beach with lots of other people, then we were alone and his shoulder was a most delicious place to nestle my head and we kind of floated, already joined, down onto sand warmed by the sun. It felt romantic, unplanned and right. There was some clumsiness about the clothes, but all in all, this time was much better. When we were finished we were no longer on a beach, but back in a public place and by not looking at each others' nakedness, maintained some dignity. Then suddenly we were dressed again, and my head was about to nestle into his shoulder and neck region again, when he said,

'I wish we didn't have to go to Majorca.'

Like a dash of cold water, it was. I mean who even likes Majorca?

I said coldly, 'We're not.'

'Not you and me, silly, that would be different.'

But then my daughter woke me up, and I lost the rest of the dream. I felt exhausted, bone weary, and I shouted at her to go back to her own bed. She cried, so I let her cuddle in with us. I tried to close my eyes and find a way back into the dream – his voice was still in my ears – but I couldn't. And time took over and all the day's trivia cluttered the surface of it till it vanished. Like dreams do.

The next week Fiona phoned to invite us for dinner. It was little unusual, we're not that kind of friends and I was surprised.

'It's for a special occasion, please come. Bring the kids. It's our tenth wedding anniversary. Me and Gary are actually going on holiday to celebrate next week, but our real anniversary is this Friday and I promised the kids a party. So please come.'

'Lovely – ten years is something to celebrate. Where are you going?'

'Majorca. My sister's having the kids. For a whole week, can you imagine? And me and Gary haven't been alone one night since the kids were born.'

Good thing I was on the phone, she couldn't see my face giving it all away again.

'Look,' I managed to say. 'We'd love to come on Friday. Thank you.'

The next dream was on the Thursday. As soon as the dream started, I experienced this tremendous relief, like I'd been waiting for this dream. And I was very clearly aware that this was a dream. I am dreaming again, I said to myself. Good, I said back to myself.

'At last,' he said.

We were in a train station, then it became an airport, then it went back to being a train station. I felt a little anxious, then I realised why. I had no bag with me – no money, no ticket, no clothes. Gary knew right away what was bothering me.

'Don't worry,' he said, and gently held my upper arm just like men did in those old movies, when women were always fainting. I leant on him, feeling weaker by the minute and he led me into a little room. I recognised it as the theatre room. Just a little unvarnished wood panelled room with a low bed. I instantly felt reassured and my old self.

'There,' he said. 'Let's just have a little rest.'

We lay down and it was the best yet. Herman was in top form. There were little flaws, of course – embarrassing noises and he practically pulled the hair out of my scalp by accident once – but none of it mattered. I think I had acquired his perspective a little. We were only human beings with bodies, anyway.

'This, Gary, is one excellent dream,' I had to tell him.

'No kidding. Move off, will you? My arm's falling asleep.'

I had always thought of the dream as my own territory, but suddenly I had another thought.

'Hey Gary, how do you know about this room?'

'Oh, I bring all my fantasies here.'

'What?'

'Just kidding. Lay back down, silly. I've only been here twice, both times with you. On the whole, it's more comfortable than the beach though, isn't it?'

'Yeah, I suppose.'

'It's going to be weird seeing you tomorrow night.'

'Don't be stupid, you're not that Gary. You're my Gary, the Gary I made up to dream about.'

'Excuse me, but I'm not.'

'Are.'

'Aren't'

'Prove it.'

'Right. Let me think. Right. I'll wear my red tartan shirt and green jeans tomorrow.'

'OK, but you won't. The real Gary probably only has ugly shirts and polyester trousers.'

'You'll see. And what will you wear?'

'I don't know. What do you think?'

'All black. Come to my wedding anniversary all in black.'

Then there was this loud banging at the door and it sounded menacing, not just someone wondering if it was in use. 'Shit,' we both said, and scrambled out a window that had just appeared and tumbled down a low slated roof into a farmyard full of rain puddles. As we let go each other's hand, I awoke. It was still a half hour till the alarm went off, and I lay very still next to my husband and tried to get back to that farmyard adventure and that feeling of kinship.

Of course it was all just a dream. For all I knew, I was so out of touch with my body – aside from child bearing and breast feeding and the physical demands of housework – that I was probably at my damned sexual peak and didn't even know it. Just went to bed too tired to do anything but sleep, and invented these stories, these dreams. None the less, I wore all black the next night to Fiona and Gary's anniversary dinner. My old black skirt, a twenties black blouse and my new black shoes. I pinned a silver heart brooch on my black jacket and thought rather well of myself. I would definitely fall in love with me, I thought.

When he opened the door to us, Gary was just Gary, of course, in his grey trousers and grey jumper. He was a little bemused and clumsy taking my jacket, but he greeted us with a genuine lopsided smile.

'You look really very nice,' he whispered, as my husband walked into the kitchen.

My heart had already sunk, though, and I found it difficult to return his smile. He was not my Gary. I guess one small part of myself had hoped.

Fiona looked flustered. There was a burning smell lingering. Her four kids seemed subdued, which for them, was something. They were wild at the best of times. Our kids went upstairs with them, but shyly.

'Come on in and have a drink. I could use one too. Everything's falling apart. The kids got hold of one of the spray paint tins from the garage and were redecorating their bedroom. Gary found them at it, got paint all over his clothes – look at them,' indicating a heap on the floor by the washing machine, 'and to top it all, while I was sorting them out, the dinner burned. To hell with it anyway. Let's get an Indian takeaway.'

She led us all into the living room and poured out four large gin and tonics. I drank my drink, said all the right comforting things, then made an excuse to go into the kitchen. There on the floor were Gary's clothes.

I had to step out the back door a minute, have a quick silent howl at the moon.

CHRISTOPHER'S ROOM

The only way I can explain it is with a cliché. Nature abhors a vacuum. Well, of course. True voids exist a millisecond before atoms of one kind or another are sucked in. Even when I delete a word on this computer, every single other character automatically shuffles itself to fill in the gap.

What's not so obvious is why I am the only one with access to the room. I am not a young child or a sensitive dog or cat. Nor would I fit into any category of individuals with psychic powers. I am a forty-six year old agnostic librarian, childless, divorced, with two budgies and a tendency to read too much fiction. I have friends, but none close; I lost the habit during my marriage and now I lack the energy. I eat well and with pleasure, I take daily walks round the park, my habits are regular and wholesome. I have never been drawn to frightening movies or supernatural stories. I have never given ghosts, for instance, a serious thought.

But then I do not believe Christopher is a ghost. That he thought I was the ghost is clear, but I am equally certain I am not a ghost. That this is my first and only existence in time. I am here and I am alive and solid. How could I be typing out these words with my fingers, if I wasn't? I will finish this account and email copies to people who claim to study subjects relevant to the room. Being a librarian is immensely helpful in finding these addresses. My computer makes me almost omniscient in the world of written words.

I am sitting in the library right now as I am no longer sure of the permanency of my home. The doors are locked here and I have peace. Not absolute quiet, because I am surrounded by hundreds of thousands of books, and all those voices can never be utterly quiet. Written words do not lie obediently on the dry page. Sterile existences cannot be the fate of such earnest and imaginative efforts. All books murmur. Very old books that no one reads anymore, or books that were never popular in the first place, these have an especially plaintive tone and can make me feel such guilt and sorrow. When one such book shouted to me, I had to put my work down and retrieve it from the masses. It was a small brown book called Poems from the Forces written by young soldiers from World War II battlefields. Heartfelt poems are words intertwined with souls. They cry out to be taken into another mind, to be heard in other ears. I read them when I can, I take home mountains of them, but I never satisfy them all. I try, but I am not a big enough receptacle to contain all the unread words.

So here I am, in my home of bound words, and I have belonged here, the library is my place. I will try to explain, as clearly as possible, Christopher and the room across the hall. Then I will go home to bed, because home as the library is to me, it does not contain this piece of furniture. I have brought provisions with me tonight, two cheese sandwiches and a flask of coffee, so hunger will not drive me away before time.

I live on the top floor of a modern block of flats. It was built five years ago and I chose it for its complete lack of character. I had had enough of old houses. I was raised in an ancient freezing cottage and spent the fifteen years of my silly marriage in an even older house in town, with stones in the walls that had been laid during the reign of Victoria. It was draughty, damp, and full of the sense of layered lives, a constant reminder of my own mortality. In an old house, you cannot fail to notice when you move about a kitchen, for instance from the sink to the stove, that you are treading in the exact footsteps of a multitude of ghostly women. I don't mean ghosts in the sense that they are still there, but that they have left something, an echo, a quickly moving shadow, that mirrors your own activities. Once, as I was taking a basket of wet washing out to the back to hang it up, this sensation of doing it, not for the thousandth time, but for the millionth time, was so overpowering I could not do it. It was too exhausting to even contemplate. I put the basket on the step and just sat the rest of the afternoon, dulled by the fatigue of overwhelming boredom.

So after I left Charlie, I bought this new flat on the top floor. I have to say I felt quite light and energetic, moving through uncluttered air and making my own footsteps echo for some future woman. I'm aware that no space in a large city is free of occupation. Before this block was built, they had to tear down twelve tenements that remembered bombs dropping and babies with gas masks. But they were only four storeys high and I am fifteen storeys high. I live in air never before occupied by humans. All of which left me completely unprepared for Christopher.

This flat is bigger than my needs. After sharing a house my entire life, I felt greedy for space that was mine and mine alone. But of course no single person, who does not have a multitude of friends, uses three bedrooms. One is my bedroom, one is full of things I do not care to look upon, but am attached to. And one bedroom I painted white, not insipid magnolia, but pure white, and I kept it clean and there was nothing in it. I liked to visit it. I found it very restful. Nobody and nothing to remind me of anybody.

The world can be a very draining place. We build a barrier to protect us from being used up. We don't even know it's there. It's a skin. My empty white room let me take that layer off for a while. I knew it was a luxury, but it was what I had instead of a family. Some people unwind in front of the box with a beer and the sound of squabbling over crisps. I had my white room.

Till about two months ago. I remember I'd taken Hugh Walpole to bed. My current read, an old red cloth-covered book called *Rogue Herries,* which was richly enjoying being read by me. It was one of those excellent rare books that had somehow slipped through the net of public consciousness, and its artfully arranged words floated free but lonely. I could feel its gladness as I picked it up. When I began to feel that pleasant aching in my bones, as if my muscles were already asleep and away somewhere, I closed my book and turned out the light. The next thing I knew, my room was flooded with light and there was a tall man staring at me. His feet were not touching the floor.

I was silenced by fear. A big piece of scream was clogged in my throat, which spasm-ed helplessly and defied my order to open and release it. Suddenly there was a heart-stopping scream and it was from him. I jumped, let out a little scream myself finally, and hung on to my sheets as if they were shields. Then he kind of whimpered, turned and ran out of the room. I heard another internal door slam somewhere near. I lay there, wondering if it was safe to crawl to the sitting room to phone the police. A man had entered my flat, turned on my light, screamed and run, and this man was still in my flat.

I tried to remember him. His hair had been funny. Like a curly wig. And his clothes, like pyjamas made of some shiny soft material. His eyes, I had to admit, had been terrified. I suddenly had a clear picture of him crouched in the dark in the white room, breathing the shallow breaths of complete panic.

I got up quietly and phoned the police. I waited on the landing outside, by my neighbour's door, ready to raise the alarm should anything else happen. When they arrived, two of them in uniform, I told them I thought the intruder was still in my flat. They told me to stay downstairs while they searched it. After what seemed hours, but was probably only ten minutes, they fetched me and said they had found nothing. No sign of entry, no intruder, nothing.

'Maybe you just heard your neighbours coming home a bit rowdy from a party.' The subtext being, maybe I'd dreamt or imagined it. Woman living alone with too many books, I could hear him thinking. His eyes glazed over in a kind of chivalrous boredom.

'We've checked all the locks and windows, everything's fine. But phone us back if you hear anything.'

I apologized and let them out and slowly locked my four locks. I made a cup of tea, feeling quite unreal, as one does at three in the morning at the best of times. I couldn't trust my judgement. Fear, the paralysing kind, was still too close in my memory. I could not afford to give in to it, living alone as I did. I lay in bed and listened. The refrigerator humming, a clock ticking, a distant siren, a dog very far away, yapping. I was just putting the light out when I realized I had left the sitting room lights on. I got up to turn them off, listening all the while, when suddenly there he was again, hovering about a foot off the floor. In his silly pyjamas, his hair all over the place, his face white and pinched with terror.

He stood in the hall, trembling, and pointed at me.

'There she is. Quick. Arrest her!'

Silently behind him, three men came into focus, exactly as if I'd adjusted the lens on my camera. From a nothing blur, they emerged sharp and as alive as pyjama man. All dressed in the same dark clothes, looking very butch but at the same time, desperately irritated. My first reaction was a deep sensation of inevitability. Of course he would reappear because I must be going mad and this was my personal manifestation of madness. A floating persecutor in pyjamas who screamed at me. And three butch henchmen. The fantasy hallucination of all divorced librarians. I had to lean against the wall to stop myself floating away, so weak was my hold on reality. Then the figments spoke.

'Where is she? Look, are you all there mate? I can't see anyone, can you Pete?'

'Can't see a thing, Gov. Just a hall, looks like to me.'

'She's standing right there, for Christ's sake,' said Pyjamas, still pointing and staring at me. Then less certainly, 'Can't you see her?'

'Look, Mister. It's late. You've had your fun and we'll let it go this time. But think twice next time before wasting our time. Alright?'

'I must be ill. I'm sorry to have called you out. I don't normally do this. I think something must be wrong with me. I'm so sorry.'

I watched as he saw them to the door. Despite everything – my fear and feelings of detachment – I couldn't help but feel a kind of sympathy for this unthreatening man, who had just discovered he was losing his marbles. I could definitely relate. I was also having problems with my vision. I had no peripheral sight, it was like looking down a tunnel at everything. I watched him lock his locks and turn back towards me. I stayed completely still and I don't even think I breathed. He shuffled along and kept his eyes down. Then, without looking up, he said, sadly:

'You can buzz off now, you're only something in my head.' Then he went into the room, my empty white room, and closed the door.

I leaned my full weight against the wall, and slid down it to the floor. I needed to think before I made any moves. I shut my eyes. I couldn't think, my mind was shut down, a mere receptor of sensory information, no cognitive abilities left. I opened my eyes again to find my familiar decor. I looked down the hall to the sitting room and my lamp was still on. I looked the other way, towards the white room, and I could almost see the door. But quite clearly, I could see a light shining from the top of the door.

Having given up on thinking, I simply acted. I threw myself towards the door, testing my boundaries as it were.

Just how mad was I? If I could invent people then maybe I could invent rooms that contained things, even though they'd been emptied. The door opened easily and I immediately tripped over a six inch step and sprawled into the room.

'Fuck.' I don't normally swear, but my shins were bruised painfully, and normality seemed to be out the window anyway. I felt quite loose and fatalistic inside. If this was insanity, then I felt prepared to meet it face on.

But what enemy was this, no challenge at all. He was curled up in the corner, his face inadequately covered with his hands like a little kid, only barely suppressing screams again.

'Oh shit, this is really it now,' he was muttering away to himself. I thought it figured that my alter ego would also swear in times of stress. Thinking I had created him gave me a certain sense of power, and I stood up and limped over to him. Around me, the walls of the room were no longer white and square, but pink and rectangular. I ignored them. Too many fish to fry.

'Excuse me, but can you tell me what's going on?'

He just whimpered.

'I said excuse me. Can you please stop that for a minute and look at me?'

I thought that sounded the right tone, authoritative but polite. He lifted his face up and for the first time, I thought he wasn't too bad looking, for a wimp. Intelligent around the eyes and mouth. He seemed to gather hold of himself and his voice when he spoke was wary but clear.

'What do you want?'

'Me? I just want to know what's going on. Who are you and what are you doing in my flat. Also, why has this floor been raised? Those are my main questions. Oh yeah, and why does your hair look like a wig?'

Figment or not, it seemed best to proceed as if we were strangers. He didn't answer at once, but seemed to shake off some of his depression and intelligent curiosity flashed over his features.

'My name is Christopher McKenzie.'

'Is it. Well, my name is Sarah. Sarah Murphy and this is an empty room in my flat. So what's going on?'

'I'm very sorry to tell you this Sarah Murphy, but this is my flat. I've lived here four years, and I've never raised the floor.'

'And the wig?' If we were going to be absurd, might as well play it to the hilt.

He unpeeled it off to reveal a perfectly pink bald head. What a vulnerable baby he looked.

'Yuck, put it back on please. That's better.'

'That's what she said too, but it didn't make any difference in the long run.'

'What are you talking about?'

'My wife, Shirley. Ran off with her evening class teacher.'

'What was he teaching?'

And so on. That was the kind of silly talk we had on the first night. We had both relaxed, as if we were both in our separate dreams and it hardly mattered what we said or did. Then a distant ringing made him leap up.

'Jesus, what's that?'

'It's my alarm clock. I've got to go, Christopher. To work. I'd better go now.'

I backed away from him reluctantly, for there'd been something cosy about the space around us. I carefully stepped down the step to go through the door. The sound of my alarm was as strange to me as it was to him, but I pretended it wasn't, and went through the motions of normality. I fully expected to enter another alien universe, anything but my mundane alarm clock and getting ready for work. But as I shut the door, I could feel the ordinariness of morning seep through me. By the time I got to my room, I was not surprised to look back and see the door opening onto a perfectly white empty room.

What followed was a typical day, and I lived it without any problems. I was busy. One of my assistants was off sick and we had two school groups in the afternoon. When I thought of the room it was with detachment. Whatever it was, it felt in my control and I was not afraid. If I was cracking up, I seemed perfectly capable of dissembling when I needed to. No one else need be aware of anything.

The next night I looked in all my rooms, including my white one, before going to bed. Everything was as always. I was deep in reading my novel when a thumping noise disturbed me. I put my book down and went directly to the room. Again, there was a light showing at the top. This time I knocked. Firmly. The noise stopped.

'Who is it?'

'It's me. Sarah.'

The door opened and there was Christopher without his wig. He didn't look as awful this time, and I told him so.

'Leave it off, who cares. Shirley's gone now anyway.'

'Would you like to come in and have a cup of tea?'

It was strange to be welcomed into a room in my own house, especially a nonexistent room, but I accepted and stepped up. Readers have few problems making leaps. He settled me in an armchair and went to fetch two cups of tea. It tasted different from mine, but very nice. I asked him what the noise had been – it was his radio – and asked him to keep it down in future as it disturbed my reading.

'In that case, could you not use your shower so early? It wakes me up.'

I was startled by his new assertiveness, but when I looked at him he was smiling in that sheepish way I would come to associate with him. I stayed rather a long time that second night. It was peaceful. Somehow his presence never felt intrusive, and yet was warmly all encompassing. He was comfortable with quiet, a quality non-existent in my chatterbox ex. There were a lot of notebooks piled on a table he obviously used for desk, and I asked if he was a teacher or student.

'No, those are just scribblings.'

'Oh, like journals.'

'No, more like stories and poems. Also half a novel.'

'You shouldn't be embarrassed.' He blushed, a give away condition I share.

'Well, it is a little embarrassing.'

'Why?'

'Because now you're going ask if I have been published, so you can say to yourself he is a writer, not just a scribbler. But I haven't been published, so I am not a writer.'

Now I blushed, because that had been my line of thought. To alleviate any further humiliation, I immediately asked to have a look at some of them. I begged. He shrugged and gestured a help yourself towards them, as if they weren't his heart and soul bared, then picked up a magazine. I began with the top notebook, prepared to find the worst and also prepared to pretend it was great. My protectiveness towards the written unread word had been honed for years. And this was what I found:

A twelve line poem about the moon, the stars and the sun which somehow, without clichés, managed to convey both irony and regret.

A five page story which contained three Victorian ladies standing by elaborately laid tables in the snow.

A novel that began: After a hard coldness, a clear warm suffusing of soil, stone and flesh.

'Christopher,' I said, and waited till I had his full attention.

'What?' He had the guarded look of an unpublished writer.

'It's OK, you know. Really. I like it.'

'Course it's OK. It's brilliant. It's just not any editor's cup of tea.'

So I'd misjudged his vulnerability.

'You've tried then.'

'A few times. I'll keep trying, when I'm in the mood.'

'Sorry.'

'Look, it doesn't matter. I enjoy doing it. No, maybe that's not the right word. I just do it.'

I thought of my unread books in the library, all the lonely voices murmuring. All those philosophers, wondering if a tree felled in an empty wood makes a noise. Do acts of creation ache to be witnessed and lodged in hearts? I don't know. Existence is a shadowy thing in a vacuum. I did what I could, as usual, and began reading his stories right away.

We had a little conversation but strangely we never touched on the obvious subjects again, like how did it happen we could see each other but no one else could. Perhaps our intimacy was enhanced by the mystery. Certainly not quite believing in the other's existence helped us lose our inhibitions. We inhabited a deserted planet, unconnected to everything but ourselves, for weeks and weeks. He wrote, I read. Sometimes I read to him from some of my favourite books and once he read me some wonderful passages by an author I had not heard of. I made a note of it to later order copies for the library, but couldn't find it on the computer the following day. I wrote a letter inquiring about this omission.

I was quite convinced I had an new type of delusionary madness, but since it didn't interfere with my life, I decided I could keep my little secret and if they did bundle me off one day to the funny farm, I could simply take Christopher with me. I was sure I could survive anything, as long as I had him. Until last night. There was a soft knock on my bedroom door. I knew who it would be. I called out to come in and as he did, my tunnel vision began again, and it was as though there were two of everything – my flat and his. Even he was semi-transparent, so I suggested we go back to his room, where we could both be solid. The white room was always the best room for us. I took some of my correspondence and a book with me.

'You don't mind, do you? This way I won't have to rush

back.'

'Not at all. Take everything you need to stay a while.'

He was always the perfect host. I had started taking things to his room and leaving them there. A favourite woolly jumper, too old for work. A few pens and books. The toothbrush was a long time in coming, mostly because I couldn't figure out where his bathroom was. If I left the room to go to my bathroom, there was no guarantee his door would be there on my return. Outside the room the flat was still mine.

So last night, I decided to take the plunge and grabbed my toothbrush. I had to ask him to show me his bathroom. He held my hand and opened a door I had assumed was a fitted cupboard. There it was, very compact and of a style I had never seen before – translucent units protruding efficiently from the wall. When I returned, he was reading one of my letters.

'Hey, find anything interesting?' Annoyed, but I had reached that stage of courtship where I extended endless credit.

'I don't get it. This envelope says your address is Westeringham, Flat 555.'

'Yeah?'

'It sounds familiar, can't remember why. But it isn't here.'

'Of course it is. And outside is River View Ave.'

'Sarah, I'm sure neither one of us understands all this, I know I don't. But one thing I know for sure is my address. Templeton House, Flat 601.'

'Oh, whatever. Call it what you like.'

'But you're right, outside is River View Avenue. Come and look.'

He went to the blinds and sprang them up. At first it all looked the usual collection of lights and cars. Then I noticed a huge black piece of sky.

'What's that?'

'Connor Towers. You know. The new development.'

'I'm sure it wasn't there last time I looked.'

'Well it's been there all year.'

'Look, I think I'd better be getting back to my flat.' I suddenly needed to cry and wanted to do this alone. Being both insane and in love was OK most of the time, but there were these sudden dips.

'Did you forget something? Your book is here.'

'No. No, it's just I'm feeling a little tired now.'

'I wasn't reading your letter. My eyes just happened to fall on the address.'

'No, it's not that. Don't worry, you go to bed.' I started to leave, toothbrush still in hand.

'Hey, I just remembered where I've seen that address.'

'Goodnight Christopher.' I began the step down to my flat.

'Westeringham. Of course! The fire. Wait a minute.'

'What fire?'

'That's why your flat is a little lower than mine. We live in different buildings.'

'I'm sure we live in different universes Christopher, unless of course you are entirely my fabrication, or I am yours. Hardly matters now. I am immensely tired. And it's possible my unreal world may need me to go to work in it tomorrow to pay my mortgage.'

He darted across the room and held on to my arm quite deliciously firmly.

'Let me go please.'

'Sarah. Listen. Westeringham burned down ten years ago. Completely gutted. I am not kidding. My building was built after they cleared it all away.'

'Please stop talking about the future in the past tense.'

'It was a gas fire. There was a huge explosion. Everybody died.'

I looked down at his hand holding my arm. It had freckles and there was a faint birth mark near his elbow. It was very real and suddenly very dear.

So here I am in the library, putting all this down for others to make of it what they will. Tonight I will enter the room for the last time. My bags are packed. Nature truly does abhor a vacuum. With nothing that needed a witness in my white room, nature pulled something from time that did. Christopher.

I hope the librarian who replaces me likes to read.

ALONE

□ □ □ □ □

MY FAVOURITE THINGS

All day, I sit. I don't have to use my hands, my legs, my mind, or, to be honest, even my eyes, which I frequently close. I fall into a dream, without falling off my chair. Less frequently, I sleep with my eyes open. I have no idea what I look like, but since no one's commented, I assume I appear quite normal. No drool. Every month when I notice my pay goes into my bank account, I breathe two sighs – one of relief and one of astonishment. How do I get away with this?

Alone? No, not alone – anything but alone. While I'm being paid to doze, hundreds of people mill quietly around me, as if I'm a mossy rock in the river and they're the current. I'm lower than them, in my chair, but they never trip over me. I notice their eyes skim the surface me, not even getting to the black suit I'm wearing, the colour of my eyes. If asked five minutes later about my appearance, I'm certain they wouldn't be able to vouch for my age or gender. I exist in another category than most material objects. But perhaps that's the point of me. I sit, and unnoticed, notice things.

For instance, I notice that the young man and woman at opposite ends of this room, are aware of each other, far more so than the paintings they are studying. Look at the way she moves, self-consciously arching her back, then rubbing her exposed neck. Yawning artificially. Look at the way he's carefully not looking in her direction when she's most able to observe his indifference. And there they go, slipping towards the door the same instant. It's a secret dance. Even they don't see how much of a dance they're dancing. I hope they've the courage to speak to each other later, perhaps in front of a Degas. Degas can have a catalyst effect. I think it's his use of red. Colours, when used correctly, can be social lubricants.

And there's the woman who looks like a lollipop lady. Her face is droopy soft as if tired from decades of kindness. I bet she bakes shortbread and stores them in Tupperware containers, in case of visitors. She's frozen in front of the Rembrandt again. Staring. Quite common, people returning to their favourite portraits. Just because someone's dead, doesn't mean you can't have a relationship with them. Certainly the rooms with landscapes have far fewer lingerers; people tend to flow steadily by meadows and mountains. It's the faces, and in particular *the eyes*, they stop for. Lollipop Lady is still staring, and now I notice the Rembrandt woman's face vaguely echoes her own, and I detect a query in the angle of Lollipop's pose. Perhaps she's looking for answers. I understand that. Why shouldn't Lollipop's answer be in the eyes of this renaissance woman? Perhaps some eyes can pull our truths out of us in a way nothing else can. Or perhaps Rembrandt wrought some miracle, and his model is not really powerless and gone. By entering Lollipop's consciousness, she may, in some sense, live on. Well, she may. No one knows these things for certain, do they? Living may be an impossible habit to break, despite the obvious practical difficulties.

I feel fidgety today. I'm going to re-cross my legs again, and it's only 12:35.

Ah! There's that man again, grey jumper, heavy-framed glasses, the one who is pretending to read the plaque below the Renoir. I have a mute rapport with him. It's obvious he's only here because he perceives it as a wholesome place to spend his lunch hour, when in fact he's so out and out lonely he reeks of it. Loneliness smells like sea water and fermenting grain, of course. Sour and sad. This man aches for ordinary human interaction, but is too shy to tap into it, so comes to a place where solitude's the norm. Look at the stiff set of his shoulders, his inability to make eye contact even with a portrait painted centuries ago, his need to read the words instead. It's obvious he hasn't the first clue how to make small talk. Perhaps he never learned because his wife did all that, and now she's gone. Dead, or away to a more outgoing man, or to that kind of independent eccentric life some middle-aged women aspire to. Ah, there he goes, in his slow paced walk as if he's here for the art, not the refuge. The irony being that hardly anyone is here for the art.

They are no signs forbidding talk, yet this is a quiet place. So I'm startled when a woman with an East European accent suddenly barks to a young man:

'You have sat on my bag!'

He leaps up and apologizes, though his expression is bewildered as there's no bag on the bench.

'It doesn't matter you say sorry, you have sat on my bag!' she insists. Her voice is so manly and her face so made up, I wonder if she is a man. Or maybe this is a virtual reality show and we're being secretly filmed.

'But there is no bag,' whispers the man.

'Ha! You tell me there is no bag, when you have sat right on it!'

I feel sorry for him, and as he passes I try to catch his eye. He doesn't notice me or my empathy, and it tumbles away, wasted.

'Loony Pole,' he mumbles.

Then, as if permission's been given for noise, a mobile phone begins to ring. The ring tone is a song; it's My Favourite Things. Instantly I can feel everyone twitch with irritation and one second later, they're all singing the words in their heads. *Raindrops on roses and whiskers on kittens.* No one's enjoying the song; it's a cultural reflex. If you were about to be executed, or married, or about to cut the cord of your first born in some dimly-lit hospital room, you would still have to sing these words if you heard the tune. Sing away in some private room in your head that has a mind of its own. *Brown paper packages tied up with string.*

A man, full lipped and well fed, finally finds his phone and hisses into it: 'Listen, I can't talk now. We need to see this man Jacob – he brought in ten kilos.'

There's a silence, while at least eight people hold their breath and freeze.

'Just stay put. Don't move and don't answer the door. I'll be fifteen minutes. Ten.'

This man then becomes the only person who notices me this month. He darts me a sharp look. I don't know what frightens me more, my sudden visibility or the ominous one-sided conversation. Then everyone begins to breathe again, and move away in an unhurried waltz. They don't fool me. In their imaginations, they're being followed and threatened violently in dark lanes, or they see kilos of heroin stashed in a warehouse and Jacob's corpse. Or, more likely, they're already editing the story to entertain their friends later, over dinner and a glass of chardonnay.

Two very long minutes later – I often study my watch, so I know about the relativity of time, how it ebbs and flows and sometimes stops altogether – all of the tension has evaporated. The room is, for a second, blank. And onto this blank canvas, walks my dream woman. My knees feel an electric jolt where they almost touch her legs. Do I look alright? Not overtly bald and middle-aged? I sit up, aim for a dignified yet reflective pose. I press my lips together, squint my eyes as if I'm finding my own thoughts amusing. Oh! This is such an important day. Not that any day is insignificant, but this woman – well, she is making this day . . . memorable. She was beautiful once, you can tell by her walk, but her eyes have that glutted look. Too much oil on canvas – I've seen it many times before. People feed on art, but you can get drunk and insensible, spending too much time here. Why do you think I avert my eyes, even nap? It's not good to look too long, and some people, like this woman (I imagine her name is Frances. Not Frankie. Not Frannie.) are more susceptible than others. People who are open, for whatever reason, should avoid extended periods in museum rooms.

Maybe I'll ease off my cloak of invisibility. She'll not be aware that I've done this, but she'll notice me and ask me the time, or the way to the Van Goghs. It'll be like she's broken a spell. I'll exist! Her reward will be my generosity and gentleness, and later, after we've drunk enough wine, she'll benefit from my immense well of passion.

'Oh yes!' she'll whisper. 'I've been waiting and waiting for such a long time.'

This is a possibility. It's something I imagine, therefore it can happen. I don't believe in rushing things, but sometimes events rush towards you and I feel capable of rash acts. I do. There are so many yawning voids in the world, for all sorts of things – absent parents, lovers, friends, cocker spaniels, armchairs, cinnamon toast made a certain way – people can be sucked into these voids, unaware of anything but the most superficial of explanations. There have been cases where small children have been sucked into puppy vacuums, and given their puzzled parents a lot of grief. Returning soldiers have disappeared into a vortex of widows grieving for other soldiers. I have a romantic love vacuum around my heart, and without doing a thing to alleviate this, I may nevertheless pull a woman into my orbit. She, of course, will have lived with a love vacuum around her heart also. I believe in the possibility of hearts calling to each other in a language unknown to the brains of men. I believe in the intelligence of hearts.

Ah, there she goes. Today is not the day. Frances will not ask me for the time. I shut that door with a satisfied melancholic sigh, and let my eyelids slip down. Tune into the whispered conversations of strangers, sentences with no beginning or end. Listen – this is what I hear, in between the silences:

. . . know what you mean, but avocados? I love them, but they're so risky. I mean how many times have avocados disappointed you? . . .

. . . what she said when I asked her if she had any regrets, listen to this, she just sat there looking like crap, and said . . .

. . . and Edie always says that, always! But I will remember to meet that train at . . .

. . . is he? Well, I still think he should get more money, after all he is the . . .

These are the noises people make when they've forgotten, in all their various strivings and distractions, that they're mortal. Their chatter channels through me, makes a single sound, a soporific rhythm. Like waves. I churn them around, taste them and become – not them, but their stories, which are too close for them to notice properly. After a while, below the voices, I hear a cacophony of heartbeats and dreams, of moments and hours, of memories and silence.

You must be familiar with that place, between sleep and wakefulness, where the meanings of words are blurred, joined, and the shapes of objects and people are blurred and joined too. I'm still not moving in my chair. My skin is tingling on the edge of unconsciousness, and my breathing is very slow. In. Out. My watch ticks silently, but my pulse notes the vibrations as if they were tolling bells. I am alive in the world, and I will go home with all of this inside me. Later tonight, when I hear distant sirens and laughter with equal detachment, this human symphony will linger yet, in the grey air of my corridors. Will sit at my kitchen table while I drink my wine. I will hum with it and not feel lonely.

IN ABEYANCE

I walk and I walk every day and one day I see a house in the middle of the fields. In a dip, so although the land around looks, even feels, flat, the house is invisible until I am quite near. I notice the rowan first, old and gnarled, at the corner of the walled garden. Enormous fronds of rhubarb are all that remain of the fruit garden. The wall has broken down in a few places and cows have been in.

An old stone farmhouse. A steading out the back. No proper road leading to it, but a narrow dirt track beyond the gate. Front door closed but not locked. Some window panes broken, old furniture glimpsed through them. I can not resist. Could never resist. An old empty house is like an invitation. Come in, come in quick while you may and see what you will.

At first he thought the Nissen hut was heaven. Dry clean blankets. A roof that did not leak, the rain hammering on the corrugated iron like a dance. All this, after the nightmare journey north. Night after night of sleeping sitting up in freight trains, in the back of lorries, on the back of motorbikes. His head dropping, then jerking awake. Twitching muscles.

Days of hiding. Or mingling with crowds, for some days it seemed safer to be seen, rather than be the one suspicious shadow.

He remembered the knot in his bowels, from eating the

wrong foods, from fear. The daily certainty of extinction. So many friends blown to smithereens, why should he be different? Nothing so far in his nineteen years had made him an exception. He was just himself, not excellent or disastrous at anything. If there was a bug going around, he got it like the rest.

The world had shrunk to a road.

Before they decided to split up for safety, there were half a dozen other soldiers, and often to pass the time, they played cards. There was one pack, bent and stained and it always seemed to be in someone's hands, sometimes his own. His hands could hold them as if everything was normal. That was a marvel and he liked to watch his hands do this, shuffle cards without trembling, while smoking a cigarette.

It took seven weeks. Surreal at times, and tense, but boring too. Hours that seemed years long, spent doing nothing but waiting and thinking, in a boring way, about dying. And that was the miracle. Instead of being dead, he was delivered to heaven on a cold grey Buchan coast. The fishing boat reached the pier just before dawn and an old man helped him off the boat. He tried to thank his saviour with his eyes, suddenly forgetting all the English words he knew except nice, from the English *Nice* biscuits someone had given him in Norway. He didn't know what the word meant, or how to say it, but the biscuits had been sweet, had melted soggily in his mouth and cheered him, and so nice meant something good.

'Nikee, nikee,' he said, mispronouncing nice.

'Right you are, mate,' said the man, who did not look him in the eye.

'Puny wee runt, think his name is Nick, that's what he keeps saying anyway,' said the man later to the policemen.

When asked by sign language if Nick was his name, he shook his head, thumped his chest solemnly and said:

'Karol. Karol Jurkowski.'

'That's Karl. Spelled with a k, I expect,' offered one of the policemen, a man who fancied himself an authority on

Eastern Europeans.

'Karl it is, then,' said the first policeman, busy writing.

He noted the different sound of his name, the hard rolling r, the absence of one vowel. He felt diminished, as if part of himself had just crumbled away. Queasy, he noted the green and brown linoleum floor, cracked and stained. And then, before he fainted, decided it didn't matter about the syllable.

The door opens easily and I am in a small dark hall. I hear scuttling sounds, only mice. The house breathes easily, empty, and I am unafraid. The room on the right has a fire-place with a built-in oven. A box bed along the wall still has the curtain drawn. A thrill goes through me, I open the cur-tains but the bed is empty. Sheets and blankets neatly tucked in, two lumpy pillows at the head. Dusty, damp, but neat.

The front door was open. This house, though not on a road, is not far from civilisation. I have only walked a few miles. Why, except for the front window, hasn't it been vandalised? Where I come from, an empty furnished house would be stripped bare in days. Even the pipes would be pulled up from under the floor boards.

A private sort of place, this. The wind is always keening and maybe it shushes people, makes them want to stay inside their own houses, be quiet. Everywhere I go, I feel I am the only person about, being clumsy and loud, drawing stares. I jar. It is not natural for me to be here, it is not my home. But since the funeral, that has been true no matter where I am. Even in my own sitting room, I hardly recognise my furniture, my neighbours; it's all strange.

I don't think about that place anymore. I'm here. I'm looking through someone else's house and it feels fine to be doing this. I open a little door off the kitchen and it's a larder, a tiny screened window at the top. Some tins of corned beef, processed peas, sardines. A few plates with heaps of grey dust mixed with mouse droppings. A milk bottle with the glass greasy and fogged.

Another door leads to the washhouse, a wooden extension out the back. There's a pump over a stone sink. A blue Elsan toilet in the corner behind some curtains, some buckets, a wash bowl, a tin bath hanging on the wall. One towel hanging on the back of the door and a mirror nailed up to face-level by the window. Back in the kitchen, I turn to the table by the wall, next to the fireplace. A metal mug. A rose rimmed plate. Some heavy-looking utensils. On the wall is last year's calendar advertising an agricultural firm. The page showing is for the month of June, 1974. It's like coming across a recent gravestone, while having a mildly enjoyable wander through an old graveyard, indulging in morbidity because it is safe to, because the sun is shining. I shiver and turn to leave because I start to feel like an intruder, like something wrong and sad and possibly dangerous is not far away. Again.

So Karl prayed. He thanked his Catholic god, a magnificent bearded man with golden robes sitting on a throne. He thanked him for the gristly bit of mutton in his soup, for the cabbage that was faintly familiar without the sugar and vinegar, for the kindness of the men and women who gave him clothes, money and work. For the wind and rain that swept around his shelter but did not touch him. He felt the bones and flesh of his body and said to himself: I am intact, not a bit of me is missing.

Why did he deserve this? If he had done nothing out of the ordinary so far, he must start now, be worthy of salvation. Wherever he stayed, no matter how primitive, he kept himself clean. He contrived to keep his clothes neat and his face shaved. He was small and sturdy and his ears stuck out, always shining pink.

When he was sent out to various farms, he worked hard. He learned to speak English. Deliberately repeating words with a questioning humble tone, so the farmers never thought he was putting on airs. He became a kind of pet.

'Get me Karl, if he's free,' was a common request.

Three days after his twenty-first birthday, the war was over. 'You can go home now, Karl old man. You can do what you like,' they said.

Home? He remembered his last sight of his parent's house, burning along with the rest. He had a little money, a few clothes and a small gold cross he always carried in his pocket. It was not an heirloom or a gift from a true love. It had no special significance beyond the fact he had found it on the ground one day walking home from school when he wasn't looking for anything, but just saw it glinting back at him. He liked the way it was so compact and smooth. He often fidgeted with it, running his fingers over the four points. The Christ figure in the middle was abstract, a mere line of raised gold, a pleasing variation for his fingers.

'Well, Karl. You've been a fine loon to work with and I wish you well,' said Alastair, one of the older farmers. He spoke slowly, unsure of how much Karl understood. He extended his hand and said: 'Good luck. I'm sure you'll be well pleased to see the last of this place.' Then Alastair had to turn his face tactfully.

'Good god, Maggie,' he later told his wife. 'You'd think the man's heart was pure breaking, the way he wept. I've never seen the like.'

I return. How can I stay away? I'm too nosy to turn from the unlocked doors and drawn curtains of silent houses. I go back, but this time with the dog, to give me courage. As I walk, I start to believe I will not be surprised if I can't find the house anywhere, that I imagined it. I'm glad I haven't told anyone. But then, who would I tell?

The door is a little ajar and I have to think hard to remember if I left it that way. Has there been another visitor? Maybe a regular visitor. I stand completely still and listen. No sound, save the gulls and crows and distant cows. The air has that moist half-rotten smell of old farm yards. I check the steading first. As I enter, a loud flapping preludes a swarm of swallows and pigeons, one of which touches my hair. I make a small noise of alarm, which startles me more than the birds.

Inside is what I expect. Huge ancient leather harnesses hang on the wall. Different sized boxed stalls for sheep and cattle, perhaps a pair of working horses. Heaps of mouldy straw and hay. Rusty tins and blue bottles of veterinary medicines stand in a neat row. A few old implements, a broken fork, a wooden barrow. Nothing useful or functioning. Someone must have been after all. Taken what was worth something, taken any animals and feed.

The light shafts through where the iron roof does not meet the stone wall. I feel peaceful. There is order here, thought has been put into it. This was a happy place, for animals at least. Or maybe this is because I am projecting my own sudden optimism. I don't know what instincts are. If they are feelings about places and people, then I am frequently wrong about them. I suppose I am ill-equipped for life if I cannot tell the difference between instincts and wishful thinking.

Alastair found Karl just in time. He was walking the road south, head down, carrying a canvas bag. Alastair pulled his Austin Morris to the side of the road and beeped his horn. Karl turned and looked, frightened, till he saw who it was.

'Hello, it is you Mr MacLeod! Fit like today?'

'Well Karl, I'm nae bad. I was looking for you and someone said you'd set off down this way. Where are you headed?'

He shrugged. 'I go. I must go, Mr MacLeod. War over, I leave.'

'Listen Karl. Call me Alastair, alright?'

'Alastair. Fine, Mr Alastair.' His face split into a smile of yellow teeth.

'Karl. I want you to come work for me. Give us a hand with the crops, the beasts. Like you been doing. Fit do you think?'

'Say again, Mr Alastair. You want?'

'You, Karl. You come with me.' He opened the passenger door, thumped the seat. 'You bide with us, Karl. Work here. Now, listen, Karl, there's no need for that. Really, Jesus Christ man, here, blow your nose.'

And that was the second miracle. He sat in Alastair's car, every cell of his body glowing, singing, leaping about in astonishment. How could it be him in this car, on his way to a home, a job?

'Maggie said you'd say yes. She's fixing up a room for you upstairs. It's only tiny, mind, but there's a wee window and it's snug. The gable end above the fire, ken. Snug.'

After peeking through the windows, I go in the front door again, keeping the dog near me. The room to the left is a small sitting room with a tiled fireplace. There are no ornaments or pictures on the wall, but a leather chair and a high upholstered sofa that was probably expensive long ago. The mice have been at it. A dead bird in the fire. The floor is wooden with no rug, save a mat by the hearth. It feels unused and empty in a way the kitchen did not.

I go up the narrow steep stairs. There are two doors. The ceiling is so low, I can't stand straight, but then I'm tall for a woman. One room is completely bare. The other slightly longer room has an iron bed with a mattress, but no bedding. On the back of the door hangs a heavy dark overcoat. There is a wardrobe and after a minute I open it. Inside are men's clothes, old fashioned heavy dark trousers and jackets, one white shirt with a black tie draped over it, all neat. At the back there's a cloth covered wooden hanger holding a blue skirt from the fifties. Faded little rose buds on it. It's the only item that's feminine.

I try to imagine who lived here, what happened. The kitchen looks like the occupant intended to return shortly, but mysteriously did not. A tidy person, probably an old man, quite small, by the style and size of his clothes. Almost two years ago, he simply did not continue his life here in this house.

But the skirt, that style from decades ago. Now that's something. Either saved for some sentimental reason, or simply left behind accidentally by a visiting auntie. No, too pretty, too girlish for an auntie. And pretty girls do not leave their skirts behind in single men's houses. Do they? Her waist was tiny, I can tell that by looking.

Maybe he wasn't always alone.

I go back downstairs to the kitchen and open the curtain again to the box bed. This time I slide my hand under the pillows and encounter something metal. A very small worn cross. Possibly gold.

Alastair and Maggie were childless and not young, and Karl was the answer to their prayers. They had a lot of land, but it wasn't great and they hadn't the money to hire anyone. He went with them to church on Sundays. He went to the auctions. For a day out once, they took him to a beach, where they sat in the lee of a dune and ate ham sandwiches and didn't talk much. On Fridays after tea, Alastair always gave him a bottle of beer and they had a game of draughts. They took turns winning.

'But you must get out on your own,' fussed Maggie. 'There's the dance this Saturday at the hall, you'll be going surely, if Alastair fits you out with some clothes. You're only young once, Karl, sure you're wanting a bit of fun.'

Young?

'There,' said Alastair as he knotted the tie with a flourish. 'You'll fair amaze the quines tonight, looking the handsome man.'

Handsome?

He winked at Karl and Karl winked back, though still not sure what all these signals meant. At the hall, there was a table with a woman pouring glasses of lemonade. On a raised platform, an accordion player and two fiddlers sat and drank from bottles. All along the back of the hall, stood rows of young men, holding their glasses and smoking. The girls were in bunches too, but they were in motion, scurrying here and there. Giggling and shrieking, arms linked. Their skirts were knee length and very full, so their waists looked tiny and their knees and sometimes thighs peeked out when they turned quickly. Their lipstick was very red. He finished his lemonade and went to the table for a refill, just for something to do. He was wondering how soon he could leave. So far no one had spoken to him.

'Hey, are you no the loon that bides with the MacLeods?'

It was one of them, broken off from her crowd. A lassie with red hair. Not immediately pretty, too skinny and sharp, but soft in her words and smile.

'Yes. I am Karl Jurkowski,' he said stiffly. He remembered Maggie's advice and smiled. 'Would you be wanting a glass of lemonade?'

'No thank you, Karl Jurkowski.' She held up her full glass and they both laughed. Then it was time to say something again.

'Would you like to dance?'

'Oh, yes please Karl. When the music starts.'

And then they had to laugh again, because he had asked her to dance and there wasn't even any music. They smiled hard at each other, then looked away in opposite directions till the music began. He didn't know how to dance, but neither did she. Even he, in his confused state, knew she was just as bad.

'Hey, sorry Karl,' she whispered in his ear, leaning so close, he could feel her breasts on his chest, her breath on his neck.

'What? I'm sorry. What did you say?'

She took his hand and pulled him outside. They stood in the late summer dusk, disturbing a nearby rookery just settling down for the night. She swayed a little, hiccupped and said: 'I'm sorry I keep stepping all over you. I've had a little something to drink, and I'm not really used to it.'

He put his hands on her shoulders to steady her and stood her away from him.

'It is alright. What is your name?'

'Jamesina. Stupid name, isn't it?'

'No. I do not think so. It is fine name.'

'No, it's not.' She sighed. 'No, you're sweet, but you don't know. You're foreign. You don't know what's stupid here. I am stupid here.' And the tears began. 'You don't know, you don't know. I am stupid and I am going to be in such trouble when I get home.'

Karl was stunned. This was his first real conversation with a Scottish girl, and it was completely incomprehensible. He did not know what? Well, everything, probably. Now she was whispering again.

'I watch you. I've been watching you a long time now. Do you never see me?'

I hold the cross, run my fingers over its worn softness, waiting for an image of its owner, but of course none comes. All I think is what a nice smooth thing it is to touch. It feels warm, but only because my hand has warmed it. I slide it back under the pillow and search for more clues. Something happened two years ago to a man. His house is abandoned. Why has no one claimed it?

This is a good distraction for me. I have not thought of myself for hours. I sit at the chair by the table and for the first time in months, I do not feel old. I am not old. I am young. I try to get a sense of who used to sit here. I am ready to believe people leave atmospheres, bits of their moods, like cast-off clothes. But how to separate myself from everything else? I feel aching loneliness, but how do I know that is not just me?

The dog is at the door, whining to be let out. I take her outside. The sun is hot and I sit under the rowan tree for the shade. It's old but the leaves are healthy. Half way up the trunk there are some carvings. Some initials. I stand to study them and their shape emerges. An echo of something I did once, well who hasn't? A heart, carved deep, and inside, initials. JM and KJ.

So who held the knife and carved, J or K? And which was the girl and which the boy? And did they love each other, or was it wishful thinking?

'Well, and when are you bringing this quine home, then?' asked Maggie. 'I ken fine who she is, and her family. Ask her to Sunday dinner.'

A week later, Karl and Jamesina stood in the garden, having just finished the dinner and needing some air. She wore her best pale blue skirt with the pink rose buds, and her white frilly blouse that just stopped short of being too sheer. Enough to let you know that, though she was not that type, she was a girl to be admired all the same.

'Ah, can we not just sit a while Karl, I'm so full.'

They sat under the rowan, minding their good clothes, with their backs to the watchful eyes of the house.

'Tell me about Poland, Karl. You never talk about it.'

'Oh. Well, Poland. Yes. We are eating different food there – red cabbage, fatter sausages. What else is there to know?'

It made him uncomfortable to think about Poland. It disorientated him. He dreamt in English now. Jamesina laughed. She was so slight, so frail, her warm full throated laugh took him by surprise.

'There is everything else. Food is nothing. I want to know the important things. Your family. Your school. Your childhood, your name.'

'My name?'

'Is it just Karl? Is that what your mother always called you?'

He felt dizzy, assaulted. Mother? Family? These were little bombs blowing up softly in his chest.

'My mother. She called me Karol. Karolski sometimes.' His voice was rough, his face flushed.

'Karolski. Karolski.'

He had to kiss her then. To stop her talking.

I could almost sleep under the tree. Seductive sleep. I've been in love with sleep recently. I close my eyes for another five minutes, then stand up and stretch, stroke the carved initials once more. I should start walking back, but the house hasn't let go. A house like this is like a face. Symmetrical, personal, knowing. Watching?

I like it.

I go and perch on the window ledge and catch the last of the day.

It rained all day, the day they married. It thrummed on the church roof, and Karl's body thrummed too, till they were safe in his – their – bedroom under the coombed ceiling. Rain and wind filled his ears and his blood pounded. The rain seemed to grow louder when she blew out the candle, then suddenly they didn't hear it anymore.

The next winter, Alastair and Maggie moved to a council house in town and gave the farm to Karl. He was going to need the extra space. Jamesina was expecting their first child. He watched her carefully. One day, just before dawn, she woke him. Smiled and said: 'Today will be the day, Karl. Our bairn will be here today.'

At sunrise, he got the horse ready to ride to fetch the midwife, but stopped when he heard her scream his name. He raced up the stairs and found her heaving and grunting, wild eyed, wet. It went from exciting to terrifying that quickly. He wanted to race across the fields, tear help from anywhere, from the sky. But she wouldn't let him.

'No, no Karl, don't leave! Stay!'

She clung on to him with an iron grip, for hours, clung and clung and pushed and made guttural noises. When her grip weakened, when her body went limp and her eyes rolled lifeless, he was still unable to leave. All his power left him and he lay on the bed with her.

Rooks are carousing and on the faint breeze I fancy I can

smell the sea, though it's a good ten miles from here. The low light lies like a golden mantle on the fields, full of wakened insects, until the sun dips behind a hill and that is that for the day.

Maybe I should live here. Inhabit this house. I can picture myself doing this. Cleaning, painting, sewing curtains, digging the garden. A nest again, with candles and the scent of fresh bread. Suddenly I need to know more, as if the prospect of living here entitles me to intrude with more purpose. I re-enter the house and this time my instinct is unerring. I go straight to the sitting room on the left. There is a small cupboard built-in under the window, and in it are some old brown envelopes of a shape not manufactured anymore. In the dying light, I am given his name. His nationality and status. A marriage certificate and her death certificate.

Displaced. The word has a hissing sound. Like wind in an empty place. I hold the old papers with their official stamps and important seals, and even now their authority makes me nervous. I put them back in their envelopes in their same order, but do not replace them in the cupboard yet.

Karl rode his bike to get his messages and didn't think of anything. The same old road, but suddenly none of it looked familiar. He looked up at a crossroads and he did not know where he was. He had to get off his bike. He didn't recognise any of it. The trees were alien, the road a strange texture, the colour of the sky, peculiar. His heart thudded. He knew he must be near home, he could not be lost, yet he could not for the life of him think where he was. And then when his mind reached for the picture of home, he drew a frightening blank. Home, home. But nothing.

Only the crows making a racket somewhere ahead, church bells ringing too, but wait a minute. What church bells? Where was he? There was no church near home, he had to get a lift in the neighbour's car to get to the church.

Karl sweated. What was he going to do? Ride to the nearest

house and ask the owners where this place was, where his home was? They'd think he was crazy. He took off his cap and wiped his face. Then he heard something, a voice, a sigh, that made sense of one direction, and not the others. He got back on his bike, relieved to follow some clue, and rode away.

I think he is probably never coming back. He has disappeared or died without a will, and the house sits, like me, in abeyance. Temporarily suspended and belonging to no one. I fancy the house agrees with me. It breathes emptiness and acceptance. It hasn't the slightest air of expectancy.

I think about taking the envelopes back to town with me, to find a solicitor, but in the end can't picture myself talking to a stranger about Karl. Or Jamesina. Let someone else, some professional disinterested person find and decipher them. I will hoard my own version. Perhaps like the house, if events live in plaster and lath, stone and glass. We live inside ourselves, mostly unaware. People have extraordinary lives we can never imagine.

THE TOP FIELD

Listen. This is so typical. I've just finished my Highers, right? My head has finally stopped hurting. And my bones feel good and my legs want to run and run. So I'm going for this walk, right, because I just have to move, and I end up in the top field, by the woods. Just before the land starts to rise again. The sun is sitting in the dip, like a puddle of heat, and that's where I plonk down. Unbelievable. You'd never guess it was Dingwall. And I start having these thoughts.

I have this terrible habit of imagining death. I've rehearsed my own death many times, as well as that of my friends and family. They always die suddenly and break my heart forever. I mean it, I can make myself cry doing this. My own death is slow with lots of tragic and dignified gestures, till I become so sick and tired, I just end. My dying words seem trivial and light, till everyone realizes their true profound significance. Then I'm quoted at parties for years to come. Some rock band even uses them for a title, thanking me on the album sleeve. My funeral, of course, is packed. The floor is flooded with tears when they play Amy MacDonald like I've requested.

So I'm sitting in this dip up the hill, right, and my bones are kind of melting into the ground, and I'm just indulging in one of these death daydreams that's more like an emotional orgy, and it occurs to me that it is really very exceedingly hot. I can't remember ever feeling the sun that way. Like it has power. And then, over my face and arms, comes this moist little breath of a breeze. Coconuty from the broom and a little pine resin from the woods. I can actually feel it with the hairs on my skin. I want to feel it more, so I pull off my shirt, and then my bra. I'm feeling a little dizzy and stunned, but nice. Much more than nice, actually. I've never done this before, but it feels perfectly normal to be baring my breasts in the top field. A tractor could come, but it won't. Everyone's too paralysed by the heat. Probably they're all sitting around naked like me. It's a funny thing, nakedness. When it feels right, it's hard to remember why we ever wear clothes at all.

My hands are stroking the grass – short tender tufts – and they stroke me back. I close my eyes, and I'm probably smiling like an idiot. I fancy for a minute that I can feel the earth revolve under me. A sort of slow persistent pulsating.

What happens next is a quirk. That's all. As random and meaningless as finding a pen when you need one. Some people believe in fate, and they even blame fate for things, but it's only the things they wanted to happen anyway. Like when there's somebody you've been fancying for a long time, maybe even dreaming about, or accidentally on purpose touching while passing and getting a delicious electric shock. And then you happen to meet that person in favourable conditions. Like he's the one who stops to give you a lift in the rain. Or you're thinking what it would be like to feel his lips just below your ear and then presto – there he is, behind you in the check out queue at Tesco. Well then, you say Yes! Thank you fate. It was meant to be.

But if fate throws you the wrong person, then you say you don't believe in fate. You say: Forget this. Right? So – there I am, laying there in the sun, communing with the earth and letting my breasts breathe, and I am ready in every pore for Prince Charming to come riding out of the woods and fall off his horse with lust for me. And I won't even open my eyes. I'll know by his touch he's the one.

Then I hear a car engine, right? There's no track up there, so at first I think it must be from the bottom road. But no, it's getting closer. I just lie there, convinced I'm a languishing blossom about to be plucked by one of my as yet uninformed true loves. I have always been in love, so there's a few of them. Then, just to be sure, I open my eyes a crack, and wouldn't you know it – it's that jerk Fergus. God, he must have radar. How the hell does he know to come here looking for me? I pull on my shirt and stuff my bra in my jeans pocket, and I'm out of the dip, looking as business-like as possible. This boy needs no encouragement.

He finally gives up driving and then he's bounding – literally – across the field to me, carrying a big bunch of daffodils. Oh. It hurts. If he has got radar, why doesn't it tell him he's not the one for me? And why don't the right ones use radar? I thank him, but hold the flowers at a nonchalant angle, like I'm carrying them for someone else, and take a lift down the hill in his old car.

I have to force all the sun out of my body, in case he misunderstands. It feels like a wave receding in me.

THE LONG MISSING

She had just emerged from what felt like a very long sleep, but was in fact 15 years of marriage. She noticed, in a detached way, that she was on holiday with her children. They were all in a caravan on a west coast beach, with the rain either hammering on the roof, or sailing by enclosed in tight dark grey clouds. In between, it was uncomfortably hot. The bay was shallow and the water heated quickly. Jelly fish in their hundreds were beached by the receding, deceiving sea. Whether it was raining or not, her children spent most of the days in the water, or on the beach, digging endless deep pits. They seemed tireless, and not at all concerned about the slippery jellyfish underfoot, or that their pits and dams had no purpose. The tides always undid their efforts, and they never cared.

It had not been a bad marriage, but deep down she had always felt they'd been frauds. From the outside, normal, but on the inside – quite often nothing, really. Not what she imagined should be there. Just two strangers rubbing along, pretending they weren't disappointed. Sometimes bickering, sometimes being grateful, but most often . . . well, it was odd living with someone who didn't seem to really know her. She had always assumed something would happen to make it stop, and in the end something did. She'd felt almost numb with relief at first; then giddy as if she'd miraculously survived a horrendous car accident – one that had seemed inevitable. A drunk driver, black ice, a bad mood. She hadn't loved her husband after all, ever. Really, she hadn't.

Now she was here, uninjured, with the rain and the beach and her children, edging into a new way of being. She felt un-tethered, light, and continuously nervous. As if she was an actress who had not quite learned her lines.

He was with his sons, in the caravan next to theirs. A small man; dark and muscular and he moved like he loved movement. Like a dancer. Her children and his blended into one tribe, after five minutes of skirmishing around a campfire lit by some teenagers who ignored them. Everyone on the site was slightly shy around the teenagers. They were at once so beautiful, and so unbeautiful. Some were skinny with bad skin, and some were overweight and short. Even the prettier girls had glaring flaws, like thick glasses or fake tan lines, but no one could look at the teenagers very long without wishing they were fifteen again. Every night, they peeled off from their families, to drink gin and vodka and beer and smoke joints, by their fire on the beach.

She watched this fire, this mating beacon, from her caravan, and when her children were not back by bedtime, she wandered down to the beach to look for them. It was difficult walking in the damp sand in the dark, so she slipped her shoes off and squinted to distinguish her own brood from the other shadows of children. They all seemed to be racing towards each other, and screaming with terror. She listened carefully for crying and heard none.

'Where are they?' she asked him, this dark dancing stranger who by fortuitous accident lived in the caravan next to hers. 'Do you see my kids?'

He had to lean in close to see her, and he said: 'There they are. Look! They're having fun. Let's leave them a while longer. They're playing British Bulldog, I think.' His voice in the dark sounded so intimate and pleased, as if he'd known her a million years and liked her inordinately. His teeth shone, and she could smell his skin. Warm and sweaty and lifesomething else. Well, he smelled of himself. A man she didn't know at all but liked. She let her eyes close momentarily. She told herself that intimacy had little to do with shared experience or memory. It was something much more visceral. If it was not easy, like this, then it was not right, and no amount of good intentions or indeed, children, would ever right it. Her marriage had been a fluke, a wrong turning; the kind of mistake that is easily made.

Much later, after all the children had been gathered like tired puppies and had their teeth brushings witnessed, she drank beer with him by the fire. The teenagers had moved on to the privacy of dunes. The two of them leaned closer and closer, telling secrets, almost touching heads. Opening more beer, till she hardly felt herself. She watched his mouth as he talked. His lips, soft and thick. Her husband's lips had been thin.

The sea at ebb tide was black and still, and there was just a sliver of moon, but still their bodies shone pale as they slid into the water. How can the ingredients for happiness be so simple? Why was the sea not full of smiling naked bodies? The shock of swimming in the freezing Atlantic, felt like life was compressing around her. She gasped and sucked in her breath and didn't say anything to the man, too full of: Alive! Now! She suddenly saw all the days of her life as if they were boxes bobbing on the sea next to her. Some were open, and some were waiting to be opened, and they all had the same capacity – the same number of hours and minutes inside. But they were not the same, because today, this box, held an eternity. Not really, of course; that was the trick. Knowing that in a minute she would leave the sea, and this would be a memory too, made her heart and throat swell. I'm here, she whispered to no one. To everyone. To everyone who had ever lived, and who was homesick for life.

They stumbled out of the sea, and her skin was tingling but not cold, and she wrapped herself in his coat and kissed him, this dark stranger, as if it was her first kiss. She'd wanted to be in love for such a long time, she could not imagine getting tired of these salty kisses that tasted of midnight swims and beer. Later, his skin on hers felt smooth and cool, and she kept thinking how he was not her husband. How glad she was, that he was not her husband. But she'd forgotten how love goes. How first kisses are always last kisses. They have to be; when the sun comes up, they change into something more ordinary. And she began the long missing of her husband.

LOVE

□ □ □ □ □

BEGIN

There was the sun, the dripping heat and there was the metallic taste in Sheena's mouth. Now she knew what caused it, it was not repulsive, but a harbinger of hope and change. A quicksilver flash that could save her.

Earlier, when she was offering flyers to the passing current of strangers, she hadn't known and the urge to spit had become so strong, she'd fled up the stairs to the toilet. Instead of spitting, she'd vomited. Sour, the enamel scoured off her teeth. But her stomach felt relieved, and she picked up her pink flyers from the floor and went back to work.

Parisian Fashions
cut rate prices
1067 Spadina, Third Floor

Paris was three thousand miles away, her boss was Turkish, she was Scottish. She'd not met many Canadians since coming to Toronto. There seemed to be a home for everyone, except perhaps coastal dwellers, of which Sheena was one. The lake could not quite answer her need for the sea. She sometimes dreamt she was home on Skye, with the Atlantic out her window, wild and familiar. Awake, a kind of claustrophobia threatened.

Some women put out their hands automatically when she gestured with her fanned out sheets. Others looked through her, made her feel insubstantial. She was wearing one of Sammy's outfits. Modelling, he'd called it. A long white linen skirt and a tight turquoise sleeveless blouse. Probably he thought it improved her chances of delivering his flyers. Better than her jeans and T-shirts.

An odd job, but no odder than most of the jobs she'd had. It was money and enabled her to live in foreign countries. Living, as opposed to visiting, felt genuine. And somehow, someday, it would all be useful. That was the theory. At the moment, empty stomached and light headed, Sheena felt as purposeless as a wind borne seed over the ocean. Random, unconnected.

She thought about the appointment she'd made at the clinic for that afternoon. The skirt band felt tight, and if she didn't pace a little, her bare feet in sandals ached. She trawled the pavement, keeping a light smile on her face. She didn't bother with the men, though mostly they sought eye contact, while she sought women's eyes.

She hadn't told Daniel. Why worry him if there was no cause?

Anyway, he was probably thinking about Natasha, the beautiful Russian woman they shared a house with, along with seven others. Daniel and herself were the only couple. They had a big bed but no place to put their clothes, so they kept them in folded stacks on the floor and a chair. The kitchen and bathroom were like all communal rooms. If you wanted a dish or pan, you had to wash it first. No one bothered with the bathroom. Somedays there was toilet paper, most days not. She had begun to keep a roll in their room.

Natasha had very dark and large eyes. She wore black and hennaed her short hair red. Definitely Sheena's superior, style wise. Natasha told Daniel he looked like John Lennon. She giggled and said John Lennon was her favourite Beatle, even if he was dead. Daniel said it was just the glasses, but smiled. Sheena had felt surprised someone like Natasha thought Daniel was worth a flirt. Was there something she'd missed, had she finally hit on it by accident? He was new to her; she was still looking at him. Was he the one?

At one o'clock, she took the remaining flyers back up the stairs.

'Here you go, Sammy. Get any customers?'

'Three lady. Two come in and leave. One, she try red dress. End up buying two. One for daughter. What you think? Hot enough today. You want Coke?'

Sammy was short and fat, with smooth olive skin that glistened. She had no idea what he thought of her. Maybe he didn't judge her at all, had no curiosity. She wondered if he'd heard her retching. She hadn't thought of that before.

'Thanks Sammy. Toasting out there, I can hardly breathe. I think I might be getting a bug. My stomach.'

'Oh, you no want sick. Tell it go away. Bug, fly out window.' He smiled, gold teeth glittering.

How did he stay so happy? He was like a placid Buddha, sitting up here in his empty shop, waiting for women to waft up the stairs on the hot air. And what did the women think, being alone with him, peeling off their cloths in the tiny cubicle to try on his dresses? It wasn't even a real shop, just a converted apartment. This part of Spadina was a smoggy noisy neighbourhood far from the cafes and art galleries. So who were these brave ladies? Both brave and wealthy, for Sammy's prices were not cheap.

Maybe they were all illicit – herself, the customers, Sammy. Frauds aping the lives of normal Toronto citizens. Maybe that was why, despite everything, she felt so comfortable with fat happy Sammy.

'Hey bug, listen to Sammy and bug off. There, I feel much better now.'

'You go change your skirt, I get ice for Coke.'

'Nice skirt, Sammy.'

'You want? For you, forty-five dollars. That half price. Direct from France, cost two hundred.'

'Sorry. How about a fiver?'

'Get out of town. You make big joke.'

The lady at the clinic asked if she wanted to wait or not. She could phone back later. No, she wanted to wait. She read the brochures on the table. Alternatives to motherhood abounded, even after birth. Trips across the border to New York were advertised. Different laws. When was a bundle of cells a human being? Several pamphlets claimed to know.

There was no air conditioning and a slight breeze of exhaust fumes strained through the window screens. While watching a fly that must have come in with someone through the door, the metallic taste re-surged and she closed her eyes to concentrate on her equilibrium. Everything in her was clouded, slow, stupid. Her name was called and she was ushered into a small room.

'I'm sorry,' said the nurse, assuming from her ring-less finger it was bad news.

Sheena left the clinic and re-entered the summer day. A long day, one which had seen her step lightly over boundaries. From Sheena the lost wanderer to Sheena the bearer of important being. Un-tethered kite to rooted tree. On the bus down Bloor, she crossed her hands over her belly and half-smiled. Around her, in the air and through the earth, she could feel a kind of sense emerging where there had been nothing but arbitrariness before. Endless options narrowed down to one, an unstoppable momentum with a unique set of routines and limits. A baby. A relief.

'But how can we? We've no money, you know,' said Daniel later, kindly not reminding her how little time they'd known each other, how perhaps she was not his choice of mother for his offspring. How much he disliked having to think about people in new ways.

She remembered when she'd first arrived. Long days of not

speaking to anyone, reading novels. Walking the streets or sitting in cafes drinking cappuccinos and eating pastries black with poppy seeds. Scanning the Star for jobs. It had been freezing. She had been cold and pierced with loneliness and boredom. When had her adventures started feeling like this, when had freedom started feeling like dislocation? She couldn't remember.

She'd met Daniel and lunged for him, to stop floating away. In the beginning, she'd watch the clock, waiting for him to come home from work. Ten minutes late seemed hours. Later, urgency melted into a softer rhythm, but there was still a sense of coming to, when she saw him. As if she was dream walking through her days.

They did not know each other, would never know each other. Their conversations were clumsy words tossed on the wind from one island to another, arriving battered and foreign. Only the clear and solid fact of their pull towards each other survived. This did not seem to require articulation or even thought.

I know this kind of news is supposed to come at a different time, she wanted to tell him. After much thought and choosing and public celebrations and mortgages and yellow painted tiny bedrooms with teddy bear borders. All safe and right.

She wanted to ask, does it really matter so much how it starts? The proper timing and reasons, these might be only social niceties. Has a child ever been born who cared about anything but love and warmth and food?

'Not now,' he repeated softly, reaching out to touch her tears.

A few minutes passed. He held her.

'I need to begin,' she whispered to his chest, hearing how stupid it sounded. Cringing.

Then Daniel did a remarkable thing. He smiled; he smiled because he couldn't help it. The pleasure was that sudden. He laid his hand across her belly, and she covered with it with both of her own. And all the rest of her life, whenever she wondered how anything had come to happen, she traced events back to this moment. Her tears, his smile, their hands.

TEN O'CLOCK TRIM

John cuts hair. That's his job. This morning he's cutting my hair.

Snip, snip, snippety snip. He looks away out the window while cutting, then back at his watch, then he looks at his own hands, lifting and cutting my faded hair.

'John, why do you wear those dark glasses?'

'To hide my laughter lines, of course,' he says.

This is not funny, not really, but John has one of those deadpan voices and I laugh. John smiles kindly and keeps snipping.

'What, you think it doesn't work? You can still see my wrinkles?'

I can't answer, I'm laughing so hard now I'm silent. I'm giddy with tiredness and badly need a strong coffee.

'Suzie, darling, try to hold still.' He holds my head still in his huge hands for a moment longer than is strictly necessary, and I sober up. His hands feel strong, stronger than any hands that have touched my head in a while, though my long marriage should contradict this. My whole scalp suddenly feels like an erogenous zone. But then the scalp is so much closer to the important bit, the bit that holds secrets, isn't it? Miles closer than, well, more traditional erogenous zones.

John notices I have stopped breathing and is holding perfectly still. He waits another three seconds, then raises his hands an inch above my head, and pauses again dramatically.

'Are you sure you're alright now, Suzie? No more nonsense?'

I nod obediently, sucking my mirth back in.

'Good. Good girl.'

John withdraws his hands completely, picks up the scissors and re-commences snipping.

'So, John, any holiday plans?'

'Do I look like a holiday type? A week in Ibiza type?'

'Sorry, I just assumed . . . what with kids and stuff.'

'Assume not! Besides, there's only one.'

'One kid?'

'Kid. And she's small too, so she hardly qualifies.'

'For holidays?'

'For being a kid.'

'But I thought being small was, kind of, well, integral to being a kid.'

He ignores this. It's as if I haven't spoken.

'You know I only have one kid and I never go on holidays,' he says in a hurt tone. 'You know these things, Suzie.'

'Yeah. I guess I forgot. It was just, you know, small talk.'

'I don't do small talk. You know that too, Suzie,' he says. 'I'm your hairdresser. I. Cut. Your. Hair.' He whispers these four syllables in my left ear, in a friendly way, and I try not to read anything sinister into the fact he is still clipping away at the right side of my head.

'God, I'm sorry John. So tell me. How is life?'

'It sucks. Otherwise fine.'

A pause, while he seems to be looking for nits, tugging my hair intimately this way and that, peering. My scalp feels itchy, I want to scratch, and John scratches the exact spot that needs scratching. A moment's contented peace. Snip snip, snippity snip.

'Terrible news this morning,' I say, trying not to small talk.

'Was there?'

'Oh! Didn't you hear?'

'Hear what, the news? I never listen to the news, never.

And I don't read the papers either. What's the point? Why do I need to know about other people's shitty tragedies and accidents?'

His lips twitch, but I can't tell if he wants to smile, or is indeed already smiling. Or is contemptuous. The dark glasses conceal so much.

'Really? Oh. I wish I lived in your world, John. No news, no stress.'

'No you don't. You would hate my world.' He says this with such masterful certainty, I shiver, in a confused post-feminist way. Shiver and mentally search for more questions to evoke masterful responses. I lean my head into John's hands, but they arch away from cradling me and reach for a comb. I inhale a sigh of exquisite frustration.

'Why do you shave your head, John? Kind of unusual for a hair dresser, isn't it?'

'To hide my receding hair line.' This, too, is delivered masterfully. 'Oh now, Suzie, don't start giggling again.'

'Sorry. Anyway, it looks OK.'

'It also disguises my grey hair.'

'Grey hair? You have grey hair?'

'Shit, Suzie, shout it out, why don't you?'

'Sorry. I thought you were kidding. I mean you don't actually look old enough.'

'I got a kid, don't I?'

'Yeah, but just one little one.'

'So, Suzie, how's that?'

'How's what?'

John holds up a mirror so I can see the back of my head. I just glance. It is way too public a place to give it real scrutiny.

'Very nice, thanks.'

'But is it what you want?'

'Uh, sure.'

'What did you want? I forgot to ask this time.'

'Just the usual. You know, John. To look young.'

'Ah. Well. Never mind. This morning in the bathroom, I'm

standing stark naked, penis a tenth of its erect size.' Pause. 'You're blushing, Suzie.'

'No I'm not. I am not! I was waiting for that. You always say that word at some point.'

'So! You couldn't remember the kid bit or the holiday bit, but the penis bit – you were waiting for it? Suzie, Suzie, what are you like?' John tisks and sighs, while his lips twitch.

'Anyway, I happened to look in the full length mirror, like this.'

He stands back from my chair and stares at his image, to demonstrate. His eyebrows signal surprise, his mouth gapes in despair, and his hands lift in a helpless gesture. He is Mr Woebegone.

'Fatal,' I say, with real sympathy, shaking my head. 'Morning. Mirrors. The whole shebang.'

'Yeah, well. It happens. I suppose you think a haircut can fix things like that,' he says.

'Can't it?'

He puts his hands on my shoulders, as if he is going to remove the nylon cloak that protects me from my own cut hair. But he does not lift the cloak, just rests his hands.

'Why do you wear that earring in your chin, John?' I ask in a dreamy voice.

'It's not an earring, moron,' he says affectionately. 'Earrings go in ears.'

'Well, a whatever. It looks like it hurts.'

'In fact, it is a bit infected.' He lifts his hands finally, cloakless. Looks in the mirror, studies his chin. Our heads are an inch apart in the mirror. I talk to his mirror image, transfixed by his proximity. I incline my head towards his. Just the tiniest bit. A tiny bit more. His lips press hard together, but no real smile. I try to imagine him smiling, and can't.

'So why wear it?'

'It hides the fact I can't grow a beard.'

'You can't?'

'Well, in theory, Suzie, I suppose I could, but it would be

thin and grey. This way I just have a bit of turquoise sticking out.'

'But it looks sore.'

'Yeah, well.' John checks his watch. Yawns. I meet his eyes, or what I guess are his eyes. His glasses are hexagonal opaque navy blue.

'My 11:00 cancelled,' he says sadly. 'Dope's so expensive these days, and customers just cancel without a second thought.'

'Oh well, keep cutting if you want,' I say. 'There's still some left. Just keep cutting as long as you want.'

'Oh, alright. Thanks Suzie.' John snips again, in a tender but aimless way. I think I can see his eyes slide shut behind his glasses. I shut my eyes too, in a little mid-morning swoon. Then he stops and plays with my hair, running his huge hands through it over and over till it's like a hedgehog. I let him. It seems a little unusual, but he is my hairdresser. Touching hair is what hairdressers do. Isn't it?

BUS STOP

Once upon a time, when the whole world thought innocence was something long lost forever and no one claimed to miss it, not really, and no one flinched at atrocities in the newspaper, or was surprised to be out of work, and everyone sighed a lot and if it was a sunny day, said 'we'll pay for it later' – in those weary times, there lived a young man called Angus McNear.

Angus is 22. He still lives on the farm he grew up on, a farm north of Inverness – distant enough so that a trip there is rare, and he's only been to the leisure centre once, and to the cinema twice. It's his own farm, with no mortgage, and 3,000 sheep all to himself, because his parent's car crashed into a lorry on the A9 when he was seven. At the time, it was a shocking tragedy. When he was older, he realised it was still a shocking tragedy, but a sadly common one. He thinks of the A9 in the same way some people think about certain battlegrounds, and thinks it deserves a memorial, like a war memorial. On his mantelpiece, there's a photo of his parents and himself building a snowman, but he doesn't look at it often. That afternoon is embedded now, and in a sense he still has parents – they just don't grow older. He was brought up by his Aunt Angusina. Yes, yes, highly unlikely. But all fairy tales are based on truth, and those are their real names.

Extraordinary fact number one: Angus McNear has, until

last night, never been drunk. Look at any survey you choose, you'll find by age of 14, most males in Scotland have been intoxicated more than once. Not Angus.

Extraordinary fact number two: Angus has never kissed a girl. Never been pissed or kissed. Unless you count Zoe last night at the bus stop. Angus, being Angus, does not count Zoe. Why? Is it because she wears skirts that fail to entirely cover her bottom, purple lipstick and her left nostril sports a turquoise star? Is it because when she took the mike last night at Hootenannys and sang 'Ae Fond Kiss' off key, she forgot the third verse and sang the second verse twice? Is it because she smells of cider and cigarettes, and laughs a soft laugh after she lands her purple kiss on his virgin mouth, last night just before he swings himself onto the bus?

No, no, those are the reasons Angus loves Zoe. Angus does not count that kiss because, although it is the pivotal kiss of his life so far, it is not an on-purpose kiss. Angus comes from a hill where they think hard about things before they do them. And so now he is thinking hard about how to find, court, and kiss Zoe properly. And then marry her.

There is nothing else in his mind but this waiting kiss. The air he breathes is fat with his un-given kisses. And his Aunt Angusina's porridge is left cold on the table.

'Are you alright, boy? You've not touched your breakfast'.

'Aye. I'm, fine. Can I have some coffee?'

'You never drink coffee, Angus. Are you alright? Sure you're not coming down with something?'

Angus slowly gives his aunt his brightest smile. She turns from the stove and gives him back the exact same slow-burning smile, with a question in her raised eyebrows. Serious, honest, bright and warm as fire, because she was born on this hill too.

Extraordinary fact number three: Places breed people, just as surely as genes are passed on at conception. Personalities are distilled from places, and this high, hard, cold mountain makes people like Angus and Angusina. The high altitude gives them their perspective, not just their view – they see the big picture quicker than the lowlanders. Rarely petty, never mean. Porous, the two of them, and trusting. Wide open to whatever the world shows them. And each night, they sleep like babies.

'I'm not coming down with anything. I'm in love, Auntie.'

'In love? How wonderful! Did you meet her last night?'

'Aye. She's a singer. Her name's Zoe.'

Aunt Angusina laughs a little and blushes, then says:

'Well done lad.'

'I know it's quick.'

'Only takes a second, if it's the right person. Bring her to Sunday dinner.'

'Aye. She'll love your roast dinners.'

He looks around the kitchen, out the window at the mountain. Angusina bustles about, grinding beans and warming the cafetierre. She's wearing Chanel no 5 and her outdoor clothes.

Extraordinary fact number four: Even in remote Highland hills, there is decent coffee and sometimes women smell very nice when they feed the hens.

Angus glugs his coffee, puts on his boots, gives his aunt's shoulders an affectionate squeeze, and heads down the hill. Hardly notices where he puts his feet, he knows this hill intimately. Walks the six miles to the bus stop, rides a bus to another bus stop, then a bus to Inverness, and marches into Hootenannys. Clears his throat.

'Zoe!' he says with gusto.

'Aye?' says Zoe, who is wiping a beer glass. She has dark circles under eyes and a love bite on her neck. She is 32, and feeling flat. This isn't what she thought her life would be. Like trudging through . . . porridge, from dawn to dusk. And that waiting sensation – waiting for her proper life to begin. A tease. She'd wither like a bud that the frost killed, before it ever bloomed. A frozen, bruised hard bud. Oh! It wasn't fair. Zoe likes to read, and her life reminds her of a book with a shiny cover, a promising first chapter, then . . . not much happening. No proper plot, no suspense, just predictable characters going round in circles. She feels cheated, almost every minute. Except when she sings. And she starts to hum right now, thinking of singing.

'You sing great, Zoe,' says Angus.

'How do you know my name?' she asks, reaching for another glass to dry.

'It's me. Angus.'

'Angus. OK. What can I get you, Angus?' She says his name stressing both syllables. Like a joke. An. Gus.

'No, seriously, it's me. We met last night, remember? I sat right there.' He points to a chair close to the stage.

'You were here last night?'

'Aye. Do you not remember? You kissed me. At the bus stop.'

'Aye, right. So what if I did. What can I get you?'

'Coke please.'

Zoe pours a coke. 'Two pounds, please.'

'Are you singing again tonight?'

'Nah. That was only because I was a bit pissed.'

'You were great.'

'Not. So not. You giving me the two pounds or not?'

Angus pulls out a wad of notes. 'I wish I could sing. My auntie, now she can sing. You'd like Angusina. She makes a great pot roast.'

He takes his coke to the same seat, and watches Zoe serve customers for the next three hours. By eight, there are so many people, he has to keep craning his neck to see her. She is looking happier now. Some pink in her cheeks. The music starts and a couple sit at his table. The girl claps and sings along. Dances in her seat. Angus introduces himself, formally, by extending his hand and smiling. At first they laugh at him a bit, but within seconds fall for his earnestness. He is too strange not to like. Just the right side of weird. He orders some food, Thai food – that's all there is. Ordering is tricky.

In the end, he just chooses a number. When 25 arrives, the couple ooh and ah, till he offers them a nibble. Angus cannot decide if it's nice or not. After the third bite, he decides nice. A bit like a Bounty bar mixed up with chilli con carne, without the beans or chocolate. He cleans the plate. His new friends order some too, and when it comes, Angus nibbles off their plates. They are buying each other rounds now, and Angus has swapped coke for beer. He cannot believe how good he feels. Better than Hogmanay and shearing day wrapped up together. The Black Isle show times a million.

Zoe has stopped noticing him, temporarily forgotten her malaise. Is approaching her beautiful part of the night, where if she is lucky she will attract attention from a man who may – who truly, madly, deeply may – be the one. The way she looks at it, the odds are very good. Look at the world – heaving with single men, and all it takes is one. Her prince is out there, no mistake.

Extraordinary fact number five: Zoe believes in Santa Claus. Or the equivalent of. A cupid who visits the inebriated, making sure true love has a chance. And this regular bout of hope lights her up like a sexy Christmas tree. It also makes her want to sing. It's midnight. The bar has stopped serving and Zoe is on the stage again. She begins with an old blues number she learned from listening to Amy Winehouse.

For you, I was the flame. Love is a losing game.

She closes her eyes, and falls into the sound of her own whispery voice. The pub is crowded and most people are talking, not listening. This doesn't matter. Zoe sings as if her heart is breaking, and Angus sits and listens. When the song ends, he stands up to clap, and whoops. Some people laugh at him, but when Zoe begins to sing again, people stop talking this time and listen to her.

To knowknowknow him, is to lovelovelove him.
Just to see his smile, makes my life worthwhile.

And when the song ends she stands still, holding the mike, seems lost. In fact, she is a little more pissed than she'd thought, and she suddenly needs the mike for support. Can she sing again? Can she remember what she has just sung? Has any man offered to see her home tonight? What the hell kind of way was this to end a Saturday night? Suddenly, Angus is on the stage, one arm around Zoe, and crooning – there is no other word for it – the words to Caledonia.

Extraordinary fact number six: Angus can sing now, because he is in love.

I don't know if you can see
the changes that have come over me
in these last few days,
I've been afraid that I might drift away ...

Angus holds the last note and lets it fade away into nothing. The pub holds its collective breath, not blinking an eye. It's eerie. Then Angus swoops into the song again, exactly as if he's diving into the burn on a humid day. The same grace and delicious release.

So I've been telling old stories, singing songs,
that make me think about where I came from,
and that's the reason why I seem so far away today ...

Another long pause. His eyes are closed now, and Zoe's are open. She looks at his profile, from her position of under his arm, which is looped heavily around her shoulders. The presumption! Did she give permission for him to act like he was her boyfriend? But she can't move, and she can't stop staring at his profile either. And for no reason that's obvious to her, because she's a bit pissed and tired with life, she remembers a long ago day, and walking to school down Montague Row. New shoes, new term, new haircut, new everything. Maybe she'll pass maths this year. Anything is possible.

Angus is smiling from coast to coast, and Zoe suddenly knows she needs to throw up. Tries to extract herself from his arm. Angus opens then closes his eyes again, and this miracle voice that did not exist before tonight, hits the perfect notes again. But it wouldn't matter if he didn't because the audience is singing along now. Everyone knows the words to this song.

Let me tell you that I love you and I think about you all the time.

Everyone has just remembered they are Scottish and that Scotland is a lot of sad things these days, and actually a thousand years of sad things, but it is also their own beautiful place.

Extraordinary fact number seven: On Saturday nights in Inverness pubs, it is impossible to be too sentimental. Where this building stands, the ghost of previous gatherings wavers, and also sings out the same song, just different words. People's hearts have been filling and emptying at regular intervals forever. Nothing really changes.

And if I should become a stranger . . .

'Gonna be sick,' says Zoe, but no one can hear her.

. . . You know that would make me more than sad
Caledonia's been everything I've ever had.

And because Zoe's had lots of practice, she vomits in a damage limitation way. Quickly ducks her head to the side, behind Angus. No vomit lands on her shoes or clothes, and she manages to grab a serviette off the nearest table to wipe her mouth.

'You alright, Zoe?' asks Angus under the applause.

'How do you know my name?'

'You told me. Last night. I'm Angus, remember? You kissed me. At the bus stop.'

Zoe squints at Angus. Thinks: Nah, won't do. Too young. Too straight. Not her prince. Pity. She lets him escort her off the stage, into the room behind the bar. Let's him find her coat.

'Well, thanks a lot Angus. You're sweet. Now piss off, OK?' With a smile – she's not that hard, Zoe. Everyone knows that.

'Now that's no way to talk to your future husband,' he says to her in dead seriousness.

'What the fuck?'

'I said: That's no way to talk to . . .'

'I heard you! You mental, or what?'

'You're just tired. And drunk. Let's get you home safe.'

Zoe protests, but the fact is he's right, she is so dreadfully tired right now. And her mouth tastes disgusting, and self loathing is lingering quite close, she can smell it. Like old urine. What word in particular did he say to make her feel limp? Safe. She lets him slip her arms into her coat sleeves, and off into the night air they go.

And they live happily ever after.

But the ending is never really the ending, right?

Not unless someone dies, but even then they can make stuff happen. And the innocence no one claims to miss these days? Of course we miss it, because there's no other way to have it, aside from missing it. Innocence always lives in the past, because we now know what happened next, and then we did not. I can tell you this: One day, Zoe will remember this phase of her life, and see that she was innocent after all. That she truly was, as Angus insisted, a nice girl. And she'll miss that. And the rest of his life, whenever Angus feels a little frightened and alone, he'll sing Caledonia. This will calm him, as if he is touching some kind of talisman. It will return himself to himself.

Meanwhile, Angus carefully escorts Zoe past the famous bus stop, over the wobbly foot bridge, and down the wet dark lanes behind the cathedral. He thinks of his hill. His house, the view from his window, his aunt's Chanel, his dog snoring by the stove. The way the air tastes just before snow. The sheep, when it snows hard at night. The way they stand so still, like a group of soft statues. As if conserving all their strength just to keep breathing. Buffering each other from the long night. Angus feels twenty years older than he did this morning. How can a single day contain so many changes? To think an impulse kiss can re-direct the flow of a life so easily. Zoe is quiet now. And she is so light and fragile, it is all Angus can do not to simply sweep her up into his arms and plant that kiss right now. But he does not. Tonight is not the night.

A GOOD WIFE

We're talking to each other about something unimportant, relaxed and unaware of each other. I'm looking at his face, watching him talk, when suddenly the room behind him slants and I feel myself slip out of being. A flicker of time-lessness. I am nowhere and nobody, except I am with him. A second later I am back in the world, shaking myself, and from that time on every time I see him I am self-conscious. My heart pounds when I think he might be near. Some days, too tired for this, I go out of my way to avoid him.

His name is James and we are both married.

My marriage is to a man, but also to a multitude of other things. Family friends, old china plates, weekend rituals, lawnmowers, photo albums, habits of sleep, domestic chores. A whole house and garden. My marriage lies deeply imbedded in our messiest cupboard. I promise to sort it out one day and it will reveal our earliest souvenirs. Old hospital plastic ID tags for newborns, the first Christmas shopping lists, letters from when we needed such things. I don't know if I love my marriage, much less my husband. Knowing, or even loving, doesn't seem necessary.

In my house are some old photographs of relatives I have never met. They're the only relatives I have and although they are all dead, I have a good relationship with them. There is a great grandmother called Violet who is especially sympa-thetic, looking directly out of the photo with clear, happy eyes. On her left, stands her husband Ted, a lovely Victorian man with a high intelligent forehead and a suppressed smile in his dimples and raised eyebrows. She is leaning on him, both arms around him, clearly comfortable touching him in front of the photographer. This impresses me. I'm sure Violet led a brave and full life. She took chances and did not shirk from strong emotion. I admire her for being so alive, even her century-old likeness shines and talks to me. So I tell her about James. I suppose Ted hears too, since they have that kind of marriage. He doesn't let on. Dead relatives always have this option.

I see James nearly every day, since we live in the same small village and have children of similar ages. I conceal my new nervousness, but one day, in the shop queue I catch an echo. He stands there, clutching his margarine and milk, and actually stutters.

'Wh . . . wh . . . where are you going this summer?'

'Orkney for a week.'

'The whole family?'

'No, Michael can't get off work till October. How about you? Are you going anywhere?'

'Oh, no place special. Camping up north near Redburn Beach. Ann doesn't like camping and it'll give her a break from the kids to just stay home.'

'You are a good husband. And father.'

We look at each other a millisecond longer than is necessary, then look at the newspapers till it's my turn to pay for my shopping. I leave, flinging a casual goodbye over my shoulder.

'Hey!' he calls. 'Wait a minute.'

I stand by the door and wait. My heart does its silly dance.

'When are you going on holiday?'

'In two weeks. The fifteenth.'

'Same as us. That's great. Maybe see you on the road.'

This is it. I have to race home to tell Violet. He feels the same way, I tell her. There is the dangerous possibility of romance in my life.

An eighteen-year-old marriage should be able to withstand a few sparks, says Violet. For heaven's sakes, what's all the fuss about? I was in love with other men my whole marriage. That's what feeling alive meant to me. I flirted, I was alive, then when it was over – as soon as he was familiar to me – I was still with my dear old Ted.

Ted nearly winks and I have to wonder if he also had infatuations, but he never opens his mouth to say anything.

Two weeks later I find myself and my children on a northern beach in that cold clear light that so dislocates me. I must like feeling dislocated, because I am forever drawn to the north and west, away from the calm normality of the east. My body feels light and strong. The children too, run with grace and beauty. The light stays in their eyes. They don't quarrel and I mostly stay quiet and let them be. They are their loveliest when resembling young animals.

I have imagined meeting him here and so I'm not very surprised when I do. When it comes to the actual confrontation, we are both embarrassed and avoid looking at each other. Is this innocent or have we contrived? Outwardly we both rest heavily on the innocent coincidence of it. It can't be fate if we planned it, and fate it must be or we are doomed, sordid pre-adulterers.

We share picnics, throw stones over grey water, pull damp clothes off shivering children and bundle them in dry. We don't talk much, no confidences or important subjects. We mention our spouses seemingly without irony. Yet there is a most extreme tension between us. I can't tell if it feels good or not. Good feels irrelevant. It ties us and holds us apart. At one point I shut my eyes to soak the sun and though he doesn't make any noise I can track his movements.

The day wanes, the world with all its limitations looms nearer. I think if nothing happens now, right now, nothing ever will. At our cars we part. We buckle the children in, then behind our cars, out of their sight, he leans towards me and I meet him halfway in a clumsy kiss. I laugh.

'I'm not very good at casual kisses,' I say, and turn to go.

'Wait,' he says.

And after an eternity of two seconds, we kiss properly. I feel myself fill up from my toes to the ends of my salty hair. I am so full of kiss. We kiss and then I nearly faint with fear. Only Violet could consume an illicit first kiss single-mindedly. I am crowded with the out stretched hands and voices of my family. And more, the sudden knowledge of James as a stranger. I am alone with him, with only my children for protection. Against what? Surely not physical threat.

Intimacy, then. Is this prospect so terrifying? Yes. Oh, absolutely. I live with distance, it's what I'm used to. Family life is about bouncing off surfaces and, at times like this, hiding.

'Have to go, James.' I give him the original casual kiss back, a quick embrace. His texture and smell imprint themselves on me, I inhale his unfamiliarity. I can barely stand straight. I smile but his eyes are sad. I can't tell what mine look like. I turn away first. Then I'm driving north to the ferry in the darkening evening. The children have nodded off in back seat. Beyond the kiss I have just had, a breath away, lays the irretrievableness of my life. Other people do this, I tell myself. And much more.

Violet, how do you live so courageously? How do you enjoy a kiss without being afraid for your life?

A kiss like that is never just a kiss, she says. Every erotic possibility can be contained in a kiss. She says this even though I am miles from her photo.

She says men like James only have one or two kisses like this in them. She won't say what to do about it. I stop the car to stretch and shake sand off. Look at my sleeping children, then find the camera and take a picture of them. The combined traits of me and my husband play unevenly on their features, so they are both separate and connected. Especially, and I am glad for this, they are separate from me.

I cannot imagine inflicting pain for this kiss. Yet it is not my husband, my children or even James I am thinking of protecting. A faithful wife may merely be a coward. I press my lips together to find the kiss still marginally there, while the permanent memory of his shape arranges itself.

The best lover you never had, says Violet.

INSTEAD OF BEAUTY

After she gives up on love, Addie decides all she really wants is a baby. A baby! A tiny person to carry around and cook lovely cakes for, someone who'll never look at her as if she's nobody. She is hung over; exhausted and taut. Outside, the July rain is un-dramatic, self-effacing, as if it knows its timing is bad. Her kitchen is humid and her head aches. A fragile day altogether, requiring great care and strength of will, and it is also the saddest time of the day – 3:00 in the afternoon. She considers her options carefully. She has nearly run out of men – Lochinellie has a certain number and no more. By the time she makes and drinks her cup of bitter black coffee, she has a short list of one. Down to the bottom of the barrel now, no mistake.

Joe Forbes, the fish man.

He is the only one with no prying family in the area, no wedding ring, and no obvious defects, if you didn't count his probable virginity as a defect. Or his perennial stink of fish, his ugliness (though his shoulders are quite nice), and his complete lack of conversation. He is the most silent and ugly and alone man she has ever met. Though now she thinks of it, Joe is curiously un-lonely looking.

'So, Joe!' she says to him that night at the bar in the hotel. Addie never wastes time, and she knew she'd find him here. Single men in Lochinellie gravitate to the bar at dusk, like single men everywhere in the Highlands, like thirsty beasts to the watering hole. 'What you drinking, Joe?'

She buys them both a pint, then lets him buy her two more pints. They sit in silence for an hour, then she tells him she wants a baby off him.

'What do you think? You like me, right?' she asks, her voice hard as hailstones, hard as desperation. Her face all rosy and her eyes excited. She could be uncannily pretty this time of night, for about half an hour. Before time was called and the lights came on full again. As if her much younger untroubled self resurfaced in some alcohol-fuelled twilight, in order to seduce. A spirit siren on a mission.

'I've seen you looking, and it's not like you've got a queue of women knocking on your door, Joe. Is it? I know you like me.'

'Of course I. Like you. What's not? To like? You're. Fun. But Addie, that's hardly the point.'

This is the longest sentence she's ever heard him say. He says the words in a halting staccato, as if English is his third language. There's a sheen of sweat on his nose.

'Aw come on, of course it's the point. If you didn't like me, at least a little, then we'd never manage it at all. I'd say you liking me is the entire bloody point, for you. You'd get a bit of experience, I'd get my baby.'

Pause, while she searches unsuccessfully for eye contact.

'I'd not be wanting any money off you. Ever. You'd be well clear of it all, really. All the advantages, none of the hassle.'

Again, she waits for his response, but he just looks emptily at his glass as if his whole stock of words has gone. She stops waiting, satisfied that his muteness is entirely appropriate, given who he is and what she is asking. She leans forward and whispers: 'I'm only wanting your sperm. And just for one night, when the time is right for me. For making a baby – there's really only a few days a month it'll work. And it's only you I'm asking. I thought about it, and you're the only one. The best one for the job. The best man.'

Joe takes a long pull of his beer and shifts in his seat. This feels like words to Addie.

'It'll just take a few minutes, actually, Joe. No need for staying the night, even. Unless you want to, of course. You might fall asleep, and then I'd just let you sleep.'

'No!' It bursts out of him with such finality, she lurches forward, already grieving this sweet fish-smelling baby. She has trouble breathing naturally, and her voice acquires an unattractive whine.

'But why? What're you afraid of? It'll not hurt, I'll be dead gentle.'

She puts her hand on his hand, which feels oily and rough, but she doesn't remove her hand. She is surprised how easy it is to ignore the oily stickiness, but lord he stinks of fish. There'd be no getting rid of that smell.

'Please, Joe. Just consider it.'

'It's. Wrong. Accidental pregnancy.'

'But it's the opposite of accidental, silly. And how can it be wrong? Everyone, but you that is, does it all the time! It's the strongest instinct there is, to make babies. Love is all crap. It's just a trick of nature to make sure the human race doesn't die out.'

Joe shrugs, finishes his pint.

'You'll be sorry. I'm great, so I am. Ask anyone.'

He looks round the pub. It's true, almost all the men drinking could probably vouch for Addie's skills. He sighs, and his sigh has longing and sadness in it. Then something happens to the room and everyone in it, and though things look the same, they are not. In fact, unseen by the customers, the barmaid has opened the back door and a surfeit of oxygenated sea air has entered the bar. Addie removes her hand from Joe's hand, and he instantly misses it. He misses it like he'd miss his own hand. He buys another round, then they sit in silence for seven minutes and drink in rhythm, each raising their pint glass and drinking at the same time. They look at the bottles behind the bar, and there is a pleasant stillness to their silence, as if the new air has induced a truce.

Joe is a word miser, and in any case, she is a lousy listener. But her muscles have wisdom and memories and don't require language. She puts her hand back in his hand, leaves it there until he wraps his fingers around it.

'Listen, I know it's a lot to ask. I'm not daft.' She doesn't look at him or the bottles now, but looks out the window. The sea is visible in the white lines of waves breaking. It is raining of course, that same thin seemingly English drizzle, with no real force. She has a sudden wish for the rain to really rain, to stop holding back. She wishes for a screaming hurricane of wind and rain, to make all choice irrelevant, to obliterate the hotel and everyone in it. She sighs and her sigh has tears of frustration in it.

'Shit, Joe. I just want a baby. It's all I can think of. I've given up on the other stuff. I'm sick to death of waiting for . . . stuff.'

Joe nods sympathetically, excuses himself to use the toilet, and when he returns, asks if she's alright to see herself home. She says yes, and he leaves her sitting there, feeling strange, with her half empty glass of flat beer and the insipid rain.

One day, a few weeks later, Joe spots Addie, standing alone by the quay in the torrential rain without a jacket. She is so strange! Looking at the sea and sky, which the rain has joined seamlessly in a tableau of a depressing summer. It's been a menopausal summer altogether; too hot then too cold, moody and intense. When she begins to turn in his direction, he quickly turns as well, and walks briskly away.

Three weeks later, early in the morning, the sun remembers its own point and sizzles. The light explodes over Lochinellie like a luminous blessing, and nothing looks dull or ordinary. Not even the rusty petrol pumps. Not even the Co-op sign with the missing letters. The whole place steams away, and Addie pulls on her favourite dress – red cotton with tiny white stars. She bounds down the road to Joe's cottage, enjoying the air on her skin, and thinks what an extraordinarily fine thing it is, some days, to be above ground and not in it. Joe is walking to his lorry, all muffled up in a fleece, as if he hasn't really noticed the day yet.

'Joe!'

He greets her by tilting his head and smiling closed-mouthed.

'Joe! What a fine day!'

He makes a noise of assent, then opens the door to his lorry and swings one leg up. She tells him this is the day they can make a baby.

'It's the best day, Joe. What time are you back tonight?'

He freezes, half way in the cab. 'I'll be gone for three days.' He pulls himself the rest of the way in, and shuts his door. Starts up the engine. Sudden glimpse of Addie in her faded red and white dress, and anxious pale face, lips red as if she's been nibbling them, with the sun giving her a halo. He salutes her goodbye, and while he checks his rear view mirror, she swings open the passenger door and heaves herself in. He stares at her, but she keeps her face forward, and is so still it is like she is willing herself into invisibility. He pauses for a moment, then pulls out into the road. She looks out the window at the boats in the harbour, notices the way they never rock the same way and the masts are always at odds. Then Joe shifts down to make the steep brae out of Lochinellie.

An hour later, after the sun slinks away in yet another huff, he offers her his jumper. She pulls it on. It's rough against her skin, and way too big, but there is a sense of relief in the roughness and bigness. They are still not looking at each other.

'Thank you Joe,' she whispers, soft as Marilyn Monroe, soft as astonishment. 'I was freezing.'

After a minute she lays her hand on his knee, and she keeps it there all the way to Carlisle. Like a piece of luck, or unexpected sun on an overcast day.

FLY

It was an oppressive day, and the sky sat on top of her head. But they had planned to take the boy fishing, so off they went. The man, the woman and the boy.

The loch was close, but somehow they had not managed to fish often. The boy had been asking to go. He caught a pike once, a huge sharp-toothed golden pike. Ever since then he'd wanted to catch a fish again.

The man, who was not the boy's father, told himself he loved to fish. But when he fished these days, he was disappointed. This was a secret. It was too late to learn some other way of being, so he kept being a fisherman even though the joy was pretty much gone.

In the car, the man talked about fishing to the boy. The woman looked out the window and tried to remember how everything looked when there was sun. Her heart was panicky and leaden, her throat ached. She glanced at her son, with a light, inquiring expression. As if saying: This is fun, isn't it? We're going fishing! She looked at the man sometimes too, but he didn't look at her. Just the rear view mirror and the road ahead. He drove quickly. She wondered when she'd become so serious. She used to be a different kind of person. In fact, she used to giggle all the time.

At the loch, they walked to the fishing place. No one else was there. The air full of thunder, and flies and midges. The man set the boy up, then assembled his own rod, and they began fishing. The boy's hook caught a few times, and each time the man put down his own rod and untangled the other line. His fingers were fat, and the line thin – yet he teased the tangle out easily. He put his huge arms around the boy, showed him how to cast, so the line was released at the right time. After a while, the man and boy fished in rhythm. With the whizzing of lines through the air, and the smooth metallic whir of the lines being wound in, there was, momentarily, grace.

The woman hoped some fish would come to her son's hook, but she feared none would. She also hoped her son didn't notice her fear. He was thirteen – what thirteen year old needed his mother to assume he wouldn't catch fish? 'We're lucky,' she said. 'No rain!' Then she couldn't bear to watch them anymore, in case no fish was fooled by her son's fly. 'I'm taking a short walk,' she said.

On and on, they fished. The man caught a few trout, threw them back. They didn't speak much. Just the occasional encouragement from the man, or one of them would curse the midges. Some birds wheeled above their heads. Thin, painful sounds. If a baby's cry could be stretched out into the sky, that was the sound. 'See that kite, he's seeing off those buzzards,' said the man, almost proud. The boy looked up, half-expecting to see the kind of kite you buy in a shop, and his line instantly tangled.

The woman walked quickly. Walking made her feel better. She walked over rough ground, heather and bog. She came to a place where it was impossible to walk, but then she found a narrow manmade levee. She walked till she came to some woods, and she could no longer see the boy and man. This felt alright for a few minutes, then she needed to see them again. She headed back, and soon she was almost running. A sense of pending doom was rising in her, and she had the feeling that whatever it was – it was not too late to avert, if only she could go faster. It was still fixable. She would try to be that other person. A better person.

But she couldn't find the levee to cross over to the boy and man – she walked back and forth, and couldn't see it anywhere. She almost cried, and then she felt stupid. What if they noticed her hurrying back and forth? She jogged all the way round to the road where the car was parked, then half ran to the shore. Too late! Too late! she kept thinking. When she got there, no time at all seemed to have passed. There they were, still fishing.

For no reason, she thought of the day they met. The way she'd felt when he kissed her the first time. As if, quite by accident, she'd stumbled upon something magical. Something the normal rules would never apply to. And she'd felt a shy stranger to herself. She'd closed her eyes and surrendered to wanting him, not caring about anything else.

'Show me how to fish, will you?' she asked the man. 'I want to learn.'

Without expression, he gave her his rod. Showed her when to let go, and how to move her arms. She couldn't see a fish falling for it. The hook looked like a hatpin stabbing a bit of feather. But she swallowed hard and kept trying, and it was good when the man touched her.

She wondered if they would come right again. Let the days fill with a multitude of forgettable saving things. Like paying bills and taking holidays and arguing carelessly in the supermarket, about what pasta to buy.

But the man had been at the end of things before, and knew for certain. He would have to remember the right words to say; there were some words, a short phrase, and it would all be over. But now his mind was too cloudy to do anything. He moved slowly, felt very tired.

The boy didn't watch his mother or the man. He didn't want them to watch him either. He was busy being 13, and hated being watched. He concentrated on fishing, despite the ache in his throat. He liked the sound the line made when it hit the water. A convincing quiet plop, like the sound a real insect might make lighting on the water. And he imagined how it must look to a trout, swimming down in the cold peaty water. The trout looking up, seeing this feathery thing wiggling across the surface. The trout wouldn't even think about it, wouldn't wonder if it was real or not. It would be hungry and want the thing that looked like food. It would lunge upwards with its mouth open, already tasting the fly.

ACKNOWLEDGMENTS

These stories have been written over a period of twenty years, and owe much to many. Particularly Laura Hird, Angus Dunn, Moira Forsyth, Janet MacInnes, Anne MacLeod, John Glenday, Michel & Eva Faber. For inspiration, I am indebted to my unwitting muses Carson McCullers and Anne Tyler. For financial assistance, I am grateful to Creative Scotland. And for patiently proofreading every version of every story and rarely screaming, thank you Peter. You are a genius.

CREDITS

Stories which have been previously published, broadcast, or won awards:

'A Dangerous Place' – winner of the V.S. Pritchett Prize 2008. Published in *London Magazine* & *Chapman*

'Etiquette of Accidents' – commended in the Manchester Fiction Prize 2011 & shortlisted for the Bridport Prize 2011

'Homesick' – *Gutter Magazine* 2011

'Rubbish Day' – *Fictional Guide to Scotland* 2003 (Open Ink). Also broadcast as 'Omphaloskepsis' on BBC Scotland 2006.

'The Bear' – *Northwords Magazine* circa 1997.

'The Room' – *Northwords Magazine* circa 1999.

'Enough Room' – *Ross-shire Journal* circa 2000.

'Home on the Road' – *Northwords Magazine* circa 1998.

'Sam the Man' – shortlisted for the Neil Gunn Prize 2000.

'Summer' – *Northwords Magazine* circa 1997.

'Wine Tasting' – *Northwords Magazine* circa 2001.

'First' – published as 'Edith and Henry', in *Boundaries* (Mouseman Press) 1995.

'The World and Things in It' – *Some Kind of Embrace* (Scottish Literary Studies) 1997.

'To Dance' – *Northwords Magazine* circa 2000, and *Written Remedy* (Luath Press) 2007.

'The Truth about Roller Coasters' – *Northwords Magazine* 2009.

'The Purpose of Photographs' – BBC radio 4, 2002.

'Persephone's Passion' – *New Writing Dundee 2009* (University of Dundee).

'Christopher's Room' – *West Coast Magazine* circa 1999.

'My Favourite Things' – BBC 4 Scottish Shorts, 2009 (oka 'The Intelligence of Hearts).

'The Long Missing' – *Cleave* (Two Ravens Press) 2008.

'Begin' – shortlisted for the Macallan *Scotland on Sunday* Competition, published in *Shorts* (Polygon) 1998.

'A Good Wife' – Chapman 2002.

'Instead of Beauty' – *Riptide* (Two Ravens Press) 2007.

'Bus Stop' – *Imagination* (Big Sky Press) 2011.

'Fly' – *Northwords Magazine* 2010.